Accidentally Family

SASHA SUMMERS

Accidentally Family

A Pecan Valley Novel

Preview of *Cowboy for Hire* copyright © 2020 by Victoria James.

Entangled Publishing, LLC
10940 S Parker Road
Suite 327
Parker, CO 80134
Visit our website at www.entangledpublishing.com.

Amara is an imprint of Entangled Publishing, LLC.

Edited by Candace Havens
Cover design by Bree Archer
Cover art by
Vitali Pechkurou/GettyImages
Alexlukin/GettyImages
Interior design by Toni Kerr

Print ISBN 978-1-68281-474-1
ebook ISBN 978-1-64063-864-8

Manufactured in the United States of America

First Edition June 2020

To Candace and Liz -
Thanks for making
me part of your family!

CHAPTER ONE

Today was always going to be a life changer, Felicity knew that. Watching her firstborn walk across the graduation stage, smiling ear to ear, was one of those slow-motion moments, a blur of happy times, milestones, and pride. Her daughter, Honor, was done. Eighteen. A high-school graduate, ready to spend the night celebrating with her friends.

Which was exactly as it should be.

This, now, leading her two kids into the emergency room, was not.

"How serious was the accident?" Honor asked, holding tightly to her hand.

"Honor," Nick, her sixteen-year-old, snapped. "You heard as much as she did."

It had been one of those times she'd wished her phone wasn't synced to her car. How could she have known the hospital was calling? How could she have known Matt, her ex—the kids' father—had been in an accident? A *serious* accident. They'd all just assumed Matt had ditched, as was the trend.

"Hold my hand, Nickie," Honor mumbled thickly, reaching for her little brother's hand.

Nick didn't say a word, but Honor didn't have to ask again.

The way her kids relied on each other was one good thing to come out of her messy divorce. They weren't just siblings anymore. They were best friends. Best friends who had no idea what was happening. It was possible Matt's replacement family was here—in the waiting room—families did that when things like this happened.

Coming face-to-face with his fiancée, Amber; her megawatt smile; and her killer legs wasn't going to make this any easier. Neither was meeting Matt's son, Jack—the baby Nick blamed for destroying their *happy* family. As much as she'd like to think Nick could keep it together, there were no guarantees. When it came to his father, Nick was equal parts hostility and resentment. The potential for reality-television drama in the hospital waiting room was a real concern.

But if the last two years had taught her anything, it was that a smile was normally the best accessory. Even when the last thing she felt like doing was smiling. Like now.

"Is that Dr. Murphy?" Nick asked.

Felicity glanced at the man at the nurses' station. At well over six feet, Graham Murphy stood out. Seeing his tall, broad back encased in green hospital scrubs was a relief. While the two of them hadn't been close the last few years, Graham and Matt had been best friends through med school and partners when Matt still had his OB/GYN practice here in Pecan Valley. "Graham?"

"Yes?" Graham Murphy turned to face them, instant recognition easing his features—briefly. His brown gaze searched hers. "Felicity." That was all. Her name, without a hint of emotion.

But he was having a hard time making eye contact with the kids, and that said so much. If Matt was okay, he'd say so. Wouldn't he? He'd offer some sort of reassurance. A smile. Something. The shock of the phone call was quickly turning into something substantial—and cold.

"I got a phone call? About Matt." Maybe he didn't know anything. Maybe—

"I'll take you to him." He cleared his throat, drew in a deep breath, and spoke. "He's going to surgery. His jaw is broken, so talking isn't comfortable. He's in bad shape, a lot of pain, but he held on to see you. Keep it positive—good thoughts, that sort of thing, okay?"

Honor was nodding, tears streaming down her face. Felicity wiped them away, pressing a kiss to her cheek.

Nick. Poor Nick. She hugged him close, his tall frame rigid and unyielding in her arms. Since the divorce, Nick's anger had grown every time Matt missed a game, concert, birthday, or holiday. While she understood, she worried Nick's fury would consume whatever affection he still felt for his father.

Graham looked at her, then nodded, leading them past the nurses' station and into the emergency room. He stopped beside the last door off the hall.

"What's best for him? One at a time? All together?" Honor asked.

"Together." The word was all Nick could manage.

Graham squeezed Nick's shoulder and went inside. "They're here, Matt."

Felicity went first, doing her best not to react to her ex-husband's appearance. But it was hard. His face was swollen and misshapen, a white gauze ice pack taped to his jaw. He was covered with several blankets, one looked like an inflated packing sheet, and each breath he took was labored and watery. He looked wrecked, in every sense of the word.

Honor immediately headed to her father, but Nick hung back.

"No crying," Matt said, the words slurred. He pressed a kiss to her forehead. "So beautiful. S-sorry…missed it. Graduated. I'm so proud. And I love you, baby girl."

"Don't talk, Dad." Honor kissed his cheek. "Mom recorded it all. You can be bored with it later—when you're better."

Matt nodded, the movement stiff. "Good." He was hurting; she could hear it, see it. "Nick?" The word a plea.

Nick crossed the room, hands shoved in pockets, jaw muscle working. "I'm here, Dad."

Matt reached up, his hand shaking so bad that Nick had no choice but to cradle it in both of his.

Felicity saw her boy's chin quiver, saw him wrinkle up his nose, the way his breathing hitched. He'd held on to his resentment for so long, he wasn't about to lose control now. But seeing him struggle hurt—so much.

"I love you, son." Matt spoke clearly, enunciating carefully. "I love you both so much."

"We love you, too, Dad," Honor said, kissing him again. "You just concentrate on healing thoughts. Good stuff. Fast cars and ice cream and puppies and—"

A nurse came in, effectively shooing the kids away while pulling the rails up on his bed. "It's time, Dr. Buchanan."

"One second," Matt said. "Felicity."

Felicity jumped. "Yes?"

Matt waited until they were alone before speaking. His gaze pinned hers, and his voice wavered. "Amber's dead. Jack." His face crumpled. "And Jack…"

Her heart stopped. "Matt, I—"

"He's alone, Felicity." His blue eyes bore into hers. "Please…" He pressed his head back into his pillows, closing his eyes. "Take him." It was a gruff whisper. "Love him."

She stepped closer, hating the crush of air from her lungs. "He needs *you*, Matt." She leaned over him. "You're his father."

His gaze burned. "I'm a doctor; I know what's happening. This is it." He spoke calmly, even as his eyes glistened. "I'm asking you to care for my son."

"Matt…" Felicity stared at him through horrible, painful tears. "Fight. You hear me?"

"Please, Filly." He grabbed her arm. "Please."

She squeezed his hand. "I promise I will. You promise you'll fight."

He nodded once, relaxing against the mattress.

"We're going now, Dr. Buchanan." The nurse brushed past her, kicking off the brake on the hospital bed.

Felicity trailed behind, numb.

"He will be okay," Honor said, taking her hand. "He's so fit and healthy. He's going to be fine."

Felicity squeezed her hand, unable to shake the dread seeping into her bones. She wanted to believe that was true. But the look on Matt's face…

"How long will the surgery take?" she asked Graham.

"It depends. A while." He glanced at his wristwatch. "I can call you if you want to go home?"

Honor shook her head. "We're staying, right, Mom?"

She nodded. "Nick?"

Nick was still staring at the doors they'd wheeled Matt through. "We can stay."

"Want to see Jack?" Graham asked.

"Jack?" Felicity frowned. "He's here? Matt said they were leaving him home with a babysitter." This wasn't a place for a baby. Especially now. Her heart ached for the little boy. For Amber. And for Matt.

Graham stared at her. "Jack…he was in the car, too."

Felicity stared at Graham, sinking further into despair. "He was?"

"Oh my God." Honor covered her mouth, bursting into tears then. "Is Amber with him? Poor little guy's got to be freaking out."

Graham looked at her but didn't say a word.

"Is he hurt?" Felicity asked.

"He's in a coma—sustained some head trauma," Graham said. "His right femur is broken and there's a lot of scrapes and bruises. But children are amazingly resilient."

"Amber can sit with him." Nick shoved his hands into his pockets, shooting a look at Honor.

"No, she can't." Felicity shook her head.

"Yes, she can," Nick argued. "He's her kid. Her problem. Not yours."

"Nick, he's your brother," Honor argued.

"No, he's not," Nick shot back.

"Nick." Felicity faced her son. "He is your half brother." She touched Nick's cheek. "And he needs us right now. Amber died in the crash." She pulled Honor close, trying to hug them both—but Nick stayed stiff. "That little boy has no one in the world except your dad. And us."

Nick stared up at the ceiling, shaking his head.

"I could use some coffee," Graham said. "Anyone else?"

"Yes, please, Graham. Thank you." Felicity looked at the man who'd once been one of her closest friends. "And thank you for being here."

"Jack's around the corner." Graham nodded. "Nick, walk with me?"

"Come on, Mom." Honor held her hand out. On her daughter's face she saw everything that was churning inside of her. Fear, determination, sadness, and the need to *do something* so the horror of the night wouldn't bring her to her knees.

• • •

Graham glanced at his daughter, Diana, sitting in the corner of the hospital cafeteria. The thick black eye makeup she wore ran in tracks down her cheeks, her chin rested on her knees, and her ear-buds were—as always—plugged in. She was mad at him—as always. This time, he'd been the asshole who was stopping her from having a life. Meaning he wasn't letting her drive five hours away with a bunch of kids he didn't know to listen to a band called Broken Souls.

She saw him, saw Nick, and wiped her cheeks. His first instinct was to go to her, to hug her, to comfort her. But she'd already told him what he could do with his instincts. *Nothing like hearing your daughter tell you to screw off to warm the cockles of your heart.*

"Coffee?" he asked Nick.

Nick shook his head, pacing back and forth while Graham fed coins into the coffee machine.

"Soda?" he asked.

Nick shook his head again, rolling his shoulders.

"Candy bar?"

Nick stopped, leveling him with a hard look. "I'm good."

He doubted that. And while the boy had every right to be upset, something told Graham it went deeper. Before his wife had died, before Matt had deserted his family, before his and Matt's practice had disintegrated, he'd known Nick well. Holidays, birthdays, summer cookouts, vacations—the Murphys and Buchanans had been close. And then life had taken a rapid nosedive, his world splintering into pieces so small there was nothing recognizable left. He glanced at Diana again, her too-skinny frame turned away from them as she held on to this latest grief with every fiber of her being.

She believed she was a 'magnet for bad-luck'. From her grandparents to her pets to her mother, Diana's life did appear to be one long strand of miserable pearls. And now, tonight.

She didn't care about Matt Buchanan. In fact, she thought the "cheating sack of shit deserved what he got." Di was very good at lashing out when she was angry—using words like a machine gun. But his daughter's temper fit tonight had nothing to do with Matt and everything to do with Graham's attempt at parenting. According to her, he was intentionally trying to sabotage her relationship with some boy who was also going to the concert. Until she'd thrown that in his face, he hadn't even known the kid existed. But once he had, he'd dragged her to the hospital with him so she couldn't sneak out and go anyway. He had enough to worry about without her pulling a disappearing act.

Nick paced in front of him, his sigh of frustration so heavy and sharp, Graham could almost feel it. He didn't know what to say. Diana had taught him he wasn't very good at talking. Or listening. But she was a teenage girl. And teenage boys were an altogether different sort of animal. "Ready?" he asked, holding Felicity's coffee in one hand, his in the other.

Nick looked at him, rolling his shoulders again. Clearly, he was not ready.

"You're going to be a junior next year?" Graham asked, sipping on his coffee.

Nick nodded.

"Still playing football?"

"Sucking at it, but yeah."

Graham smiled, assessing the boy. He was tall, over six feet, and spare—more long-distance runner than linebacker. Imagining Nick buried beneath kids bigger and bulkier made Graham wince mentally. "I doubt that," he said.

Nick shot him a look. "Come to a game next fall.

See for yourself."

"Okay," Graham agreed.

Nick glanced around the room. "That Diana?"

Graham nodded.

"She okay?"

Graham shrugged. "She's having a rough night." Considering what Nick was facing, his daughter's hysterics and drama over not getting her way were embarrassing. She was upset over a concert. Nick was upset over the possible death of his father.

Nick's laugh was hard, forced, and angry. "Seems to be going around."

"She's going to be at Pecan Valley High School this fall." She'd been kicked out of St. Thomas Catholic school for smoking in the bathroom. Pot. Because smoking cigarettes wasn't edgy enough.

"Freshman?"

"Sophomore," he murmured, staring at his daughter.

"I always thought she was way younger than me," Nick said. "Maybe I will get a soda."

Graham fed some change into the soda machine.

"She's into the whole goth-grunge thing, huh?" Nick asked. "That's new."

Graham didn't argue. It was new for *Nick*. But Diana had been wearing smudged eyeshadow, poking holes in her lip, and listening to music that sounded like animals being disemboweled for almost two years now. "I'm hoping it's a phase."

Nick took the soda. "Thanks."

Graham smiled. "I should get this coffee to your mom. You don't have to come—"

"I do," Nick argued. "She's acting all strong, but

I know she's not. Dad's made a career out of pulverizing her heart into mush for a while now."

Personally, Graham agreed 100 percent. But Matt Buchanan was fighting for his life right now, so it didn't seem like the right time to say as much. "Here." He handed the extra cup of coffee to the boy.

Nick peered into the cup. "She likes cream."

Graham glanced around the stark, institutional cafeteria. The serving line was closed, no sign of cream or sugar packets to be found. "Well, that sucks."

"She'll probably drink it," Nick said.

Graham glanced at Diana again, but she stayed as she was, facing away from him, so he followed Nick from the cafeteria and back to the ER to be informed that Jack had been moved to the ICU.

"He's stabilized," Graham explained, pressing the third-floor button on the elevator. "That's good."

"Why is he in a coma?" Nick stared at the cup of coffee.

"They were going at least sixty miles an hour. Then they weren't. The human brain isn't meant to withstand that sort of impact. Sometimes it shuts down the body so it can heal." Graham knew it was a piss-poor clinical explanation, but Nick seemed to accept what he said.

"Will he wake up?" Nick's voice was tight, thick.

"I don't know." He wished he had answers. He wished he could erase this whole nightmare for Nick and Honor. He knew what losing a parent could do to a kid—he saw it regularly. The only difference was neither Nick nor Honor could blame Felicity for Matt's death. Unlike his own daughter.

The elevator doors opened, and he asked for directions to Jack's room. The closer they got, the more Nick's posture stiffened like he was preparing for battle.

Honor was sitting in a chair, staring blindly at the muted television set.

"Where's Mom?" Nick asked.

"She went to the bathroom," Honor said. "Is that for me?" she asked, reaching for the soda.

"Nope," Nick argued.

"Share?" she asked.

Nick sighed, offering her the bottle.

Felicity came in, her face scrubbed free of makeup and her long hair pulled back into a ponytail. She looked young. And like she'd been crying.

"Coffee?" she asked, taking the cup from Nick with a smile. "Perfect." She sipped the black coffee, her face revealing nothing. She walked to the head of the bed and stared down at the toddler. "He looks so much like you, Nick. It's…amazing." She smiled at them. "You were never this still, of course. Even when you were sleeping, you'd toss and turn and make noise." She sipped her coffee again, wrapping one arm around her waist. "It's cold in here, isn't it? Do you think he's cold?"

Honor leaned forward, resting her hand on Jack's arm. "He feels okay, Mom."

Graham couldn't begin to imagine what Felicity was thinking or feeling. He'd lost his wife, Julia, but they'd all known it was coming. There had been no loose ends or messes to clean up. He lost her knowing she loved him, that she knew he loved her. It hurt so much that he'd wanted to die for a while, but from missing her—not from things left unsaid.

This was nothing like that.

Matt had destroyed his family, willfully putting them all through hell. And now he would leave them with a reminder of that.

Felicity stood, all five feet, two inches of her, with no sign of buckling. She'd gone to the bathroom, had her cry, and pulled herself back together. He didn't remember much about the weeks leading up to Julia's passing, but he was certain he hadn't handled it half so well.

"Sorry, no cream." He nodded at her coffee.

She stared into the cup. "I didn't even notice." Her blue eyes met his, held. "Thank you, Graham."

There were tears in her eyes. And damn but he wanted to hug her then, to tell her they'd survive this, that things would go on, even with a hole in the heart.

"Dad?"

Graham turned to find his daughter peeking in the door. "Hey, Diana, you okay?"

She pushed off the door, her smudged gaze sweeping the room. "Yeah. I guess. Hi, Mrs. Buchanan. Hi, Nick. Honor. Guess tonight is totally sucking for you guys. I-I'm sorry."

Felicity was hugging his daughter before he realized she'd moved. "Thanks, Di. 'Sucking' is exactly the right word."

Graham saw the look on his daughter's face, saw

the yearning when Felicity drew her close. So why did she keep him at arm's length? And why wouldn't she let him call her Di anymore? It didn't matter. He wanted her to have affection, even if he couldn't be the one to give it to her.

"Can I...I don't know...do anything?" Diana glanced at Nick, then Honor.

"We're watching a marathon jewelry sale on the Spanish channel," Honor said. "Come on in."

Diana brushed past him, barely acknowledging his presence now that she'd been welcomed in. "Heard anything?" Diana asked, resting her hands on the footboard of Jack's hospital bed.

"No, just waiting," Honor said, scooching over in the hospital chair. "Wanna sit?"

"You graduated tonight, didn't you? You look great. I like your hair," Diana said, sitting close to Honor. "Man, that's got to be great. Getting out of here. Freedom. All that."

"Yeah." Honor's smile was tight, her gaze wandering to her mother and then to Jack. "Sort of forgot."

"Right. Yeah. Crap. Well... The accident is all over the news, you know? I don't understand why they don't put more lights out there on that road." Diana sniffed, her attention on Jack. "Poor little guy."

Graham agreed. The strip of road curved sharply along the edge of a hill, with minimal visibility. This wasn't the first fatal accident on that stretch of road, and it probably wouldn't be the last.

"Do you know what happened? I mean, what's the news saying?" Honor asked, shooting him a nervous glance.

"Just that they swerv

"They? You mean D

Nick snorted. "Carel

"Nick." Felicity's to

isn't the time."

"No?" Nick's voice

tal, Mom. On Honor's

swerved into oncoming traffic?

"Nick, please." Felicity's tone was soft, soothing. "Come on, hon. Everyone is tense."

Diana was staring at Nick. "I get that you're upset, and you totally have every right to be pissed, but—"

"You do?" Nick nodded. "You get it?"

"Yeah. I. Do." Diana slid from the chair, her hands fisting at her sides. "I hate that this happened as much as you do."

That was exactly the wrong thing to say right now—even if she meant well. "Diana," Graham put in. "Let's not make tonight harder than it already is." Which was also the wrong thing to say—so, apparently, she got it from him. But the words were out, and the damage was done.

"I didn't do anything." Diana's face turned bright red as she held her hands up. "How am I going to make it harder? How about I make it easier and leave?" And she did.

Graham ran a hand over his face, shaking his head. "I'm sorry." He sucked in a deep breath. "She's sort of wound up."

"You don't need to apologize." Felicity was frowning at her son. "She meant well."

taring up at the ceiling.

od, frowning at her brother. "Nickie,
ne only ones having a bad night, you
she sighed, brushing past her brother. "I'll
k to her. Just…" She paused. "Find me if
e's news on Dad?"

"You don't need to go, Honor." Graham smiled.
"She's my family. You stay here with yours." He
nodded at Felicity and went off in search of his
daughter.

. . .

Honor stared at her phone. Message after message
kept popping up. Everyone in Pecan Valley knew
her dad had been in an accident—and they all
wanted details. Even Mr. Fabulous himself, Owen
Nelson, had called. She'd ignored his call, as always,
but he'd left a voice message. Not that she'd
listened to it—or any of the voice messages for that
matter. Somehow, that would make all this…*real*.

Still, the texts kept coming in. Her fingers hovered over her screen, frozen. What to say?

My dad's in surgery.

My dad's baby mama is dead.

My baby brother's in a coma.

She looked at baby Jack, sound asleep. Not
sleeping. The poor thing was in a coma. A *coma*.
The last time she'd seen him—the only time she'd
ever seen him in person—had been his baptism.
Nick refused to go, so she'd gone alone. Alone-
alone. Dad's friends weren't Dad's friends anymore,
for the most part. Not the ones Honor knew,

anyway. Which was weird
Mom's friends, either. Whe
lo... thing else lost in the di...
... had been an adorabl...
felt exactly ... Before the d...
ready to go home... way as ...

And then there'd be... A... ...fully beautiful, model-in-a-bikini gorge... and mesmerizing.
She'd tried to include Honor, sort of. But it was
clear she was having a hard enough time with the
whole mom thing with Jack. Figuring out where
Honor fit hadn't been a top priority.

That was the only time they'd had together. Last
Christmas, their Christmas with Dad, things had
"come up," and she and Nick had stayed with Mom.

And now, there wasn't time to get to know
Amber.

She swallowed some of the soda she and Nick
were sharing. It was sweet, too sweet, making the
back of her jaw tingle.

"I thought we were sharing," Nick said, grabbing
the bottle.

She shrugged, smiling at him. She held up her
phone, showing him the growing list of notifications.
He nodded.

"You, too?"

"Yep." He sighed, sitting on the arm of the chair.

"Sort of nice," she said.

"Sort of annoying," he returned, finishing off the
soda.

"It's nice." Her mom smiled, smoothing the
blankets over Jack. "We're lucky to have people

out us."

watched the sure movements of
knowing just how calming her to... Not
Poor Jack. He didn't have a mo... able. And
having her mom around would b throat, making
Dad... A hard knot lodged
her breath unsteady.

Dad would be okay. He had to be okay.

"You want another soda?" Nick asked, interrupting her thoughts.

She shook her head, standing and stretching. A quick glance at the muted television told her the way-too-smiley saleslady was still selling jewelry. Sitting here worrying wasn't going to do any good. "Maybe a walk?"

"You two go." Their mom nodded. "Stretch your legs."

Nick didn't argue when she hooked arms with him and led him down the hall. He didn't say anything. Because he was just as freaked out as she was. He'd never admit he was worrying about Dad. But she knew. Nick said he hated Dad, and maybe he did. But part of him still hoped their dad would come home and somehow everything would be okay again.

"You gonna keep it together?" she asked softly.

"What, pretend Dad isn't an asshole because he had an accident? Or be cool with pretending his kid is somehow worth my time when I was never worth his?" Nick stopped, staring down at her. "Can I say no? Because I'd like to say no. And maybe, 'screw you, Dad.'" His eyes glistened, but then he tore his gaze from hers and stared at the hers. Small. Motionless.

She knew nothing about Jack.

Did he have a middle name? A favorite toy? Or blanket? Food allergies? What words did he know? What sort of temperament did he have? He was probably walking. If he was anything like his siblings, he was running by now. Her gaze traveled over the thick white plaster cast that started right beneath his breast bone.

Something about how still he was, how pale, terrified her.

"Your little fingers are cold." She rubbed his hand between both of hers and scooted closer, smoothing the blankets over him. "How about we get you some more blankets? Sound good?" She pressed the nurse's button, pulling her vibrating phone from her pocket as she did so.

Her mother—known to everyone simply as Mimi—and Matt's most devoted hate-fan. Felicity glanced at Jack, the clock on the wall, and the picture of her smiling parents on her phone in a matter of seconds.

The nurse's voice came through the speaker. "Yes?"

"Can we get some more blankets, please?" she asked.

"Sure." The static clicked off.

Felicity stared at the phone. She might as well answer. If she didn't, the calls would just keep coming. And, it would be nice to have them here— with her and the kids.

"Hi, Mom," she answered.

"So, how was it?" Her mother was all singsong

enthusiasm. As much as her parents had wanted to go to Honor's graduation, Matt tended to bring out the worst in her mother. They'd decided to celebrate with her later—so there was no chance of ruining her graduation day.

The irony wasn't lost. "It was lovely. Honor looked gorgeous, lots of smiles and—"

"What's wrong?" her mother's voice sharpened. "And don't try to hide it from me, Filly. Something's wrong, I can hear it in your voice... Shush, Herb, I can tell when our daughter's upset."

Felicity smiled, imagining her father attempting to pacify her mother. "Well, a lot, actually. Nick and Honor and I are fine. But Matt was in an accident. We're at the hospital."

"Turn the car around, Herb. Head to the hospital." She paused. "No, no, the kids are all fine. But they need us."

"Thank you, Mom." Felicity's relief was instantaneous.

"Have you eaten?" her mother asked.

"I can't remember." Had the kids eaten? Tonight had been such a whirlwind of activity, the pregraduation chaos, the ceremony, this...

"Well, we'll take care of it when we get there. Have you heard from Charity? She was flying in tonight. Never mind, we'll call the house and see if she's here yet. Don't you worry about a thing." There was another pause. "Dad says to stay positive. We love you, Filly."

In all the chaos, she'd forgotten about Charity. Her sister had so wanted to be here for Honor's graduation. But a storm in Chicago had grounded her flight, and Felicity hadn't checked in to see where she was or when she might arrive.

"Love you, too." Felicity hung up, standing when the nurse carried in a few blankets. "Thank you. His little hand feels so cold."

"This one is fresh from the warmer." The nurse handed her the top blanket first.

It was toasty and soft, exactly what a toddler would want to cuddle up under. She covered Jack, tucking the fabric close.

"Anything else?" the nurse asked.

"I honestly don't know. I feel so…useless." She shook her head. "Is there something I can do?"

The nurse smiled. "Talk to him. Use his name. Some studies say patients can hear us. I'm sure he'd like that." She placed the rest of the blankets on the foot of the bed and left.

Does it work if the patient has no idea who is talking to them? Jack had never met her. He wouldn't know who she was. Even if she had come up in conversation, he was too young to remember or care.

Realistically, Matt and Amber wouldn't have mentioned her. Matt had been so consumed with Amber that everything before her sort of faded away, including his other kids. Their recitals and games, birthday parties and special events were no longer noteworthy to Matt. She'd tried to plead their case, remind him that Nick and Honor were great young people — well-liked, smart, respectful, hardworking… That they needed their father.

She drew in a deep breath, closed her eyes, and shook out her arms and hands.

Stop. Those wounds weren't healed enough to start picking at them.

Besides, there was no point going over it again. No point in getting herself worked up. Jack was what mattered right now. She couldn't stand seeing anyone hurting, especially a baby who had done nothing to anyone.

"Your daddy will fight for you, Jack. He loves you so much…" Her voice broke. Felicity sucked in a deep breath, choking on a mix of anger and desperate sadness. Matt owed it to Jack—to all of them—to be strong. To stay.

"In no time he'll be right here, talking to you and holding you close." More than anything, Jack needed someone to know he existed, someone to hold him and assure him that life was a wonderful adventure he'd share with people who loved him.

Matt was that someone.

"But, since he can't be here right now, I will be. Okay?" What choice did she have? When Matt was better, she'd walk away. Her kids, her family, didn't need any more emotional conflict.

"I'm Felicity, Jack," she murmured, stroking the silky-soft golden curls at his temple. "I'm…I'm a… friend of your daddy's." She wiped blindly at the tears she didn't know had started. "I'll stay right here with you, don't you worry." She cradled his little hand in hers, squeezing gently—hoping he felt it. The urge to hold him close, to rock him, washed over her. But he was too fragile for that now. That stark white cast was a vivid reminder of that fact. "I'm right here."

"Felicity?" Graham stood in the doorway, a cup

of coffee in each hand.

"Oh, hey." Out of instinct, she wiped her face, stiffened her spine, and assumed as carefree an expression as possible. *Positive thoughts, right?* It's not like crying would do any good.

But something made Graham set the two coffee cups on the bed table and pull Felicity up and into an awkward hug.

Except it wasn't all that awkward. It was warm. Strong yet gentle. It offered comfort, something she desperately needed. Something she didn't want to admit she needed. She clung to it—to Graham. His arms tightened just enough for her to lean on him. So, she did, burying her face in his shirtfront and breathing deep. He held her up until the sting of tears and crush of panic had receded.

The instant she stepped back—cold, hard reality was waiting.

"Sorry," she murmured, taking the coffee cup he offered her. Damn her shaking hands.

"Don't be." His brown gaze held only sympathy. "You don't have to be strong for me."

He was trying to be kind. But being strong was her only option. Though, tonight was definitely testing her. As tempting as it was to fall apart and let him hold her for a while longer, she couldn't. She was the rock, Miss Calm, the glue, the rational one. One slip might send her crashing to the floor, and she wasn't sure she could get back up again. Instead, she sipped the coffee, too hot to taste. "Diana okay? Nick can be a little…challenging."

"He's having a hell of a night. You all are." His gaze searched hers before shifting to his coffee.

"Diana is the queen of challenging. And drama. I have to remind myself how much she's been through for someone so young. But there are times when I don't know how to *handle* her."

Felicity heard the bone-weary defeat in his voice. Graham Murphy had always been a good guy. When their families were young and their friendship was solid, he'd been one of those super hands-on dads. And Diana had adored her daddy.

Clearly, something had changed.

When Matt left and Graham's sweet wife entered hospice care, the world had come apart. Piecing it back together was, for all of them, an ongoing process. "Parenting is exhausting, isn't it? Parenting teens takes it to a higher level, I think. I don't remember being a difficult teen. I'm sure I was. Aren't all teens? It's a requirement, isn't it?"

Graham smiled at her. "Somehow, I don't see you ever being difficult."

"My parents might disagree." But most of their trying teen stories were focused on her wild little sister, Charity, and her adrenaline-seeking brother, Zach. Felicity had never been a risk-taker or a rule breaker. And she'd never felt like she was missing out, not really. "Where is Diana?"

"She's sleeping over at a friend's house. She's not a fan of hospitals, in general."

Why would she be? She'd spent so much time here when her mother was sick. If she was in Di's shoes, she'd do whatever she could to avoid being here.

Graham studied Jack, crossing the room to get a closer look at the toddler. He scanned the monitors.

"His vitals are good. That's something. Lots of wait and see in his future."

The future. Right now, that was measured in minute-by-minute increments. She sipped more coffee, wishing she could absorb its heat through osmosis.

"Nick and Honor go home?" he asked.

"Just a walk. They want to stay, of course." She moved to the other side of Jack's bed, watching his little chest rise and fall slowly. "I can't seem to leave the room. He's too little to wake up alone. And he looks so much like my babies…" Could she do this? If…if Matt didn't pull through… No. Not touching that. She changed gears quickly. "I know with work and Diana, you need sleep. If you need to go, you can."

Graham didn't say anything, so she looked at him. He was studying Jack. "I have a patient upstairs who will probably deliver tonight." He ran a hand along the back of his neck. "I checked in after Diana left. Mom and Dad are fired up and ready, but first babies like to keep everyone guessing."

Upstairs, a baby was being born. Someone's birthday. A new family, full of hope and love and dreams. Life went on. It was an oddly stabilizing realization. Felicity smiled. "That's really wonderful news."

Graham looked at her then, a slow smile creasing the corners of his brown eyes. He'd always had a nice grin. That hadn't changed.

She pulled one of the two chairs closer to Jack's bed and sat. "We could all use some good news."

"Mrs. Buchanan? I'm Dr. Sayeed." Dr Sayeed

stepped inside Jack's room. "Graham." He glanced at Jack.

"Sam." Graham's tone was stiff, drawing her full attention.

"I was Matt's surgeon." Dr. Sayeed spoke calmly. And it rattled her nerves. "We knew there were some internal injuries, but they were more extensive than anticipated."

Graham's jaw muscle flexed, and his brown eyes locked with hers.

Matt had known. It took effort to breathe. To stand.

Dr. Sayeed looked between her and Graham, prompting Graham to move to her side before he went on. "I'm afraid I have bad news…"

. . .

Charity Otto stood in the doorway of her childhood home, confused by the lack of people, music, and partying. Yes, Pecan Valley wasn't a social mecca, but it was barely eleven. And it was Honor's big night — worthy of celebrating. Charity had plans to make the night unforgettable. These plans included the setting off of illegal fireworks, waking the neighbors with obnoxious party blowers and air horns, and — if her parents and sister didn't freak out too much — providing the graduates bottles of celebratory champagne.

"Hello?" she called out. "Family of mine?"

She tugged her large wheeled suitcase into the foyer, put her brown paper bag of contraband on the floor, and closed the front door behind her.

"Felicity?" she yelled, flipping on the lights.

The door hadn't been locked, so someone had to be home.

Or not.

Pecan Valley meant community watch groups and nosy neighbors. Living in one of the biggest, oldest houses in town and being part of a family that had helped settle this region of the Texas Hill Country meant their family was more closely monitored. It was one of the reasons Charity had left town the day after her high school graduation. She wasn't going to live under a microscope. She was going to live.

"Nick? Honor?" She flipped on more lights. "Wowsers, Filly, good job." She stood, appreciating the remodeled kitchen.

Dad would never have allowed the changes made to his family home. But it wasn't his home anymore. After Felicity's divorce, Mom had convinced him that Felicity and the kids needed a place to start over. The fact that she'd never been a fan of the big dark house might have helped as well. Once Mom had found the perfect fishing cabin, perched right along the lake, Dad had handed over the keys without blinking an eye.

And Felicity had worked her magic, renovating the hundred-plus-year-old home from the roof to the floors. Lighter, airier, less cluttered…it looked great—a real, livable showplace. The family pictures over the thick wooden mantle were mostly the same, with the addition of Nick and Honor's most recent school pictures.

Charity lingered, stunned by how grown-up they

both looked.

"Oh, Felicity, you're gonna have more heartache over him," she murmured, picking up her nephew's picture. He looked just like her brother-in-law at fifteen. Matt had been around before Charity was in her first training bra or thinking of boys as anything other than a pain in the butt. A view Matt had only reinforced the last few years. It'd been hard watching her sister's heart get shredded. And sad to lose a man she'd considered her brother. "Let's hope you only *look* like your dad."

She moved on to Honor—she had high hopes for Honor. The girl was a solid mix of old soul and childlike wonder, kind and smart-as-a-whip. Gone were the kooky glasses and braces. Now she was a gorgeous young woman who'd be attending college on a full academic scholarship, far away from the confines of Pecan Valley.

"Hello?" she yelled, jumping when Praline and Pecan came thundering down the stairs. The golden-striped cats wound between her legs, purring ferociously. "Hi, guys. Where are the human inhabitants?"

She shrugged out of her jacket, kicked off her heels, and flopped onto the couch—the early morning flight and hours of waiting in the airport catching up with her. "Looks like it's just us girls." Praline and Pecan immediately crawled into her lap, kneading and headbutting her until she had one tucked under each arm. She sighed, resting her head on the back of the couch.

Might as well enjoy the quiet. Once the family arrived, quiet would vanish and the questions would begin. How was work? Where had she been last? Had she met any interesting people? And, most importantly, how long was she staying in Pecan Valley?

"I'm not going anywhere," she murmured, continuing to give the cats a solid rubdown. "If Filly's okay with it, I'll be rooming here with you guys." The time for living out of her hard-sided suitcase had come to an end. No more stamps in her passport. No more travel or tours or adventures. "I'm a lady of leisure now, guys. Exploring all my options." At least, that was the answer she planned on giving when people asked.

The truth? That might not go over so well. Her hands strayed to her stomach. She wouldn't be able to hide her baby bump for much longer—which meant she needed to come to terms with the whole pregnancy thing and stop thinking about her hometown as a place to escape from. Her family was here, and since she had no idea how to raise a kid or be a responsible adult, she was going to need them.

"Who wants ice cream?" she asked the cats. "I could go for some pecan praline." She laughed as two sets of identical copper eyes stared up at her. "Or plain old vanilla."

She stood, pulled her phone from her pocket, and headed into the kitchen. Two messages from her mother. Nothing from Felicity. She frowned, pressed play on her mother's first voicemail, and opened the freezer.

"Jackpot," she said, pulling the tub of neapolitan from the shelf.

"Hi, Charity, it's your mother." Her mother's voice filled the kitchen.

"Hi, Mom. I know it's you." She smiled as Pecan jumped onto the counter.

"Felicity told me your flight was delayed, so I thought I'd check and see if you needed your father to come and get you. How late will you be? We're having clear skies here. Can't wait to see you. Oh, and you'll never guess who asked about you. Braden Martinez." Charity spooned a large bite of ice cream into her mouth as her mother drew in a deep breath. "Braden, you know, the one you went to homecoming with. He looked so very pleased to hear you were staying for a short visit…"

"Maybe not so short," Charity muttered, spooning in another delicious mouthful.

Pecan mewed pathetically so Charity put a dab of ice cream into a bowl and offered it to the cat. Praline stayed by her feet, wailing loudly.

"Okay, okay," Charity said. "Guess you have the better manners, don't you? No cats on the counter." She gave Praline her own bowl.

"…so, let us know. And be careful, please. There was a story about a young woman being abducted from an airport. She traveled for her job, too, and no one realized she was missing for weeks because…"

Charity rolled her eyes. "I'm here, Mom. Where are *you*?"

The message ended.

"It's so quiet," she said to the cats. "My ears are ringing. Are yours?" She pressed play on the next voicemail.

"Hi, Charity, it's your mother. You're probably on the airplane now, but please call when you land. There's been an…incident. We're all at the hospital.

Now's not the time for details. Oh… Please call me. Love you, Charity. So so much." And then the message ended.

Charity stopped eating ice cream. Her mother was never—ever—short-winded. So that was the first red flag. The second, her mother lived for spilling details. Not a one. But the last flag, the big one: they were *all* at the hospital. Something bad had happened.

In five minutes, she was on the road to the hospital, puzzling over possibilities.

It wouldn't be Dad. Mom wouldn't have been able to call her if it were—it would have been Felicity on the phone.

Could it be Grams? Was her great-grandmother back from her widows' group cruise down the Rhine? Again, Mom seemed too calm for that to be the case.

So, who?

She didn't want to think about the kids. But it was graduation night. Accidents happened.

I'm such an idiot. She thought about the bottle of champagne sitting on the floor in the brown paper bag. She was trying to be the cool aunt. *An idiot.*

The roads were quiet. No traffic. She sat at the red light, her fingers tapping in irritation. Did she really have to sit here? No one was coming. No one. At all.

She put her foot on the accelerator and rolled through the intersection.

Red and blue lights came to life, the siren scaring her so much that she jerked her rental car and bounced off the curb.

"Dammit!" She hung her head, waiting. And still, the knock on her driver's window made her jump.

She rolled down the window.

"Evening," the officer said. "In a hurry?"

She nodded, trying to sound calm. "I'm headed to the hospital."

"Emergency?" he asked.

She nodded, glancing up at the man shining a flashlight on her. Beyond a large, dark shape and a glare in her eyes, she couldn't see much. "According to my mom, yes. I just flew in from Chicago."

"Wait. Charity? Charity Otto?"

She held her hand up, trying to see. "Yes?"

"Well, hell, Charity, let's get you to the hospital."

CHAPTER THREE

Felicity stared straight ahead, her anxiety rising faster than the elevator they were riding.

"Is this weird for you?" Charity asked, rolling the collapsible storage cart full of recyclable shopping bags back and forth. When they'd been growing up, Felicity had always known when Charity was nervous or upset by how much she fidgeted. Since she'd offered to come with Felicity to Matt and Amber's apartment, her sister had been on full-fidget mode. Spinning her bangled bracelets, tapping her fingers on her thighs, brushing through her long strawberry-blond curls with her fingers. Constant movement. It was oddly comforting.

"I'm guessing it's really weird," Charity added.

"Yep," she agreed. Weird didn't begin to describe it. This was...enemy territory. He'd left her for this.

Matt. Matt who was gone forever.

She had yet to come to terms with what, exactly, that meant. But she'd had no choice about coming here. Thinking about Jack waking up to a stark, empty hospital room full of hovering strangers with nothing familiar to soothe his fears was all she needed to go through with it. Surely Jack had some special blanket or toy in his crib he'd want when he finally opened his eyes.

The Porsche key fob was heavy in her hands.

Not from the keys but from the size of the keychain. It had been Amber's—Amber's shiny convertible and Amber's keys. Keys to a shiny convertible that now belonged to her daughter.

For now, she'd use the keys to enter Amber's apartment. Amber and Matt's apartment. Where they were going. Now.

"This sucks," Charity whispered.

"It does. All of this." She glanced at her sister. "I'm really glad you're here."

"Of course." Her mischievous grin warned Felicity her sister was up to no good. "Did you really think I'd miss an opportunity to see *her* stuff? I mean, come on, she was a husband-stealing bitch, but her wardrobe was always on point."

Charity had easily revealed her initial obsessive rage over Matt's desertion. He'd been a big part of her life, too, so she'd unabashedly stalked Matt and his other woman on social media for a while.

Apparently, Amber posted selfies and happy family pictures daily, adding little digs here and there about landing her doctor, how expensive her upcoming wedding was going to be, and her always impressive record-breaking pharmaceutical sales.

"You know you can't have any of her clothes." Felicity glanced at her sister. "Right?"

"Felicity, come on. I won't keep them *all*." She batted her eyes. "Honor could have the rest. She'd be the best-dressed freshman on campus."

Felicity rolled her eyes. "No." Selfish or not, the idea of bringing Amber's things into her home was more than she could handle right now. Besides, she wasn't here for clothes or, much to Charity's disappointment, reconnaissance. This was about Jack. With any luck, they'd be in and out before her anxiety got the best of her—or Charity managed to sneak out part of Amber's wardrobe.

"At least think about it," she pleaded.

She didn't say a word. Arguing with her sister never ended well for her.

"I'll take the silence as a maybe." Charity sighed. "Has anyone been located? Amber's family, I mean. Anyone at all?"

"No one." Felicity swallowed. "Matt's friend Robert Klein, Rob the lawyer, is looking into it."

"Rob Klein? The one Mom slips into conversation whenever possible? Single. Handsome. Ready to settle down. She's not even trying to be subtle." Charity shook her head. "Wait, Rob was white-teeth guy? Matt's golfing buddy? I remember the teeth."

"Yes." Felicity smiled. "About the golfing. I don't remember the teeth."

"How is that possible?" Charity asked. "Other than that, he was sorta cute. Too bad he's a lawyer."

Felicity wasn't sure what to make of that, so she picked up the original thread of conversation. "Anyway, he's trying to track down anyone connected with Amber. With the reading of the will coming up, it's important to have Matt's…Jack's family present."

The elevator doors opened, and Charity stepped out, pulling the cart behind her. But Felicity froze. There was nothing right about this. Nothing.

"We're in and out," Charity said, holding out her hand. "You can do this, sis."

Felicity stared at her sister. "I can." But it was more a question than anything else.

Charity nodded. "Totally."

Felicity blew out a deep breath, took her sister's hands, and let Charity pull her down the hall to the door that read 503. She froze again, staring at the gilded numbers on the door.

"Let me." Charity pried the keys from her fingers, unlocked the door, and pushed it open. "I'll go first." She paused. "If you want, I can get everything, Filly—"

"No." Enough. It was just a room, an empty space. She had to stop letting the past affect her. Especially now that everything was different. "This is ridiculous. I'm fine." Still, it was hard to walk over the threshold.

"Holy shit." Charity was already hurrying across the completely white living room to stare out the floor-to-ceiling windows. "Talk about a view."

Felicity was too busy wondering how they managed to keep everything white with a toddler running around. There were no toys, no babyproofing, no books—no sign that a toddler lived here. It was gorgeous, in a stark *Architectural Digest* sort of way. High ceilings. Open concept. A massive abstract painting over a fireplace—a white marble fireplace. "It's very *white*," she murmured. And cold.

Charity laughed. "It's sophisticated, Filly."

Felicity shrugged and headed into the kitchen. The kitchen was the heart of her home—the place they all congregated on stools and around her beloved wooden farm table. This was all clean lines and chrome. It looked pokey.

She pulled the cart behind her, opening cabinets and drawers, pulling out all the child-size utensils, bowls, sippy cups, bottles, and bibs she could find, filling one grocery bag to the top. The refrigerator was empty, minus a few jars of organic baby food and some almond milk. Was the almond milk for Jack? Did he have digestive issues? Matt didn't. That left Jack. Or Amber.

"Charity," she called out. "We need to find Jack's vaccination records. And any medical stuff— his pediatrician's name would be even better." The steel front of the refrigerator was blank, no magnets, no notes, nothing. "His birth certificate. All that stuff."

"Maybe in her office?" Charity called back. "Looks like *she* worked from home a lot. I'll see what I can find."

"Thank you." She already felt like she was trespassing. Digging through Amber's things, learning about Amber and Matt's life—thank God Charity was here. She flipped off the kitchen lights and tugged the wagon down the hall. The exterior wall was mostly windows, giving her a clear view of the outside world. A world she didn't belong in. She hurried along, eager to find the nursery.

Considering how very white everything was, the grouping of photos on the interior wall stopped her. Amber and Matt on some snow-covered mountain somewhere. They'd gone to Paris and Italy… A picture of Amber pregnant. And one of the three of them. She knew Matt's smiles like the back of her hand. These were real smiles. He'd been happy in this new, whitewashed world.

It hurt like hell. It shouldn't matter that he'd worn that same happy smile for her. But, dammit, it did. There had been so many smiles and special moments and fun travels and real-life struggles they'd made it through together. Seventeen years, a substantial length of time, and there wasn't a shred of evidence here that those years had existed. They'd been erased, leaving his past as blank as these walls. How empty that would feel to her. Whatever pain he'd caused her, their children deserved his presence in their lives. So she'd refused to take down family pictures or, as her mother pleaded, to physically cut him out of them. She couldn't pretend they'd invested that time, love, and energy into a life that never existed. It had, and she treasured those memories.

Holding on to the hurt and blame and anger now didn't make any sense. Whatever had happened between her and Matt was done. She wanted to let go. She needed to—so she could move on.

"I found a box with Jack's name on it. Amber must've had OCD; you should see her office. Upside, she was super organized." Charity peeked out of the room and saw her staring at the pictures. She joined her. "Ugh. Filly, don't. Do you honestly think he was going to stay with her? Forever?"

"I don't know." Felicity took the picture of Jack and his parents off the wall. He'd want to know who his parents were. "I never thought that way, you know. Matt was gone. If he had come back— how would I have been able to live with him?

There'd always be this fear he'd leave again…" She took a picture of Matt and Amber and tucked the photos into another bag. "It doesn't matter now, anyway."

"You know what I think?" Charity asked, joining her in the hall.

Felicity glanced at her sister, smiling. "I'm not sure I want to know."

"You do." Charity nodded. "You really do."

"Go on." She could hardly wait.

"First, I know she had a boob job." Charity leaned forward for a better view of Amber's perky chest.

Felicity laughed. "Charity…"

"That was mean, so sue me. But it leads me to number two. Which is, you're gorgeous—natural boobs and all. I think it's time you started to act like the beautiful, amazing single woman you are. You need to put yourself out there." She stared her sister right in the eye. "Date."

"Sure." Felicity shook her head and walked down the hallway, peering into each room, searching for the nursery. "We're not having this conversation right now."

"I'm not going to let up on this." Charity trailed behind her. "I'm worried about you."

"And dating will make you not worry about me?" She groaned. "It's not like I've had to fight off all the interested men." Which was a relief. Just thinking about dating terrified her.

"You're not exactly giving off 'available' vibes."

"What does that even mean?" She shot her sister a look and pushed open a door on the right.

"Do you go anywhere without your kids? Other than PTA meetings or church or the family business? You know, places single men go?" Charity paused. "Wait, this is Pecan Valley we're talking about. Tell Widow Rainey. She'll have a screened list of interested, respectable men in no time."

Find a single man herself, or put her fate in Widow Rainey's hands? She wasn't sure which option was more terrifying. The last door opened into the nursery. "Finally." She blinked, eyeing the less-than-warm room. "What did Amber have against color?"

The nursery was just as white as the rest of the apartment. White curtains with a black-and-white-checked border hung in the window. A black-and-white-checked rug lay on the floor in front of the crib. Above the crib, Jack's name was stenciled in bold block print. A white rocking chair sat in the corner, complete with one black throw pillow. And his toys were stored in black-and-white bins on white painted shelves. Even his linens were white.

Except one. Felicity's lungs deflated at the sky-blue blanket shoved into the corner of the crib. Tiny gray sheep leaped over white fluffy clouds. She didn't have to touch the blanket to know how soft it was—it was exactly like the blanket Nick had when he was a baby. How many times had she and Matt scrambled to find the thing that soothed Nick when he was teething? Or washed it until it was threadbare, only to stitch the beloved blankie together for just a little bit longer. Retiring it had been a milestone for the whole family.

Seeing that blanket, knowing Matt would have

had to search for it, tugged at the thinning strands of her self-control. She gripped the blanket in her hands and stared at the oh-so-familiar print. This meant something—but she'd never know what.

Because Matt was gone. Not with Amber, not traveling or off living a new life…but gone. Forever. And the reality of that crashed into her. She'd hoped there was time. Not for her, but her kids. He'd come around again, miss them, want them back in his life—she'd believed that. And when that happened, he would have done whatever it took to make amends for the damage he'd caused. But now…

Matt's gone. The words pressed in on her, the piercing grief sudden and undeniable. It hurt to breathe. Gripping the crib, blinking back angry tears, swallowing down all the sadness and frustration she'd been battling since leaving Matt's hospital room was nearly impossible.

How could she ever make this better? For Nick and Honor and now Jack?

"Maybe Amber was color blind?" Charity asked.

Felicity jumped, staring at her sister.

"You okay?" Charity's gaze fell to the blanket she was holding to her chest. "Oh, man…" She sighed. "I remember that thing."

"It's not Nick's." She cleared her throat. "It's like his…but… Grab a bag and help me." She folded the blanket and tucked it into her bag.

Charity didn't argue, thank God. Maybe she could sense just how close Felicity was to falling apart. Her sister was more like their father in that department—avoiding uncomfortable conversations and honest, awkward emotional sharing at all costs.

The two worked in companionable silence for the majority of the morning. She put the toys from Jack's crib into a separate bag, hoping they had special meaning to the baby—enough to help him through the shock of waking up, anyway. Once his closet and drawers were packed up, they loaded his tubs of toys onto the cart and took apart the crib, using tie-downs to keep it together.

"You should have asked Dad to come." Charity helped her carry the crib down the hallway to the front door.

"If Dad had come, Mom would have come. And that would have made this unbearable."

"Do the kids know yet?" Charity's blue eyes met hers. "That Jack will be a part of your family until things get sorted out?"

She shook her head. "Sorted out" made things sound simple—easy—the opposite of the situation. But then, her sister knew nothing about Matt's request. If she told Charity, it would be out there, real and scary. Besides, saying it out loud was tempting fate, so sharing wasn't an option. Not yet. Not until she had no choice.

Hopefully, Rob-with-the-white-teeth would locate some of Amber's family. She hoped they'd be wonderful, big-hearted people who'd eagerly welcome Jack into their family, not just because that would make their lives infinitely less complicated but because that's what the little boy deserved.

"You don't think they'll figure it out? With this?" Charity patted the crib. "Or the mountain of baby crap we'll be toting into the house. Or the fricking awesome convertible that will be in your garage, which you are going to let me drive home tonight, since all of this won't fit in your car?"

Felicity didn't have it in her to argue. "I'm taking it minute by minute here, okay?" She pointed at a panda bear sitting in the corner. "Can you grab that?"

Charity lifted it. "Oh my God, do you know what this is?"

"A panda bear?"

"Smart-ass," Charity shook her head, turning the toy over. "It's one of those nanny-cam things." She opened the Velcro down the back. "It's got one of those SD cards in it. Right…here." She pulled the small computer card from the back of the toy. "Guess they didn't like their babysitter?"

"Or they wanted to see what they were missing while they were at work? Hopefully the answers we need will be in the box you found. If not, you can do your sleuthing and see what's on the nanny cam. It would be nice to hear from someone who knows the little guy." She stared at the panda, wondering what he'd seen and heard in this room—and why he was here to begin with.

• • •

"Dr. Murphy." Adelaide Keanon held the door wide in invitation. "I wanted to speak with you about Diana's progress."

Graham and Diana's counselor had very different ideas about what "progress" meant. But Adelaide was his only glimpse into his daughter's life, so Graham kept his opinions mostly to himself.

"She's under quite a bit of pressure." Adelaide sat in her overstuffed wicker rocking chair, leaving Graham the floral-covered loveseat.

"How so?" It was summertime. The only thing he'd asked of his daughter was a part-time job. And that was only to get her out of the house and away from the kids she'd been hanging around with. "We agreed leaving her unsupervised for long periods of time was a bad idea."

"I think it's gone beyond that point, Dr. Murphy." She opened the drawer of the small cabinet beside her chair. "Between the cutting, the anorexia, and the depression, I think it's time to readdress sending her to Serenity Heights for a short stay." She held out the full-color brochure covered in smiling, well-adjusted-looking kids. Their absolute normalness was a slap to the face.

"I'm not sending her away for six weeks." He stared at the woman.

She stared right back. "You need to go through her room again before you make that decision."

He pinched the bridge of his nose, the roar of blood in his ears making it hard to think.

"She mentioned your prescription sleeping pills." She paused until he was looking at her again. "Her depression has ahold of her right now. The boy, from the party? Apparently, he broke up with her."

"You're telling me she's going to try to kill

herself?" He didn't say *again*. He didn't have to.

Adelaide had come into their lives after Julia died. Diana's hunger strike had put her in the hospital hooked up to a feeding tube—under psychological observation. Graham had been beside himself, completely out of his element. He'd lost his wife. He couldn't lose his daughter, even if she wanted nothing to do with him. Dr. Adelaide Keanon was the only person Diana would talk to.

"I'm saying she's in crisis." Adelaide studied him. "How are you?"

He shook his head, studying his hands to keep his frustration in check. There was nothing worse than being completely and utterly helpless. This was his daughter, his baby, the person he loved above all else they were talking about. *How was he?* Was she fucking serious? "I don't have an answer for you at the moment."

Silence filled the office. What if he was wrong? What if Serenity Heights could help? If Diana needed this place... No. He couldn't do it. If he deserted her there, she would never forgive him. He knew it.

"I need another option." He cleared his throat. "Something. Anything. Give me something else?"

Silence returned as she studied him. "Take a leave of absence. Get away, have a vacation—find a way to connect with her. The two of you live under the same roof but, as far as I can tell, you are strangers to each other." She leaned forward, elbows on her knees. "But I'm not sure that will give any long-term solutions. When the vacation is over, and you come back, I worry she'll slip into the same familiar patterns she's set for herself." She held the brochure out again. "Diana refuses to let go of her anger, Graham. You know that. If she does, she'll have to deal with her grief and pain. Her anger gives her a sense of control—we've talked about it a hundred times."

"We've been talking about it for three years." He bit out. "Why the hell isn't she getting better?"

Adelaide smiled. "It's not that easy. The wounds to the human psyche heal when the person is open to it. Diana doesn't want to because she's not ready for the work it will entail."

Graham pushed off the loveseat and shoved the brochure into his coat pocket.

"Please make sure there's nothing in her room she can harm herself with," Adelaide said, unfolding herself from her rocking chair. "She's upset—not thinking. Inclined to making foolish decisions."

He nodded.

"Will you think about checking her in?" she pushed. "For her own good?"

"I'll think about a leave of absence." He swallowed, already making a list of what he'd need to do to make that happen.

Adelaide Keanon sighed. "As I said, there's no guarantee that will change a thing."

"You think locking her up with a bunch of strangers so they can talk about their problems and addictions will? She's a child. I'm her father. It's my job to protect her. I have to try everything before... before I consider what you're suggesting."

"Sending her there is protecting her, Graham.

From herself." Adelaide held the door open for him.

He left, considering his options: punch something, yell at someone, or drink enough to dull the constant ache in his chest. He may not understand his daughter—but he loved her. If there was the slightest chance he could avoid committing her, he would. It wasn't like he'd have to close the clinic. The office Matt had opened in the city could send one of their docs. He'd schedule a conference call tomorrow and have things in place before the end of the month.

He pushed through the doors of the hospital, head down, lost in thought.

"Graham?"

He looked up, inches from slamming into Felicity. "Hi."

"Hi." Those green eyes swept over his face. "Everything all right?"

He forced a grin. "Long day." And he still had to go home and dig through Diana's room. God only knew what he'd find. He reached into his pocket for his keys. Nothing. He patted his coat, shoved his hand in, and pulled out his keys—the brochure for Serenity Heights, a pack of gum, and his hospital badge falling to the ground.

Felicity was stooping before he could stop her.

"I can get it," he murmured, kneeling beside her to collect the gum.

She handed him his badge, reaching for the brochure at the same time he did. For some indiscernible reason it was important she not see the damn thing. His business was his business. He and Diana were struggling, but they'd be okay. He snatched up the brochure and stood, hoping like hell she hadn't seen what it was.

He helped her up, fully aware of the way she was looking at him — and choosing not to acknowledge it. "Checking on Jack?" he asked.

She nodded. "Still no change."

He already knew that. "I peek in on him whenever I can."

"You do?" She smiled. "Of course you do."

He swallowed, overwhelmed with loneliness. There was a time he could have told this woman anything. Not all that long ago, he and Julia and Matt and Felicity were a team, of sorts, navigating marriage and parenting together. Right now, he could use a team.

"You and Diana should come by the house, Graham." Those green eyes were searching his. "If you have time?"

He would have time. Soon. For a long overdue vacation. With his daughter. And it scared the shit out of him. Not that Felicity needed to be burdened with any of this. As tempting as her invitation was, he knew Felicity had enough chaos without introducing Diana into the mix. "I appreciate the offer but—"

"Don't 'but' me, Graham Murphy." She was smiling. "Say yes. I have a feeling we're both charting unfamiliar territory here. Maybe, I don't know, we could spot each other?"

She meant it. He could tell. The weight crushing his chest lightened the slightest bit.

"Okay?" she asked, placing her hand on his arm

and lightly squeezing.

Saying no was the right thing to do. He should say no, smile, and walk away. Instead, he nodded. "Okay."

"Good." She squeezed his arm lightly. "No need to call." She let go of him, already headed inside. "You and Diana are welcome anytime, Graham."

He stood, watching until she disappeared inside—her long auburn hair and light-blue dress swallowed up by the automatic hospital doors— taking the brief sense of lightness with her.

CHAPTER FOUR

The last four days had convinced Felicity that everyone she knew had secretly decided the last eighteen months of her life hadn't happened. No, Matt hadn't married Amber, but he hadn't been married to *her* when he died, either. Once word of Matt's death got out, something changed. He was once more her beloved husband, town doctor, pillar of the community, and Honor and Nick's adoring father. Honor took it in stride. Nick did not.

Once the funeral was over, the kids deserved a break. She wasn't sure where or how, but it might do both of them some good to have a change of scenery. Maybe Charity could take them someplace exciting, let them laugh, grieve…be.

But first they had to survive the funeral.

The day was hot and rainy and gray, so oppressively humid her black dress stuck to her back. By the time family and friends were done sharing their fondest memories of Matt, hostility was rolling off Nick. She took his hand, needing the contact as much as he did. Between the throb in her head and the stifling heat, she was just as ready for this to be over as Nick.

Well, close to it.

Once the service was over, the town descended on the house to continue their support. No one seemed to realize that all Felicity and her kids wanted was to be left alone. She kept smiling, accepting food and hugs of sympathy. Nick was surly and rigid, while Honor did her best to intercept and divert.

Charity, thank God, made running interference for the kids her top priority. Hopefully, Nick wouldn't blow up on one of the well-meaning citizens of Pecan Valley.

She carried another tray of food into the kitchen, searching the laden counters, island, and table for room. She gave up, gently laying the tray on top of a cake plate and rifling through the kitchen cabinet for two aspirin. The band of pressure around her temples was expanding—and tightening. What she wouldn't give for a hot bath, some wine, and lots of peace and quiet.

"I think these have pecans," Charity said, backing into the kitchen toting a massive dish. "Pecan raisin cookies and some zucchini bread—with pecans."

Pecans were important to Pecan Valley—so important that most residents figured a way to incorporate them into everyday recipes. Sometimes it was delicious. Sometimes, it wasn't. Felicity cocked a brow at her sister. "It's nice."

"It's weird," her sister countered. "Was there some sort of time warp I missed on the flight? I mean, I'm not going to turn down the food, but how did this happen? You aren't married to Matt anymore, right? You're single. Available. Unattached to Dr. Douchebag. Sorry, guess I can't do that now that he's…" Charity broke off, her smile dimming. "Well, sorry."

Dr. Douchebag. Felicity didn't know whether to laugh or cry. "It's the town, I think. Someone dies, the town feeds their family. Since Honor and Nick are his only family—and Jack—they're doing what they feel is right." Felicity wiped down the sink faucet, finding things that needed to be done in the kitchen to escape the curious, if well-meaning, residents of Pecan Valley. "We take care of one another—through good times and bad. One of the reasons I love this place." It was a reminder—for herself.

"I say we kick everyone out and you indulge in some seriously hard liquor." Charity slid onto one of the bar stools. "Nick definitely looks like he could use a drink."

"My sixteen year old?" Felicity sighed, wiping the marble countertop with vigorous strokes. "I think that might be a bad idea. Besides, I need to head back to the hospital soon, anyway."

Charity frowned. "No, you don't, Filly. You *need* to stay here. Your kids need you. Grams is with baby Jack. She has it under control. As long as she's got her knitting basket, she's happy."

Felicity leaned forward, resting her elbows on the counter. "Maybe." But there was no *maybe* about it. Charity was right. "How did my little sister get so smart?"

Charity's eye roll was epic. "I've always been smart. And since you're actually listening to me, I'm going to add that you need a rest." Charity took her hand. "And, probably, alcohol. If I remember things correctly, a couple of drinks and you're out like a light. Might do you some good."

Felicity pushed off the counter, stretching her back and arms. "I can't. Not yet."

"Why? If Jack wakes up and you're asleep, we'll wake you up." She sighed. "Seriously, Filly, how much sleep have you had in the last five days?"

Felicity didn't answer.

"You're not going to be much help to anyone if you're a zombie." Charity kept on. "You'd probably scare the shit out of Jack, too."

"Girls." Their mother came in. "We have guests. You two can run and hide later."

Charity rolled her eyes again, slid off the stool, and waited for Felicity. "Guess it's a good thing you're not taking a nap because *I'm* not going out there alone."

Felicity led the way, her cheeks aching from her pinned-in-place smile. She had to. Yes, everyone was here to be supportive, but they were watching—closely. She'd been on the receiving end of sympathetic looks and whispers before Matt's death. Now, she'd progressed to murmurs of "poor Felicity," followed by lots of "bless your heart." Matt's death was shocking, but she'd lost him eighteen months ago. It was the kids she was worried about.

"Stay strong," Charity whispered, hooking arms.

If she fell apart now, people would read into it—and her little sister was reminding her of that. More drama should be avoided at all costs. Especially for the kids. "Will do."

After another hour of playing the perfect hostess, she glanced across the room to see Nick creeping up the stairs as slowly as he could, taking care to dodge the squeaking board, before disappearing from sight. *Good*. He had the right to some time to himself.

After today, this week, they all did. Not too much, not enough to get lost in grief, but just enough.

Gauging that might be a problem.

Not five minutes later, Honor was making her way up the stairs, offering a small wave before making her escape.

"Excuse us, won't you?" Her mother led her from a group of nurses who had worked with Matt to a small tribe of hat-wearing women that Felicity knew well. "Gram's widows' group is here. Come say hello. They brought pecan sticky rolls."

Felicity accepted hugs and lipstick kisses on the cheek. These women had been a part of her life since before she could remember, and she was thankful for their presence here today. Not only did the widows' group have stories and "tidbits" to share about everyone in the room—they had strong opinions on who should be doing what and why. It was expected and oddly comforting.

"Felicity, honey, we stopped by to see your grams at the hospital before we came, and we have an idea," Widow Rainey said, taking her hands. "There's not a lot to occupy a bunch of old biddies like us—"

"Except doctor's appointments," another widow said.

"And bingo," another added, her gigantic black and tulle hat resting at an impressive angle on her head. "Can't give up bingo."

"Fine, fine," Widow Rainey continued. "What I'm trying to say is, we'd like to help you out with little Jack. We can all take turns watching him while he's sleeping. That way you're not chained to that hospital. You've got family that need you and a life to live. We don't mind waiting."

"You hear that, Felicity?" Charity gushed, joining in. "I'm not the only one worrying over you. I was saying the same thing to her."

Widow Rainey nodded. "I know you don't like to burden others, Felicity. And we all admire how well you've handled *things*, but I don't know of a soul in Pecan Valley who wouldn't offer up a little time to watch over that baby and take a bit off your plate."

Felicity's eyes burned, badly. And her hands, still clasped in Widow Rainey's hands, were trembling ever so slightly. "I don't want to impose—"

"It's no imposition, honey," one of the women said.

"Not at all," the jaunty-hat woman continued.

"Wouldn't have offered if it was," Widow Rainey finished. "We'll start tomorrow. Here's what we've worked out. But you just let us know if you need something else."

Felicity took the graph paper, lined and labeled with a flowing, tidy script. In the margin, each of the ladies' names and phone numbers was listed. "I…I can't thank you enough."

"Well, then, that's that," Widow Rainey said, releasing her hands and turning to look at Charity. "I hear tell you got an escort to the hospital by Pecan Valley's sheriff, Braden Martinez. Not here a few hours and you're already causing trouble." She chuckled. "I see Braden's here, Felicity. Isn't that nice?"

The question startled her. But then, conversation with Widow Rainey was always a little dizzying. "Yes…" Felicity managed, her gaze finding the man in question.

"When did he get so hot?" Charity whispered for her ears only. "He sure didn't look like that in high school."

Felicity swallowed a laugh. Braden Martinez had *always* been devilishly good-looking. Charity had been too focused on getting out of Pecan Valley to notice anything good about her hometown. But Sheriff Martinez appeared to be just as smitten with her sister as he'd been back then, his heavy-lidded eyes returning to Charity again and again. Poor Braden. Her little sister was more heartbreaker than homemaker—it was who she was.

"Your mother says most of Pecan Valley's dropped by to show their respect. Your family is loved, Felicity." One of the widows patted her arm. In seconds, the widows went back to spilling all of the secrets of Pecan Valley.

She kept her smile in place, appreciating the support but ready for a little less community love. Right now, she wanted to follow her kids upstairs and—maybe—have a nap.

• • •

Honor sat in the large, wingback chair before the picture window. Before Granddad and Mimi had moved to the cottage, this had been their room. *The haunted room.* That's what she and Nickie called it. All dark wood, spooky corners, and thick, hide-behind curtains. Perfect for a ghost. Or monster. The sort of place they'd play rock-paper-scissors to avoid going to when Granddad or Mimi had asked them to get something. And, if they lost and had to go in there, they'd run as fast as they could—terrified something would jump out of the dark to get them.

But after the divorce and they'd moved in, this had become Mom's room. She and Nick had both supported their mother's plans to gut it. Now it was all whitewashed wood; frilly linens; open space; cream, lavender, and cornflower accents; and an old crystal chandelier. The three of them spent hours together here, sprawled across the floor for homework or piled up on her bed to watch movies or talk. It had become a special place for them all. So, it made sense she and Nick were here, seeking escape from the craziness downstairs.

Nick sat on the foot of the bed, his shoes kicked off, shoveling a massive piece of chocolate cake into his mouth.

"Chew," she murmured.

Nick shoved the remainder of the cake into his mouth.

She laughed, shaking her head.

He grinned, chocolate covered teeth and all.

"Do *not* get that on the bed," she warned, grimacing as he made a huge show of licking the frosting off the plate. "Classy."

He finished with the plate, set it on the floor, and flopped back on the bed. "Think we'll still take a vacation?"

Honor stared out the window. The skies were turning dark, a summer storm rolling in. "I don't know, Nickie." There was a lot she didn't know.

Summer had just started. She had three months before she was supposed to move to Austin for college. It wasn't enough time. She'd known exactly what she wanted since before she could remember. The Otto family had run the town pharmacy from the very beginning. She wanted to carry on her mother's family tradition—as a pharmacist. Her full scholarship had guaranteed that would happen. But now leaving seemed wrong. How could she? "Where would you go?"

"The beach. Mom always loves the beach," he murmured. "Fishing, maybe."

The lump in her throat caught her by surprise. But so had Nick's answer. Their father had taught Nick how to fish, wading out in the Gulf of Mexico to catch red drum, black drum, sand trout, and hardhead fish. Nick had always complained about going, said he hated it, but in the end he always went. And Dad had always said he lost twice as much bait as the fish they caught, but that hadn't mattered. It was about their time together.

"Sounds fun," she managed.

"A break would be nice. Away." He shrugged. "Far away from all this *crap*."

She understood. The texts and phone calls had died down a little, but her world was still upside down. Things like going to the lake, parties, hanging out with friends—or going on a date with the ridiculously persistent Owen Nelson weren't important. But, with Jack in the hospital, she wondered if a vacation was a possibility.

"When do you start working?" she asked.

Nick had spent the last two years working at the local summer camp as a counselor.

"Not sure I'm going," he answered. "I heard they're trying to hire older kids now, for insurance purposes. Besides, Granddad said I could work in the store this summer."

Honor chewed the inside of her lip. Her mom was worrying about Nick—everyone was worrying about him. Where Honor had held on blindly to hope that they'd eventually find a place in their father's life, Nick's heartbreak had twisted into something ferocious and angry. And Dad couldn't make any of this better now.

Because Dad isn't just off-with-his-new-family gone. He's gone-gone. Forever. Dealing with that was…impossible.

"Are we hiding?" Their mother appeared, closing the door behind her.

"Yes," Nick said, unmoving on the bed.

"Sorry, Mom. They just keep coming." Honor wrinkled her nose.

"I know they do." Her mother shook her head. "So does the food."

"Looks like a storm is rolling in," Honor said, pointing out the window. "Maybe everyone will head home?"

"Or stay until it's over," Nick argued.

Honor saw the smile her mother shot Nick. She looked beautiful in black. Tired, sure, but they all were. Still, she was there for them. Always. Until recently, she didn't realize just how important that was. They were a team, the three of them. A wave of love washed over her, for her mother and her brother.

"We can hope they head home," her mother said, pulling the clip from her hair. She sat beside Nick, running her fingers through her long auburn hair.

"There is some good news. I think we have enough food to last through Christmas."

"So, we're good for a zombie apocalypse?" Nick asked.

"Or a regular apocalypse, even," Honor added, climbing on the bed beside them. "Zombies are so overdone."

Their mom laughed. "Either sort, we've got food. I need to load up the freezer in the garage, too. Waste not—"

"Want not," she and Nick chanted in unison.

"Can I eat any of it?" Nick asked.

"You're not allergic to pecans, Nickie," Honor reminded him.

"She's right." Their mom sort of melted onto the bed, sighing.

Honor lay down at her side, grinning as Nick scooted up the bed until he snagged a pillow.

"I might be," Nick argued. "If allergic means I think they taste like dirt."

Their mom laughed, making Nick smile and easing some of the weight Honor had been shouldering since the night of her graduation.

"We'll sort out the with-pecan from the pecan-free, just for you. And, if you promise not to tell Grams, we might even toss some of it." Mom's voice was soft, her yawn bone weary. "I love you guys." She pressed a kiss to Honor's temple, then Nick's. "I'm here, okay? I know things are tough, I know you're sad, but I'm here. We'll get through this together. You know that, right? Whatever you need."

And just like that, things were a teeny bit better. She believed her mother, trusted her. "Okay," Honor murmured, resting her head on her mother's shoulder.

"Love you, too, Mom," Nick said, his voice already thick with sleep.

Honor watched her mother's eyes drift shut; her breathing grew deep and steady. She pulled the quilt up over them and let her mother's breathing, her brother's light snore, and the gentle tap-tap of the rain lull her to sleep.

• • •

"I don't want to go." Diana stared at him, not bothering to hide her frustration. "They don't care if I'm there."

"We missed the funeral. The least we can do is pay our respects." Graham stared at her, floored by her outburst. "We're going."

"I'm not." She crossed her arms over her chest.

"I wasn't asking." Graham tucked his wallet into his back pocket and reached for his keys. She'd been spending far too much time closeted in her room, plugged into her earphones and video games. Getting her out of the house would do her some good.

After his meeting with Dr. Keanon, he'd spent every minute he wasn't at the office with her—much to his daughter's frustration. Every night, when she showered, he searched her room. He'd recovered the sleeping pills, some of Julia's expired pain pills, and a bottle of whiskey he'd never seen before. He didn't say anything about the confiscated items to Diana and, if she missed them, she was smart enough not to say anything to him.

He'd yet to tell her the reason he'd spent a few nights working late was because he was taking a six-week hiatus to delay the inevitable fallout. At this point, he was running on fumes. "We're going."

"Fine." She smiled and her eyes narrowed. "I'll go." Her tone left no room for misunderstanding. She would go and make every second a nightmare.

His patience was at an end. He sighed, running a hand over his face. "I'm not sure when we got here, Di, but I'd really like to figure a way back. You're my daughter and I love you—"

"Right, you love me. You want me to be happy. That's why you're making me go to a funeral for some cheating asshole whose son hates me. That makes sense." Diana was a master eye-roller.

"I might not approve of everything Matt Buchanan did, but I do respect and care about his family. For crying out loud, Di, you know how it feels to lose a parent."

"Stop calling me that," she snapped. "I do know. Every day. My mom is gone because you let her go." Her face was bright red. "So, you're taking me so I can start a dead-parent club or something equally pathetic with the Buchanan kids? Sounds amazing. Where do I sign up?"

Graham counted backward from five, the sting of her words easier from time. "I'm taking you because they came when your mom died. Because it's what friends do."

"We're friends now?" she bit back. "Mom's dead and Dr. Buchanan's dead and now we're all suddenly friends again? Oh, wait, I get what this is. Why not, she's hot and you're both single."

What? Was she serious? He tried to keep his face blank, but she was so good at pushing his buttons. He was the parent, dammit. She would listen. And he would control his temper. "Diana, enough. I'm not sure why you've decided to dislike the Buchanans, but they're nice people. Nice people who've suffered a loss. Kids who used to be your friends and who've lost their dad. So, yes, we're friends again— because they could use some." He cleared his throat, admitting, "And so could we."

Diana stared at him—her red lips pressed tight. "I never said I didn't like them."

He waited.

"I just don't understand why they suddenly matter?" she asked.

"I'm not sure why they stopped mattering. I'm sure that was my fault. We were friends before, close. You, Nick, and Honor... I know you remember." He hoped she remembered.

She stuck her chin out, crossing her too-skinny arms over her chest.

"Would it be so bad to have them back in our lives? Be there for them?"

She stared at him, her eyes huge and dark in her pale face. Her posture eased, barely, just barely. "Fine." She surprised him, walking to the front door. "Then let's go."

Her mood swings were relentless, but he was getting what he wanted so he wasn't going to argue. Any attempt to engage in further conversation ended when she plugged into her earbuds. He let it go, driving through the rain, hoping the visit wouldn't be a colossal disaster. The last thing he wanted to do was add to Felicity's stress level—or her family's.

In the last few days, his admiration for Felicity Buchanan had only increased. He'd run into her at the hospital a few times, various members of her family in tow. Felicity was a powerhouse, a gentle, caring powerhouse. She steered her family seamlessly, smoothed feathers, offered support, with a smile.

Sitting with her at Jack's bedside, he'd been struck by a memory. A past vacation, his family and Matt's had been at the beach. The kids were building a sandcastle and Felicity was strolling along the beach, hunting the ever-elusive sand dollar. Julia had pointed out how beautiful Felicity was to both men. She'd been right, as Julia normally was. And when Matt had whistled at his wife, she'd covered her cheeks and smiled—embarrassed and awkward and charming. He'd never been jealous of Matt. He had Julia. But he'd always thought Matt had been damn lucky.

The day Amber Strauss walked into their practice with her pharmaceutical sample case, mile-long legs, and megawatt smile, he'd felt the air ripple between her and Matt. Still, he'd held on to the belief that Matt loved his family too much to do anything stupid. Attraction was tempting, but what Matt and Felicity had was real and special.

Then Matt had given his family up and left Felicity alone to pick up the pieces.

While he was losing Julia.

When Julia got sick, Felicity helped out. Her funeral? Felicity had taken care of so much. After, he'd been useless—ignoring her calls and avoiding her drop-ins.

In his grief, he'd deserted a dear friend. He realized that now. And felt like an ass. If he could do something to make this easier, he would. *Because having a workaholic whose kid is on the verge of being institutionalized around is just what Felicity and her family need.* Maybe this was a bad idea. He parked his car and stared at the Otto-Buchanan house.

"It's not raining," Diana said, looking out the window. "Soo...are we going in?"

He nodded, regretting that he'd forced the issue.

Diana was out the door and hurrying up the stone walkway, glaring at him when he didn't pick up the pace.

"Dad?" Diana stared at him, oozing impatience.

"What?"

"Are you going to knock?" she asked, sighing.

He knocked.

Charity Otto opened the door. "Graham, I thought you'd passed the point of needing to knock on the door years ago. Hi, Diana? Look at you, rocking the goth-smolder thing. Nice to see you guys." She frowned. "God, is it okay to say that? Considering the circumstances?" She shrugged. "Come in, eat, please. Seriously."

Graham followed Diana inside, closing the door behind them. "Guess we are running late?" The house was empty.

"Sort of." Charity smiled. "The funeral was this morning, everyone just cleared out, and my folks are at the hospital with Jack. I'd say your timing is *perfect.*"

Graham smiled. Charity's sarcasm was surprising—and amusing. "We'd meant to make the service but—"

"Dad was birthing babies," Diana offered.

"A far preferable experience, I'm sure." Charity smiled. "All healthy?"

Graham nodded.

"That's way happier than hanging out in black, trying to come up with nice things to say about... him." Charity shrugged. "Did I mention you should eat? A lot. We could feed the town for a week. Seriously. Follow me."

Graham did, smiling when they found Felicity, Nick, and Honor gathered around several tubs of ice cream. "If this is dinner, Diana and I might stay."

"Yeah, we have like two celery stalks and something growing mold in Tupperware. I vote ice cream." Diana took the spoon Honor offered.

"Bowls are optional," Felicity said, squeezing around the table and offering him a bowl. "So is real food, Graham. We have real food, lots and lots of it, if you want me to make you something more substantial."

"I don't want to be a bother," he murmured, trying not to let Diana's comment about Felicity get to him. But it was there, impossible to ignore. Felicity was attractive. No, she was beautiful—radiating a sort of warmth that was impossible to ignore. Everything about her said "woman" in a way that made a man sit up and take notice. And yes, he noticed. He wasn't dead. But that had *nothing* to do with why he was here.

Her green eyes met his. "Gives me something to

do," she explained. "So, please, let me cook for you."

"Especially since you haven't eaten all day," Diana added.

"Take a seat, Doc Murphy. Mom's the bomb in the kitchen," Nick said, before shoveling ice cream into his mouth.

"Is that a serving spoon?" Graham chuckled.

"He's a growing boy," Honor said, grinning.

"This is awesome. Here I thought it was going to be all crying and talking about Dr. Buchanan and all sorts of depressing shit," Diana said, happily scooping strawberry ice cream into a bowl.

Everyone stopped to look at his daughter. How did she not hear herself? It was like her thoughts just forced their way out of her mouth without a filter.

Felicity burst out laughing. "I'm in favor of avoiding depressing shit."

Diana nodded. "Right on."

"And while I appreciate the vote of confidence on my cooking skills, I'm being lazy. Tonight, my *cooking* will consist of warming things up." Felicity opened the refrigerator and started pulling plates, trays, and tubs out. "Ham? Turkey? Meatloaf? Lasagna..." She lifted a lid. "Pasta salad. Green salad, Jell-O salad...some sort of pudding thing—"

"*That* sounds tempting." He laughed.

Felicity smiled at him. "Careful or that's all you'll end up with."

He held his hands up. "I'll take whatever you're serving... Whatever's easy."

Felicity's gaze inspected the various tubs and plates on the counter, then pulled a plate from the cabinet. "How about a little taste of everything?"

He nodded, sitting on one of the bar stools while Honor called Felicity over.

Charity was staring at him, smiling. "How are things, Graham? I feel like I haven't *seen* you in years."

"You haven't," Graham agreed. "Around Nick's fifth birthday?"

"That sounds about right." Charity's smile faded. "Not the best godmother—or aunt for that matter."

Graham shook his head. "I'm no better."

"Looks like you picked slackers for your kids' godparents, Filly." Charity winked. "We could buy them each a car. Maybe that would make up for it?"

Graham laughed.

"Guess you're the only OB/GYN in Pecan Valley now, huh?"

"No. We have a new doctor at the clinic. Solid. Experienced. Soft-spoken. Dr. Veronica Luna." He couldn't have handpicked a more qualified and competent physician. "Or you could go to my competition. Dr. Marissa Delaney and Dr. Hannah Jorgansen opened a practice."

"Choose between a mean girl I went to high school with and the wife of one of my dad's fishing buddies?" she asked. "No thank you. As far as I'm concerned, it's you, this Dr. Luna, or a drive into Austin."

Graham grinned.

"Awesome." She sucked in a deep breath, an odd expression crossing her face. "Guess that keeps you busy. Open this for me?" She held out a wine bottle and opener. When he took them, Charity put a wineglass in front of him. "Drink?"

He shook his head as he opened the bottle. "Driving." But it was tempting.

Charity nodded. "Someone was talking about you today."

"Oh really?" he asked, absently twirling the cork from the open wine bottle. Felicity's laugh drew his attention. She was listening to the kids, looking almost relaxed. Whether or not that was the case was another story. He'd begun to realize just how good she was at shielding her emotions from the rest of the world. It had to be exhausting.

"Yep. Widow Rainey." Charity sounded downright giddy.

That got his attention. For Widow Rainey, matchmaking ranked right up there with knitting and quilting and getting into everybody else's business. She meant well; she did. But this…*dating*? He wasn't interested. He wasn't ready. Apparently his gentle, but firm, attempts to dissuade the woman from finding him a "compatible partner" were useless. No surprise, really.

Even if he was, there was Diana. He didn't know if it was possible for his daughter to dislike him more than she currently did, but he had no interest in finding out. "I'm pretty sure I don't want to know." He set the cork on end, doing his best not to sound irritated.

Charity nodded. "Exactly. Not that she named names, but she has someone in mind for the good doctor of Pecan Valley."

Great. Graham rubbed a hand across the back of his neck.

"He's so not interested." Diana jumped in, stealing a roll from his plate. "She's been trying to set Dad up for a while now. I keep telling him he needs to get out more. I mean, look at him—he's totally a hottie. And he's obnoxiously focused. And loaded."

His daughter was giving him compliments...sort of. "Um, thanks?" But now Honor and Nick, Charity and Felicity were all studying him openly, and he didn't like it.

"OMG, Dad, you're totally blushing." Diana giggled.

He stared at his daughter, seeing his baby girl, giggling and carefree, with no trace of her normal hostility. He smiled back, etching everything about that moment into his mind.

"Well, this got awkward." Nick grabbed the ice cream tub, turning to Diana. "You play *Black Ops*?"

"Um, do I? You wanna get your ass kicked, lead the way," Diana said, sliding off the kitchen chair.

"Can't we play *Mario Cart*?" Honor asked, following them. "You know, something without exploding body parts or weapons of mass destruction?"

"Whatever happened to board games? Like Clue?" Charity asked.

"Nah, come on, Aunt Charity. I bet you can kill-shot zombies like a boss." Nick nudged his aunt, teasing. The kid had a great smile.

Graham sat watching as the kitchen emptied of everyone but Felicity and him. "Who knew ice cream was the cure for teenage angst?"

"I'm afraid the effects might be temporary. But I'll take what I can get." Felicity laughed. "Hope you don't have any plans because it looks like you're staying for a while." She slid the plate in front of him. "Once Nick gets plugged in, it's all over."

"Diana's the same." He didn't mind staying. Better than going home, waiting for the opportune moment to search his daughter's room for any cause for concern. Additional concern. Worrying about his daughter had become a twenty-four-hour occupation. This was as close to a break as he was going to get.

"It'll do him some good. Diana, too." She looked at him, thoughtful, as if she had more to say.

He waited, wanting to know what she was thinking. But she only smiled and went back to tidying, and he turned all his attention to the plate she'd made for him. It was piled high. He shot her a look, loving her answering impish grin.

"I hate to throw food out." Her hands smoothed the plastic wrap over a tray of brownies.

"You can't expect me to eat all of this?"

"You can do it. According to your daughter, your pantry is bare." She glanced at him, opening the fridge. "You have to take care of yourself, for her. You know that, right? She watches you."

"Glares at me." He swallowed a bite of turkey.

"That's impressive." With his fork, he pointed at the strategically packed shelves of her refrigerator. "You weren't kidding about the food."

"I'm sending some home with you. That pudding thing for sure."

He laughed. "Just what I wanted."

"I thought as much." She closed the refrigerator door and faced him. "No matter how she acts—

Diana, I mean—she's paying attention to what you do. Probably more than you realize. I know it's been a while since we talked but…how are you?" That green gaze locked with his.

"You're asking *me* how I am?" Her question made him feel like an even bigger ass. He and Diana had been doing this dance for a couple of years now. Felicity, her kids, were facing a whole new sort of hell. "Shouldn't I be asking *you* that question?"

"You go first," she pushed, a furrow forming between her brows. "Graham?"

"I'm hanging in there." Which was true. "Every day it gets easier." Which wasn't true but he couldn't bear to unload on her.

"Good. Julia wouldn't want you to hold on to the hurt. You know that." There were tears in her eyes. Because she'd loved Julia, too. "She loved seeing you both happy. She'd want that now."

The lump in his throat doubled in size, preventing him from answering her. It had been so long since he'd allowed himself to think about Julia beyond the sickness and loss.

"I'm sorry." Felicity covered his hand with hers. "It's none of my business and I—"

He stared down at her hand, covered it with his. The touch was casual enough, but it meant more than she could understand. Affection of any sort was no longer commonplace in his life. And her hand was so soft and warm in his. "Don't be. You're right. It's a good reminder." He smiled at her. "Need more of them."

She nodded. "Definitely."

He blew out a long, slow breath, sliding his hands

away from hers. Somehow, he'd gone from being the comforter to the one being comforted. Which was the last thing she needed. "Want a ride to the lawyer's next week?" he asked before taking a bite.

"That would be great." Her gaze darted to the kitchen door. "I keep hoping Amber has some long-lost sister or aunt, someone to take Jack. Is that wrong?"

Graham shook his head. "The kids don't know about Matt's request?" He couldn't blame her. How the hell did you have that conversation?

"No." She sat on the stool next to him, propping herself on her elbow, and whispered, "I'm scared. They've had a rough two years. I've tried to reassure them they will always come first because, for me, they do. And now... I can't make them love Jack." She shook her head.

"But that baby boy... None of this is his fault. He's just a baby. A baby with no one to love him." Her green eyes searched his. "I don't know what to say to make this okay. If I can make this okay. Honestly, I'm not *okay* with this—any of it. But I'm trying to be."

"Say that," Graham said. "They know you love them. They might not take the news well initially, but they'll understand. They're good kids." He hoped like hell he was right. Honor would step up, ready and willing to be Jack's sister. But Nick? It could go either way.

"Want anything else?" Felicity asked.

He glanced at his plate. "I'm stuffed."

"You didn't eat much. I can make some coffee, too, if you like?"

"That's not necessary."

"I know, but I don't mind. And I want some." She waved off his words, putting dishes away. "Charity mentioned the widows' group has made you their newest project. I think I know who the widows have picked out for you."

"Is there a way to kindly refuse Widow Rainey's services? An unsubscribe or opt-out option?" But now he was curious.

Felicity laughed. "You don't want to know?"

He shrugged. "Not really. But if you want to tell me…"

She smiled, leaning against the kitchen counter. "My sister. Charity."

"Huh." Graham glanced at the kitchen door. Charity? There was no denying she was pretty. But her sister wasn't on his radar. Did he even have a radar anymore? Outside of his daughter, there were no women in his life. Maybe that was wrong? He was forty, not eighty. In a few years, Diana would be gone, and he'd be older—and still alone. But Charity? No. She wasn't the settling-down sort, and he wasn't the carefree, world-traveling type.

"It's okay for you to live, Graham. You know that, don't you?" Felicity pulled mugs from the cabinet and filled the coffee pot.

"I guess." Was there a woman strong enough to take on his broken heart and his damaged daughter? And, if there was, could he love her the way she deserved? "I'm not sure I can." He looked at her. "I don't know where I'd start…or if it's worth it."

"I get it." Her sad smile gutted him. "There's safety in not putting yourself out there—in not being rejected or left. I'm not sure I'd survive having my heart ripped out again." She forced a smile and shrugged. "But we should try? Shouldn't we? At least that's what my mother, my sister, Widow Rainey…everyone keeps telling me."

Graham chuckled. "You, too, huh?"

"The joys of small-town living." She poured the coffee. "Cream? Sugar?"

"Black. And thank you."

"Brave man. I make it super strong; you've been warned." Her green gaze met his. "It's really nice having you and Di here."

He was still contemplating her words when her phone started vibrating, ending their conversation.

"Hi, Mom…" She paused. "What? When?" She stared at Graham. "No…no… I'm on my way."

Graham stood. "What's wrong?"

"Jack. He's awake." She took a deep breath.

"I'll drive," he offered.

CHAPTER FIVE

"Where are you going?" Charity paused in her hunt for munchies. Her sister's pale complexion and Graham's clenched jaw were signs all was not right with the world. Again. She'd come home expecting it to be the same boring, predictable place she'd been so eager to leave years ago. How she wished that was the case.

"Jack's awake," Graham said, shrugging into his coat. "I'm taking Felicity to the hospital."

"I'll hold down the fort. Diana and Nick are having way too much fun blowing each other up to interrupt." She held up the bag of Cheetos and pack of red licorice laces. "With enough sugar, they probably won't even know you're gone."

"Are you sure?" Graham wavered.

Poor Graham. He was all serious and responsible. Like Felicity. And, after listening to Diana, it was clear he and her sister probably shared something else: the need to go out and have some fun. If they were really lucky, they'd get laid. Big time. Talk about a stress reliever. Why two good-looking singles would choose to remain sad and celibate didn't make any sense.

Her gaze darted from one to the other, the ideas bouncing around in her mind all good ones.

Her sister.

Graham.

Oh my God, yes. Move over Widow Rainey, I'm

all over this matchmaking thing. "Sure, I'm sure. If they get burned out on video games, we'll find a horror movie to watch. Or something."

Felicity hugged her. "Thank you."

Graham handed her his card. "In case you need me." Oh, she was going to need him, all right. But for reasons that had nothing to do with his daughter. There was something dependable about Graham Murphy. And since she had no idea what she was doing, she needed a doctor she trusted. She'd already called to make her first prenatal appointment, and she was counting on the whole doctor-patient confidentiality thing—for the time being. Her family couldn't take one more hit at the moment.

"Feel free to, you know, go have a drink or see a movie or something afterward." She stared right back at them. *Too much. Way too much. Tone it down, Charity.* "What? Maybe we could use a break from you two? Ever think of that? Maybe giving them a night of video games, horror movies, and junk food away from their parents is just what *they* need?" She sighed.

"We'll be back as soon as we can." Felicity shot her a look.

Her sister was so off her game. Good thing she was here to help things along.

Graham nodded and held the door for Felicity. Because he was a gentleman. Exactly what her sister deserved—for a change.

Charity peeked out the front glass door, watching as they hurried down the walkway. Sometimes, life could suck. Those two had had more than their fair share of sucking. As Graham's black luxury SUV pulled away from the curb, she hoped they'd take her suggestion to heart. A few shots and some heavy petting might just help them both relax.

Her sister was the strongest person on the planet, but she had to be running on fumes. Not that Felicity would say so, or confide, or lean—she was way too into the big-sister protector thing. Still, Matt had been dead five days. In those five days, her sister had been saddled with his funeral arrangements, keeping her kids' spirits up, and the whole "when will the ex's illegitimate love child and destroyer of her niece and nephew's happy family wake up from his coma?" thing.

Charity felt for the baby, she did. But her loyalties were here, to Nick and Honor, and Felicity, too.

She grabbed a bag of sour-cream-and-onion chips and added it to her pile of snacks, then backed out of the kitchen. "Who's hungry?" she asked, flopping onto the couch beside Honor.

Honor was watching the bloody melee on the television, a growing look of disgust on her face. "This is horrible. I keep jumping."

Nick chuckled. "You should try it. Definitely calms the nerves."

Charity snorted. She was pretty sure trying to shoot a zombie before it bit into you *wasn't* relaxing. At least not her idea of relaxing.

"Right?" Diana added. "Dad took my game away because of the whole pot thing. It sucks, big time. Which is why I have lots of sleepovers."

Charity didn't say a word. She wasn't sure how to read Diana yet. Was she really messed up? Or was she acting messed up for attention?

"Pot?" Honor asked.

Diana nodded, taking a licorice lace from Nick. "It's no big deal. It was one joint. One. The school totally flipped out and expelled me."

"You were expelled?" Nick looked skeptical.

"Why else do you think I'm going to your school next year?" Diana rolled her eyes. "Dad can't buy my way back into any of the private schools. Why he thinks I'm better off at a private school versus a public school is beyond me. Where does he think I bought the pot to begin with?"

So, the real deal then. Not that she was going to judge the girl. She couldn't imagine how hard it would be to lose a parent. There had been plenty of times during her school years when she'd wished her parents would leave her alone—disappear even. But death? Permanently losing one? She couldn't imagine that.

Was this one of those times she should act like an adult or not? Felicity would probably pop off some after-school-special message that would instantly and forever change Diana's outlook on life into some happy rainbow-and-cupcakes-kitten thing. But Charity didn't know how to do that. She didn't know how to be a mom. The kid in her belly was getting a raw deal. She needed to start taking notes on Felicity's parenting style.

"Is my dad still in there with Felicity?" Diana asked, nodding at the kitchen door. "What are your thoughts on that?"

Charity perked up then. This kid was smart.

"On what?" Honor asked, covering her eyes as Nick did some horrible exploding, stabbing thing to a group of virtual zombies and the screen went red. "Gross."

"My dad. Your mom." Diana waited.

Nick clicked a button on his controller, pausing the slaughter. "What about your dad and my mom?"

"I don't know. I think, maybe, they should get together." She shrugged. "You know, my dad's as cool as a dad can be. And your mom is awesome."

Nick stared at Diana like she'd sprouted another head. "Like dating?"

Honor giggled. "Nick, Mom has been alone for a long time,"

"I know that." He leaned back against the couch. "Dad really screwed her over. I figured she'd stay single. Wouldn't blame her if she did."

"She's way too young and pretty, Nick," Diana argued. "Better she and my dad get together than some other loser."

Charity's heart broke a little bit for her nephew when she saw the look on his face. "Would that bother you?" she asked.

Nick glanced at the kitchen door.

"I like the idea," Honor spoke up. "If Mom's happy, I'm happy. Right, Nickie?" She nudged her brother.

Charity ruffled her nephew's hair, feeling the need to soothe Nick's ruffled feathers. "I'm pretty sure neither of them is thinking about dating—each other or anyone else."

Diana sighed. "Which is sad. I mean, life is too fricking short to be alone and miserable all the time."

Charity smiled at Diana. "That's where you're

wrong. Neither one of them is alone. Your dad has you, and my sister has these two. And I'm pretty sure you guys make them very happy."

Diana's gaze fell from hers, her black-tipped fingers picking at the crocheted trim on the throw pillow in her lap. "Yeah. No. Not in my house. My dad hasn't been happy since my mom died." She shoved the pillow aside. "We ready?" she asked Nick.

Charity felt horrible. This was what happened when she tried to be all wise and maternal. She stuck her foot in it. Big time.

"Yeah." Nick nudged a controller in her direction. "You can spawn in, be on my team."

"Cool," Diana said, smiling at him. "Let's kick some zombie ass. Come on, Honor."

"Fine." She took another controller from Diana. "But this isn't going to be pretty."

"It's a zombie-hunting game. It's not supposed to be." Nick sighed a long-suffering sigh that had Charity giggling.

But thirty minutes later, she'd reached her threshold for kill-shots and sniping and zombies running at the screen.

Everyone was occupied. Now was the time to do what she'd wanted to do since she found the nanny cam in Matt's apartment. She didn't know what she was looking for or why it mattered, but it did. Maybe she needed proof that Amber's social media posts were a cover-up. Maybe she wanted to know Matt missed his real family—even a little. She carried her bag of sour-cream-and-onion chips into Felicity's home office and stuck the nanny cam video card into the slot on Felicity's computer.

Most of it was Jack napping.

Upside, she now knew Jack really loved his blue blanket with clouds and lambs all over it—Nick's blanket. He held it in one hand and sucked on the thumb of his other hand. It was adorable. Poor little guy. It wasn't his fault he was a home-wrecker.

She pressed fast forward. Other than napping, there were a few bits and pieces of diaper changes. Matt rocked his son, but she didn't want to watch that. She remembered all too well the kind of father Matt had been to Honor and Nick—before he became a walking cliché.

She stopped the recording a few times, but nothing exciting happened. Until it did. Amber walked into the nursery. She was wearing to-die-for heels and a glamorous and perfectly tailored suit. She walked toward the crib and peered inside. Jack was screaming.

"He's coming," Amber said. "Daddy's coming." She reached in and patted the baby awkwardly. "Matt? What's the holdup?"

"Pick him up, Amber," Matt answered, some-where off-screen.

"I'm in my work clothes," she bit back.

Matt appeared, wearing scrubs, his jaw covered in a heavy stubble. He reached into the crib and picked up Jack, who instantly plugged his thumb into his mouth and calmed. "This is all he wants."

"Don't lecture me again, okay?" She was upset. "I'm not cut out for this. We *need* a nanny."

"I agree." He was patting Jack, rocking the boy in his arms. "But a nanny won't be twenty-four seven.

We need to make time for each other and our family. Both of us. It's important."

"So is my career. You knew I wasn't one of those women who thinks her greatest achievement is her children. That's not who I am." Amber crossed her arms over her chest. "That's Felicity. And you left her, remember? Something about how she always put the kids first? How she stopped making time for you? Stopped taking care of your needs." She sighed. "You picked me, Matt."

Matt was quiet for a beat, then said, "Felicity is a good mother."

"I'm not? Are you kidding me? Why do you think I've interviewed so many nannies? Why I've fired three of them? I want the best for Jack." Amber cut him off. "Stop trying to make me the bad guy, Matt. I've never changed. Ever. I'm beginning to think you have."

Matt didn't say a word.

"The way you're acting… I need a break. We both do." She sighed. "Go to Honor's graduation on your own tomorrow. Take Jack with you. You and Felicity and the kids can all be one big happy family again."

This happened the day before the accident? It made the argument ten times worse.

"Fine." Matt's voice was tight.

Amber stood there, shaking. "That's all you're going to say?" Apparently, she hadn't expected Matt's answer. "You don't want me to go?"

"Tomorrow is about my daughter, Amber." He cleared his throat. "I've been a shit father for the last year, but that's going to stop now. My kids, all of them, deserve to have a father. I want to be there for Honor. Maybe get Nick to…look at me—to start…"

"Another choice *you* made, Matt." She sighed. "I can't be here. I'll… I don't know what I want anymore. I don't know about anything." She walked out.

Matt sat in the rocking chair with Jack, barely flinching at the sound of the front door slamming.

"She'll be back, Jack. She always comes back." Matt spoke clearly, no hesitation. "But she's right, and I need to tell her I made the wrong choice."

Charity jumped at the crash behind her. She spun around to find Nick in the door, a pie splatted on the floor at his feet. But the devastation on his face, the yearning and regret, tore Charity's heart into a million tiny pieces.

"Nick." She was up, reaching for him, pulling his stiff body into a tight embrace.

"It's cool, Aunt Charity." He patted her back, shrugging out of her hold as quickly as possible. He stooped, raking the squished pie into the metal pie pan. "Guess they made up, huh, since they were all coming to Honor's graduation. One big, happy family."

"Nick—"

"Can we order pizza?" he asked, standing, eyeing the residual pie stickiness on the floor. "And rent that horror movie you were talking about? The shark-storm thing? After I mop."

If he didn't want to talk about it, she wouldn't push it. But this was *so* a big deal. Technically, it was her fault her nephew had just had his heart ripped out again. How did she make this better? Could she? It was too late for Matt to fix things with Nick—but it had to ease some of Nick's rage knowing his father had wanted to. Didn't it?

Or, shit, had it just made it a million times worse?

"Order whatever you want," she said. "My wallet's in my purse. I'll clean it up."

Nick nodded, cradling the pie pan against his chest as he headed back toward the living room. He looked so like Matt. Acted like him sometimes. The pre-deserted-his-real-family-for-a-bimbo Matt she'd thought of as her brother. Her heart twisted again. He'd regretted leaving his family... He wanted to tell Amber as much. She wasn't sure whether she hated Matt a little less or a whole lot more.

• • •

Felicity could hear Jack as soon as the elevator doors opened. Crying. Inconsolable.

"I should have been here," she murmured to herself.

"It wouldn't have made a difference," Graham answered, his hand catching hers. "Breathe, Felicity. Be calm. You can't be everywhere at once. He's awake, but he doesn't know who you are. You know he's yours now. He doesn't." Graham's brown eyes held hers.

He was right, of course. Jack would have woken up screaming his head off whether or not she was at his bedside. He didn't know her. No matter what the lawyer said at their upcoming meeting, this little boy wouldn't see her as his mother—she was a stranger.

But, stranger or not, she couldn't bear the sound

of his crying. She squeezed Graham's hand before letting go. The closer they got, the louder his wailing became. She sucked in a deep breath, put a smile on her face, and walked into the room.

"Oh, Filly, he's in a state," Grams said when she spotted them.

"Don't worry. He's a little disoriented." A nurse was checking his chart. "Give him some time, and he'll settle down."

Disoriented? More like terrified. Of course he was. Waking up alone in a strange place. Not a familiar face in the bunch. Her heart ached for the baby boy.

The nurse smiled. "I see you brought some of his things. That might help. Does he have a favorite toy? Or a blanket? Something familiar."

She carried the bag full of Jack's things to the bedside, praying something inside worked. "Here's hoping," she murmured, the little boy's bright red face worrying her. "Can I hold him?" she asked the nurse. "I don't want to hurt him."

The nurse smiled. "Hugs are encouraged but we don't want to move that leg too much."

Grams moved so Felicity could sit on the edge of the bed. "Hi, Jack."

Jack stopped screaming long enough to look at her with huge light-brown eyes. Brown, not blue or green. Light brown. Amber's eyes.

She smiled, smoothing the curls from his forehead. "I've been waiting to meet you." She touched the tip of his nose. "I'm glad you woke up."

He sniffed, his chin wobbling, before he pressed his eyes tight and began to fuss again.

"Hey, hey now, little one," she soothed. But Jack turned his face into the pillow, away from her, and crossed his arms over his chest.

"You can cry." She continued to stroke his forehead. "I'd cry, too, waking up and not knowing what was going on."

Her grandmother squeezed her shoulder.

Felicity smiled up at her. "Grams, I'll stay now. Thank you so much for sitting with him."

"I'll be back tomorrow, Filly—with the other ladies." She pressed a kiss to her cheek. "It'll all be right as rain, you'll see. Keep on loving him; he'll come around in no time."

Felicity hugged her grandmother goodbye, praying she was right. She didn't like feeling helpless. And right now, she'd never felt so helpless. With a wave, Grams left, and Felicity started rubbing Jack's back. Offering comfort, through touch, was all she could do.

"Let's see what we have here," she said, opening the bag and pulling out a few things.

Jack had no interest in the purple hippo or the soft truck that beeped when you hugged it. He ignored the board book on dinosaurs, too.

"I can go to Matt's condo tonight and bring back more options," Graham offered, watching from the foot of the bed.

"I think Charity and I already cleaned out the nursery," she murmured softly.

Graham sat on the opposite side of Jack's hospital bed. "Was it bad?"

There was no point pretending she didn't understand his question. She glanced at him, wrinkling her nose before rifling through the bag for other options for Jack. "It was something I hope never to experience again." She pulled out a toy plastic phone and the blue blanket covered in lambs and clouds.

Jack stopped screaming, grabbed the blanket, and tucked his thumb in his mouth.

"Well." Felicity smiled at the little boy.

"Looks like a winner to me." Graham's chuckle was soft.

Jack was staring at Graham now, sniffling and wary, but no longer screaming.

"Does he know you?" she asked.

"No." Graham leaned forward, his peekaboo attempts warming Felicity's heart. "Matt pretty much cut all ties to Pecan Valley once he moved to Austin." He kept his voice playful, all his attention focused on the toddler.

Jack kept sucking his thumb, his eyelids growing heavy.

"Should he be tired already?" she asked. There was so much she didn't know, it scared her a little.

"Perfectly normal," Graham assured her. "His body has been through a lot of trauma. And he's a little guy. He'll tire easily for a while. Once he dozes off, I'll see what I can find out about his prognosis and treatment plan."

"Thanks, Graham." She drew in a deep breath.

His brown eyes bounced to hers, his smile crinkling the corners of his eyes nicely. "If you need anything, or if I can help out somehow, tell me, okay? I'm here."

He had no idea how much his offer meant to her. Not that she could burden him with any of her baggage—but still. She nodded, swallowing back the sudden tightness in her throat.

Jack pulled his thumb from his mouth and squealed, a frustrated sound that startled them both. He tried to sit up, but the cast was too restrictive, keeping him flat on his back and triggering another batch of tears.

"Bet that cast is no fun," Graham said, reaching forward to pick up the blue-and-black-striped tiger toy Felicity had pulled from her bag. "It'll take time to get used to." He made a silly face.

Jack blinked, his uneven breath and tear-streaked cheeks tugging at Felicity's heart. "I'm so sorry, little guy."

Jack glanced her way, his scowl almost comical. Clearly, he preferred Graham. He tugged the blanket tighter and resumed furiously sucking on his thumb.

"You like your blanket?" She smiled. "Nick had one just like it. Nick's your big brother." She paused, studying the little boy whose gaze fixed on her face. "When he was little, he carried it everywhere he went. It got frayed and dirty by the time I managed to get it away from him." She ran her hand over the edge of Jack's blanket. "Your daddy called it his germ mat."

Jack tugged the blanket from Felicity's touch and turned his face away from her. From this angle, he could be Nick, with his golden curls and his round cheeks working away as he sucked his thumb. Silence washed over them. Felicity did her best to keep thoughts off the life she'd lost forever. It had taken her a while to come to terms with her divorce, but she had. Now she was a wiser, stronger, and far more cautious woman than she'd been before. But that was good, wasn't it? So she wouldn't be blindsided the next time something unexpected cropped up.

Like this.

No. She'd been blindsided anyway.

Little Jack's chest rose and fell steadily, the quiet easing him into a peaceful sleep. For now. But when he woke up again, she'd still be a stranger. His favorite blanket could only do so much.

"Sometimes I miss this." Graham kept his tone soft and soothing. "When a pacifier or a favorite toy could fix almost everything."

She nodded and sat back in her chair. Infancy, toddlerhood—they'd been golden years that she'd enjoyed with every fiber of her being. Teenagers were different. She studied Graham Murphy. He was raising a teenage daughter on his own. And not just any teenage daughter. Diana was a mess, broken and screaming for attention. She knew Nick struggled with his emotions from time to time, but Diana— well, you couldn't live in Pecan Valley without hearing things. And Diana Murphy's antics came up often. From her suggested relationship with a no-longer-employed coach at one of the private schools in a neighboring town, to her pot possession and expulsion from the small Catholic school in Pecan Valley—Diana seemed bound and determined to leave a wake of destruction behind her.

"Diana was an easy baby." He continued, almost as if he'd read her mind. "Quick to smile and laugh." He glanced at her, the vulnerability on his face too raw to stay quiet.

"She's testing you," she murmured softly.

"And I'm failing." He paused, hesitating before he added, "I don't know how to change that or even if I can."

It was impossible to imagine what he was describing. No matter what they'd been through, she and her children were close. At least, she hoped they were. If Matt had taught her one thing, it was people's perspectives varied widely. She thought they were close—close enough to know when her children were in distress. Diana was clearly in distress, quite possibly the sort of distress that needed professional help. "Don't be offended, okay, but have you thought about counseling?"

"I'm not offended." Those brown eyes met hers, raw and bleak. "She's been seeing a psychiatrist since Julia died—after she tried to kill herself the first time."

Felicity tried not to react. Diana had tried to kill herself? Multiple times? And he'd had to deal with that on his own? "Oh, Graham…"

"Her psychiatrist wants to admit her to one of those rehab places." He cleared his throat. "Like sending her to that sort of place will help her. Maybe it's the best thing for her, but my instincts tell me it's not." He blinked and his voice was thick. "If I send her away, she'll hate me even more. I'd be deserting her—the way I did her mother."

Surely, he didn't believe that? "You never deserted Julia, Graham." He'd been at his wife's side through her entire cancer ordeal.

"I let her die." The words were harsh. "I gave her permission to stop fighting." He sat back slowly, his gaze settling on the sleeping boy. "That's the way Di sees it. I gave Julia permission to let go and stop fighting. I took her mother away."

Felicity watched Graham—the way he rolled his head and ran a hand along the back of his neck. Diana was too young to understand how lucky she was to have this man for a father. Or how much her actions and words hurt.

"While I was obsessing over losing my wife, my daughter was losing her mother." He cleared his throat again. "It took me a while to realize that I'd been self-absorbed. Like Matt, I abandoned my daughter and my responsibilities." He looked at her then. "I won't do it again. I can't risk it."

It was on the tip of her tongue to argue with him. He wasn't Matt. But she knew what he meant. Adults didn't have the luxury of immersing them-selves in their own emotional experiences—not if there were children in the mix. "Adulting sucks sometimes." She smiled at him, relieved when he smiled in return.

"You can say that again," he agreed. "Might sound wrong, but Jack's the lucky one. He'll never know what he lost or what he's missing."

She leaned forward, taking the little hand in hers. Graham was right. Jack's leg would heal and what-ever memories he had of Matt and Amber would be hazy at best. He was so young. That was some sort of blessing.

Nick, Honor, and Diana? They understood all too well. Their wounds would take years to heal. And the guilt she and Graham carried for wounding their children?

Would they ever recover from that?

CHAPTER SIX

Graham stared at his phone. It wasn't a familiar number, which immediately set off warning bells. Diana. Always Diana. She'd said she was volunteering at the library today—then waited for him to drill her with questions and details. Instead, he'd called the library on his way to work and confirmed she had signed up to volunteer. Not that volunteering ensured she'd stay out of trouble. He drew in a deep breath, paused in the hall outside the next exam room, and hit redial.

"Hello?" He nodded as one of the nurses walked past, escorting a very pregnant Mrs. Guajardo into exam room five.

"Hello?" He didn't recognize the voice. "Graham? Graham Murphy?"

"Yes," he snapped. "If you're selling something, I'm not interested—"

"No." A high, feminine laugh. "It's Romi Takahashi."

He blanked. Did he know a Romi Takahashi? No one sprang to mind. But the name was familiar.

"Miss Takahashi—from St. Thomas Catholic School. The assistant principal. But, please, call me Romi."

The school Diana had been expelled from. "Yes." Now he knew exactly who it was—he'd spent enough time in her office. But it didn't clear up why she was calling him now. Diana was no longer enrolled there. And it was summertime. "How can I help you?"

That laugh again. "Don't tell me Eileen Rainey didn't call you?" She paused. "She gave me your number. Said something about you mentioning having coffee with me but…were too shy to call?"

No, she hadn't told him. Because Widow Rainey knew good and well he'd never said anything about having coffee with Miss Takahashi or any other woman in Pecan Valley, and he would have told her so. Again. He closed his eyes and swallowed the litany of curses that rose up. "She did?"

"Yes." An awkward silence ensued. "So, anyway, I'd love to have coffee. If you're free?"

No, he wasn't. "Coffee?" He was flattered but… "Now's not a good time."

"Well, not *now* now. Of course. I meant, sometime in the near future." She paused. "I was really flattered you'd ask, after Diana and…well, you know."

Technically, she was the one asking—but he didn't point it out. He was still doing his best not to blow a gasket. It wasn't Miss Takahashi's fault. He didn't know how the hell Widow Rainey gotten his number, but this was a problem. Widow Rainey was relentless and, clearly, she hadn't listened to his objections. *Not good.* He'd never thought to guard his number. Considering his profession, most of his patients had it. He might have to rethink that practice going forward. "I'll have to check my schedule and get back to you."

"Sounds great, Graham. How's Diana doing?"

"She's fine." He didn't miss the nurse's pointed

look from the clock to the patient's door. He under-stood. None of them wanted to work late. Again. "I'm sorry to cut this short, but I'm at work—"

"Oh, right, right. Some people have to do that job thing through the summer, too." She laughed again. "I'll let you get back to it. Looking forward to hearing from you soon."

"Right. Bye." He hung up and stood, staring at the exam room door. Clear head. Work mode. He took a slow, calming breath, grabbed the chart, and entered the exam room. "Good afternoon…" The name threw him for a loop. "Charity?" Charity Otto was the last person he'd expected to find in his office.

"Surprise," she said, her cheeks a bright red.

He scanned over her paperwork. Charity Otto was pregnant. And alone—two things that didn't add up. Where was Felicity? Or Mrs. Otto for that matter? "Yes." He glanced at her, then back at the chart.

"I'm pregnant," she whispered. "I'm just as shocked as you are."

He smiled his professional smile, ignoring the list of questions he was mentally assembling. She was here as his patient. As such, the only questions he should ask were pertinent to her and her baby's health.

"You can't tell anyone, right?" she asked, fingers pleating her examination gown. "I know you and Filly are getting chummy, but I'm wanting to wait a while on my baby bombshell. I think the family is dealing with enough at the moment, don't you?" It was a sincere question—as if she wanted his opinion.

"You're my patient. Unless you give us permission to share information, all of this remains here."

He studied her, noting how uneasy she was. She looked young. And scared. "You're almost three months along?" he asked. "You won't be able to keep it a secret for long. Pregnancy is emotional enough without keeping it a secret. You have a supportive family. You should tell them, Charity, so they can be here for you."

"I'll take that under advisement, Doctor." The paper on the exam table crackled as she swung her legs back and forth.

He began a quick exam, listening to her heart and lungs before reading over her chart. "Your numbers are good. Blood work looks great. Are you taking prenatal vitamins?"

She nodded.

"Eating well?"

She shrugged. "If that means eating everything in sight, yes. I'm eating very well."

He smiled. "No. That's not what I meant. Focus on eating quality food—foods that will give your baby the vitamins to grow big and strong."

Her skin paled as she nodded. "My baby. I can't tell you how bizarre that sounds," she whispered.

"Unplanned, then?"

"Oh yeah." A nervous giggle. High. Forced. "I met Sergio when I was working as a private tour guide in Florence. He sort of swept me off my feet. Seven weeks later, his wife comes knocking on our apartment door." She shrugged. "Turns out his missus was someone important enough to get me fired. I hocked the diamond ring Sergio gave me after his faux proposal and made my way home."

Graham had no idea what to say.

"I know. Crazy, right?" Her hands gripped the edge of the exam table so tightly her knuckles whitened.

Scared, alone, and hurting, then. "I'm sorry." He meant it.

She smiled even though her eyes filled with tears. "Graham, you're the sweetest guy." She wiped her eyes with the back of her hand. "If I hadn't already decided you and my sister are soul mates, I would so be crushing on you."

"Not you, too," he murmured. First Diana. Now Charity. No. Felicity deserved better.

She perked up. "Me too, what? Don't tell me Filly made a move? I'm so proud of her. I mean, I sort of mentioned what I was thinking but I didn't think she had it in her—"

"No moves have or will be made." They'd talked about him? Was Felicity interested? What would he have said if she had? He pressed his eyes shut. *Get a grip*. What was wrong with him? He was forty, not some knobby-kneed high school kid. He shut down that line of thinking before it took root. "I'm not interested in dating. No matter what you, Diana, or Widow Rainey think."

Charity groaned. "Oh. Who did she sic on you?"

"Some assistant principal." He shook his head. He was not going to discuss this with her—she was his patient now. "It doesn't matter."

Her brows rose. "It does if the woman's going to give my sister competition."

He crossed his arms over his chest. "If you're going to be my patient, we need to lay down some ground rules."

She crossed her arms and stared back. "I'm not good at rules, Graham."

He ignored her. "When you're here, you are my *patient*. Meaning we're not going to discuss things that aren't related to your pregnancy."

She frowned at him. "But when I'm not sitting on paper, wearing some naked-backed robe thing we can still be friends?"

He wasn't sure how to answer that. "It might be best for you to see Dr. Luna, Charity. Because of the…the family connection."

She stared at him, her legs swinging rapidly. "You mean connection between you and my sister."

"This isn't going to work." He pinched the bridge of his nose. Six o'clock couldn't get here soon enough. Maybe an hour at the gym would ease some of the kinks out of his neck and back. But if that were true, the last year of near-daily hour-long workouts would have his stress under control. Clearly, that wasn't the case.

"Fine. Fine. I'll stop. I don't want to see Dr. Luna." She sighed. "I'm scared, Graham, okay? Freaking out. Don't pawn me off on some strange dude."

"Dr. Veronica Luna," he interrupted.

"Right, still. I'd rather see you. So, I'm deter-mined to get you and my sister hooked up—but at least I'm up front about it."

He stared at her. Hooked up? She sounded like Diana. Uncensored and unapologetic. Still, the idea wasn't bothering him the way Romi Takahashi's phone call had. No, something told him he would have reacted very differently if Felicity Otto-Buchanan had called him. And he wasn't sure that was a good thing. "If you can act like a patient, I will be your doctor. Agreed?"

"Yes, totally. Agreed." She nodded. "But outside your office, all bets are off."

• • •

Nick ran his hands through his sweat-slicked hair, heart hammering in his chest as he ran along the near-dry creek bed. No one hovering around, acting like he was going to explode. If one more person asked if he was okay, or gave him that *look,* or said they were sorry, he was going to lose his shit.

But that would give everyone in this pathetic town something else to say about his family. And that was the last thing his mom—any of them— needed.

Diana said she had something that could help. Why he was listening to someone who was even more screwed up than he was, he wasn't sure. But now he was running the dry creek bed at two in the morning to meet her where all the potheads hung out to get high. He was that fricking desperate. Because his dad was an asshole.

Dead now. A dead asshole. And the fact that his asshole dad's death hurt this bad pissed him off.

He couldn't shake it. The anger. His phone kept blowing up with texts to hang out, go see a movie, or game online, but Nick ignored them—ignored the phone calls and tweets and snapchats, too. They didn't get it. He couldn't hang out and act like everything was normal. Unlike his friends, he knew the truth: life sucked. It was cruel and pointless and believing anything different would get your heart stomped and your dreams trashed.

Over and over again.

"You came." Diana was sitting at the edge of the pipe, her skinny white legs all but glowing in the dark.

"Yeah," he said, gasping for breath. He pulled at the hem of his shirt, sweat gluing the fabric to his chest.

"Jesus, Nick." She pushed off the ground. "You ran here? You *are* crazy. Come meet everybody."

Everybody was three people. Some vaguely familiar overweight girl named Beth, with bloodshot eyes and a see-through shirt. A guy Diana called Whack, who had acne scars and a chip on his shoulder.

And Lane. Lane Aisley. Lane was a major prick—everyone at school knew that. The asshat lived to piss people off.

This was further proof that life wasn't fair. If it were, this waste of a kid would have died, and his father would still be here to piss him off and ignore him.

Breathing in hurt. Something jagged lodged in his throat.

Lane had a joint in one hand and a half-empty bottle of whiskey in the other—as if Nick needed more proof that the guy was a complete tool. But something about Lane's face, his cocky smile, made Nick's hands clench. Planting his fists into Lane's face, again and again and again… Stopping would be the problem.

He pulled at the hem on his shirt again and rolled his neck.

"Chill. Here," Diana said, holding out the lit joint. "I promise, this will help."

Getting high wasn't going to do a damn thing—except get him high. But screw it, he needed a break before he did something really stupid. The sweet cloud of smoke flooded his lungs and then he breathed out slowly—through his nose.

"Feel anything?" Diana asked, watching him.

The full moon overhead cast shadows over everything. Diana's smudged dark liner made her eyes look like holes in her pale face.

"No," he murmured, his tongue thick in his mouth. Anything? Try everything. Too frigging much. He was sick and tired of choking on all the things he didn't say. Wound tight with all the things he ached to do but didn't.

Diana smiled. "Sure." She took a long drag off the joint. "You can cut the crap, okay? It's me."

Maybe that's why he was here. With Diana, he didn't have to try. He didn't know why she was pissed at the world, but they had that much in common. Considering she was a total nut job, that wasn't exactly comforting.

He stared beyond her at the others. Lane was watching them, that smug smile creasing his face. His fist, on that face—he could almost feel the force of the blow, see the way Lane's head would pop back. He'd fall, down, down... And Nick would be the one smiling.

The images stretched and twisted, throwing off his equilibrium. The world slanted, the corners softening and blurred.

"I get it." Her smile was hard. "I *so* get it."

Wait, what? She got it? "No. You don't," he pushed back. She had no idea what he was going through.

She ran a hand through her hacked-off black hair, scratching her too-thin forearms with black-tipped nails. "Whatever." She took another hit. "If you're going to be an ass, you don't get to share my weed."

He sighed and stood, staring up at the star-laden sky overhead. The sky was dropping, pushing down on him and swallowing the air. If this was her idea of relaxing, she was more messed up than he'd realized. This sucked. Stars were moving. Or was he moving?

"You think your dad is up there?" Diana asked, swaying slightly and holding out the joint.

He took another hit, breathed in deep before eventually answering. "Nope." His legs were giving out so he sat at the edge of the pipe, the sky slowly descending until he couldn't move. Was his dad there? Close now, close enough to touch—if he could reach out. He didn't. "No way."

She sat down, hard, beside him. "My mom is."

He nodded. The ground was moving. "Your mom was awesome. Her peanut butter cookies. The best." He wanted one. No, he wanted a plate of them. All the memories he had of Mrs. Murphy were good. She was up there in the stars. Stars that were falling, leaving big white streaks in the sky. "Think she can see us?"

Diana leaned back, resting on her elbows. "I sure as hell hope not."

"Diana," Lane Aisley called out. "Come here."

Diana sat up. "The boyfriend calls."

Diana had self-destructive tendencies, but… That *tool* was her boyfriend? Maybe she didn't know he was all about hooking up and sharing the details with anyone who would listen. The guy was a douche. She needed to know that. He should have beaten the crap out of the loser when he had the chance. "Bad idea," was the only warning he managed. Everything was heavy. It was hard to focus on anything.

"I'm all about the bad ideas, Nick." She was blurry and wavering, but she was staring at him. "We both know being good is a dead-end street." She sighed. "You've never done this before, have you?"

Weed? No. Never. But he didn't make a sound.

"You gonna be okay?" she asked, reaching up to ruffle his hair.

Those words again. Why did people ask when no one wanted an answer? No. He wasn't okay. No frigging way. But no one wanted to hear him scream or see him punch the wall of this concrete pipe until his knuckles were shredded and breathing was possible again. Right now, the world was spinning too much for him to do either. All he could do was hold on to the edge of the concrete tube, hold on or fall.

"Here," Diana said, nudging him enough to throw him off-balance. "Shit, Nick… Lean against the wall."

Somehow, he made it to the side of the pipe. Head back, eyes closed, he held the cigarette she'd pressed into his hand but didn't take another drag. Through the fog, the same shit was waiting for him. His father, Jack, his mom and sister, his inability to

make things better or get away from everything.
And sadness. He wanted to run, to keep running
until he couldn't think or run anymore. But
movement, now, was an impossibility. And it scared
the shit out of him. He was too high to leave, too
high to drag Diana home, too high to stop the hot,
angry tears from spilling down his cheeks.

• • •

Honor rolled over and looked at her phone. It was
almost five a.m., and Owen Nelson was calling her?
"Are you kidding me?" she groaned. Did he not get
the whole silent treatment thing? Fine. If he needed
her to say the words outright, she would. "Hello?"

"Good morning, sunshine. I found something
that belongs to you." He was whispering.

"Are you drunk?" she asked, rubbing the sleep
from her eyes.

He chuckled. "I'm not. But your brother is.
Wanna let me in before that old lady next door calls
the cops on us?"

"What?" Honor sat up and covered her other ear.
"Nick?" she whispered, pushing her tangled red hair
from her face. "He's been drinking? With you?"

"Yes, to the first one. No, to the second. I found
him when I was out running." He paused. "We're
outside and he's heavy."

"Back door," she heard Nick add, voice slurred
and thick.

"Coming." She was already hurrying across the
landing, down the stairs, dodging Pecan and Praline
as they leaped up hoping for breakfast, and through

the living room to the french doors at the back of the house. Outside was Nick, his arm draped around Owen's neck, bleary-eyed and looking like hell.

"What's going on?" she asked, opening the door. "Nickie, are you okay?"

Nick glared at her. "Seriously?" he growled.

"He's stoned. Whiskey, too—I can smell," Owen said, practically dragging her brother inside. "Threw up a few times on the way."

"Sorry, man," Nick mumbled.

"My shirt." Owen glanced down. "And my shoes. But he's doing better since he downed my water bottle."

Honor adored her little brother. But this… On top of everything else? Fury kicked in, hard and fast. "I can't believe you…" But her voice was rising so she broke off and clapped her mouth shut. When there wasn't the fear of their mother discovering them, she was so going to lay into him.

"Honor," Nick groaned. "I know I screwed up, okay? Not gonna happen again. I need to sleep it off."

"Shut up," she hissed. "You are not going to wake up Mom, you hear me? She has enough to deal with right now. So be quiet before I…I lose my cool." Hands fisted, she glanced at Owen. "Why are you smiling?"

He shook his head, but his smile never wavered.

"This way," she hissed, sliding across the floor in her fuzzy socks. "Fifth step squeaks," she said, pointing at the step as she led them to Nick's room.

She glanced back, angry and worried and completely clueless about what to do next. Was Nick okay? He looked terrible. All gray. His lips were white. And he was covered in sweat. Did he need a doctor? Sleep? A kick in the ass?

"He'll be okay," Owen said.

She frowned. How did he know? Did he have a vast knowledge of being stoned and the aftereffects? And why was he smiling at her like that?

"In here," she said, pushing open Nick's door.

Owen helped her brother to his bed. "Going down," he said, lowering her brother slowly to the mattress.

Nick lay back, both hands pressed to his head. "This sucks."

Good. Serves you right. But she couldn't very well yell it at him the way she wanted to.

"Thanks, man." Nick clasped Owen's hand in that weird angled handshake thing guys did to look cool.

"No prob." Owen put his hands on his hips. "That shit's bad for you."

"Yeah," Nick groaned.

"I get you're wound up, though. So, starting tomorrow, you're going to the gym with me." Honor's anger was temporarily derailed by Owen's offer. He did have the body of a professional athlete—all muscle. And he moved like one, too. Not that she'd spent a lot of time noticing. She hadn't. Everything about Owen Nelson made her squirm. He was too pretty, too popular, and too…too confident. He'd always loved being the center of attention. And people loved making him the center of attention, so this newfound selflessness didn't make sense.

"Okay?" he asked, still waiting for some sign from her brother.

Nick gave a thumbs-up.

"Good." Owen waited until Nick nodded before leaving. "You owe me shoes."

Nick's chuckle ended in a groan.

"Shh," Honor reminded them.

Owen held his hands up and headed her way, lingering in the door—beside her. Way, way too close to her.

She stepped back and whacked her head against the doorframe.

"Careful," he whispered, his hand sliding between her head and the doorframe. "Don't want to have to carry you to your bedroom."

Tingles covered every inch of skin. He was close. And big. And staring down at her with a totally different smile on his face. She didn't know what it meant but the hot, tight burn in her belly was delightfully foreign and totally unsettling.

"He's going to be okay?" she murmured. "No doctor or anything?"

"No," Nick groaned. "Sleep. Lemme sleep."

She glared at her brother.

"Sleep should do it," Owen whispered, his gaze never leaving her face.

Which was good because she was wearing a massive T-shirt, zebra-striped socks, and had crazy bed head.

"I should go." When he wasn't trying so hard, he wasn't nearly as obnoxious.

"Yes." She nodded, leading him back down the stairs. It was only when she was pushing open the french doors that she realized he could have shown himself out.

He paused in the doorway. "You're avoiding me?"

There was just enough rumble to his voice to make her toes curl in her fuzzy socks. Against her better judgment, she looked up at him and held her breath.

"I'm leaving for boot camp in a few weeks. After that, you'll miss me."

He'd been a thorn in her side since the day he'd moved here. Freshman year. English class. He'd been assigned the seat in front of her. From there she'd seen what sort of guy he was. From his constant flirting with every girl in school to the way he relentlessly teased her, Owen Nelson became her nemesis. Everything about him pushed her buttons. She was pretty sure he knew that—and liked it.

Now he was leaving. Miss him? Her lungs felt heavy. Why would she miss him? "I doubt it." Her voice wavered.

"Ouch." He pressed a hand over a bulging pectoral.

She swallowed, too aware of him. "But tonight, this morning, I mean… Thank you for this."

His fingers brushed a curl from her cheek. "That hurt to say, didn't it?"

She was smiling at him. Why was she smiling at him?

Owen's hazel eyes swept over her face, the hint of real emotion surfacing on his model-worthy face. "I knew you'd be worried about him."

Meaning he'd done this for her? No. That wasn't at all what he meant. Was it?

"I'll whip him into shape before I leave. I need

someone to work out with anyway. If you're okay with that?"

She nodded, doing her best to stop smiling at him.

He drew in an unsteady breath. "We need to go out." It was the softest whisper.

Say no. Say it now. And tell him to stop asking. She swallowed. "Why?"

He grinned. It was a heart-stopping sort of grin. "Because I'd like to spend time with you. A lot."

He did? "Why?" She repeated, not nearly as resistant to the idea as she should be.

"Shh," he reminded her, but his grin grew. "Why *not*?" His gaze held hers. "Good memories to take with me when I leave."

He was leaving. Joining the Marines, like her uncle Zach. Meaning she wouldn't see him again for a long, long time. Like Uncle Zach.

"Please," he added. The word was soft and husky.

"Owen." A little voice inside shouted *yes*.

"Honor." He cocked his head, stepping closer. "Why is it so hard to say yes?"

Because he was all about the hunt and she was the one—the only one—who'd turned down *the* Owen Nelson. And now? She didn't have time for this. For him and his smile and the way he was getting to her. "Why is it so hard for you to accept my no?" Why couldn't she sound certain? Instead of all soft and wavering and lame. *Because I'm lying and I'm a terrible liar.*

"I would, if you meant it." He reached for her again, his hand warm against her cheek. "You know what, Honor Buchanan? I've made sure I have no regrets so far. You're going to mess that up. Because us, not happening… I'll regret that every day."

He was staring at her, waiting. But she couldn't back down. Not after three years of eye rolling and staying strong. How could she?

Because she really wanted to. *Oh my God, I do.* "Fine," she muttered.

"What?" he asked, his thumb sweeping lightly across her cheek.

"You heard me." She shot him a look, but there was no hiding the shiver his touch caused.

His grin was back. "I heard you."

That grin was a warning. This, he, was a bad, bad idea. "But…things are sort of messed up right now."

"I got that." His eyes searched hers as he stepped closer. "I'll call you. But that means you have to answer the phone." Another step. If he leaned in to kiss her…

The overhead lights clicked on.

"Honor?" Her mother stood there, staring back and forth between them in shock and mounting concern.

Her mother waited for an answer and, for the first time in her life, Honor didn't have one. The truth was there on the tip of her tongue, but she couldn't do it. The last few weeks had been hell. Adding more stress and worry went against everything Honor believed in. She would make sure Nick didn't pull this sort of crap again. And, if Owen was serious, he would keep Nick out of trouble—for her. Her mother didn't need to know. Maybe.

"Mom," Honor managed, her voice high and thin. She was scrambling for an explanation. She was in her nightshirt, with a boy, in the dark… "We didn't want to wake you."

Her mom's owllike eyes blinked. "Oh?"

Way to really *freak Mom out.* She sucked in a deep breath and took Owen's hand in hers. "Owen. You know Owen, don't you?" She cleared her throat.

Her mother nodded, eyes on their hands.

"Well, he and I…" She shrugged, smiling nervously.

Owen squeezed her hand. "I was out for a run, Mrs. Buchanan. Just stopped by to say hello." He chuckled. "I forget not everyone is up at this hour."

Her mother's posture eased the tiniest bit. "Running? At this hour?"

"Yes, ma'am. I leave for boot camp in a few weeks. Trying to get myself on schedule and in fighting shape." He smiled his win-over-the-teacher smile. "I apologize for stopping by uninvited. Had to see Honor—miss not seeing her every day at school." His fingers threaded with hers, setting Honor's nerves to tingling. "Best way to start my day."

Honor's heart was thumping in her chest. He was good. Oh, so good. Good enough for her to wonder what that would be like—for him to feel that way about her.

"She has that effect on people." Her mother smiled. "You're welcome to join us for breakfast, Owen. After your run?"

Her mom was a goner. Not that she blamed her.

"I appreciate the offer, Mrs. Buchanan, but I have work today. It was nice to officially meet you."

"You're welcome to drop by this evening if you'd

like. Just let me know what works." Honor knew she was freaking out over walking in on her daughter in her pj's with a hot guy, but she was doing her best to act cool because she was the best mother ever.

"I'm sorry I woke you." Those warm brown eyes locked with hers. "I'll let you go back to bed."

Like that was going to happen. Her head and heart and…all of her were in a tailspin. She swallowed. "'kay."

"I'll call later." His fingers tightened around hers, then slid free. This shivering from his touch thing had to stop. She enjoyed it way too much. "You have to answer your phone," he whispered.

She nodded, his smile making her flush warmly.

"Bye," he said, waving at her mother, winking her way, and leaving through the back door.

Her mother's arm slid around her shoulders and pulled her close. "Wow," she said. "He's sort of… grown-up."

"We're the same age, Mom." But she knew what her mother meant. Owen was wow.

"And Owen is your *boyfriend*?" she asked, squeezing her shoulder.

No. No way. The idea was laughable. "Yep."

"And he did *just* stop by?" she pushed.

Honor glanced up at her. "Yes."

Her mother relaxed then. "I know you're an adult, Honor. I know you're responsible and young and, apparently, in love. Just promise me you'll be careful. Okay?" She touched her cheek.

Careful? Was she talking about sex? Sex? With Owen? Even if she did forget that this was all a big cover-up for Nick's stupidity, which she wouldn't, there was no way she'd ever contemplate sex with Owen.

All right, fine. Maybe. But she barely considered herself a decent kisser at this point. It wasn't like she'd had a ton of experience. But Owen? He was probably a pro at kissing. Probably sex, too. Not that she'd ever know—or that she wanted to know. She didn't. At least, she didn't think so.

CHAPTER SEVEN

Charity sat beside Jack's hospital bed, doing her best to finish reading the storybook without getting hit in the face with whatever projectile the toddler was heaving at her. Good thing he was too little to have good aim.

"Good one," she said, leaning to dodge an empty juice box. "Your dad was backup, backup quarterback, I think. That's a nice way of saying he was a benchwarmer." She tried smiling at the red-faced toddler. "I liked him. Then. *He* always liked me."

Jack didn't look like he believed her. Or like he cared. He stretched and flailed but when he couldn't reach another missile from his bedside table, he burst into tears. Even with her limited knowledge of babies and toddlers, she knew a tantrum when she saw one.

"I know the feeling," Charity said, setting the board book on the bed and standing. Should she comfort him? Talk to him? Run from the room? Honestly, the last option was the most appealing. "Grams is coming, okay, little dude. I get it. You don't want me here."

Felicity had received a surprise call from Matt's lawyer and, since Grams was running late, she'd been forced to sit with baby Jack. She was pretty sure the kid hated her. He was staring at her, white-blond curls standing on end, flushed cheeks and quivering lips. Poor little guy was pathetic.

"Come on, Jack. I'm really not that bad, I promise." She smiled.

He threw the board book at her.

"What's all the racket about?" Grams asked, waddling into the room with her massive knitting basket hooked onto her arm. "You torturing the boy or what?"

Charity smiled down at her grandmother. At eighty-one, the woman was just as feisty and active as women half her age. "You know me."

"I know you've never been fond of children," Grams answered, reaching up to pat her cheek. "Which is why I've given up hoping you'll provide me any great-grandkids. Guess I'll have to count on your brother for a good half dozen—to make up the difference."

Charity swallowed. *Oh, Grams, you have no idea.* "Think Zach is a little busy saving the world right now, Grams."

"He'll come home eventually. I told him to get a move on. I'm not going to live forever," Grams argued.

"Yes, you will," she sassed right back. "Jack's in a bad mood. Maybe it's just me. But the nurse is bringing him some applesauce and Jell-O." She tried to mimic the singsong voice she'd heard both Felicity and Honor use. "Yum-yum."

Jack peeked through his fingers at her.

"And it's not that I don't like kids," Charity argued. "They don't like me." Which was true. Even Nick and Honor had been wary of her when they were really little. But then, she'd been wary of them. Once they were walking and talking, it was cake.

Which meant the baby growing in her stomach was in serious trouble for the first two or three years of life.

"Charity?" Grams was looking at her, waiting.

"What?" she asked. "Sorry."

"I'm the one hard of hearing, girlie." Grams paused. "I asked if you'd gone to see Maudie at the travel agency. You know, to get a job. I bet she'll sell you her business, too. She's been wanting to retire for years."

"Why hasn't she?" Charity asked. "Who even uses a travel agent anymore?"

"Not everyone likes putting their financial information into those dang computers, Charity Ann." Grams was incredulous. "All those hack-men out there, stealing your identity and crashing your credit goals. I travel all the time, and Maudie O'Meara is the only person I trust to make sure I'm safe and taken care of."

Charity couldn't stop smiling at her grandmother. She was a piece of work. Exactly the way she wanted to be when she was eighty-one years old. "I love you, Grams, you know that?"

"What's not to love?" she asked, grinning up at her. "But don't change the subject. If you're staying put, and I hear you're thinking about staying put for a while, might as well make yourself useful—especially if you're going to be another mouth for Felicity to feed."

Charity paused then. Grams was right. She needed a job. Preferably one with benefits. Even though the idea of being caged behind a desk in a small office right off Pecan Valley's quaint and cliché

Old Town Square made her skin crawl, there weren't a ton of options. It wasn't just her anymore.

"Do you have Maudie's number?" she asked.

"You go on down and see her." Grams waved her aside. "She's been hoping you'd stop by since she heard you were in town."

"Okay." It's not like she'd been back that long. What had it been? Two weeks? Not quite? Was that all?

"Good." Grams sat beside the bed and dug through her bag. "I finished her doilies, too, so you can take them with you." She held up a brown paper sack.

"Anything else?" she asked.

"I'll text you if I think of anything." Grams smiled as the nurse came through the door. "Well, lookee here, Jack. Snack time. I hope they brought enough for me."

"I did, Mrs. Otto." The nurse smiled. "And I have good news. The doctor thinks little Jack will be released soon. Maybe a day or two."

Charity was pretty sure that wasn't necessarily good news. "I'll tell Felicity."

"He's not going home with Filly, is he?" Grams asked, shaking her head and making the same disapproving click she'd made since Charity could remember. "His mother had no people?"

"So far, no one has popped up. But I think they're looking." If there was any justice in the world, someone suitable would turn up. Hopefully her sister would come home tonight with good news. "I'll let you two enjoy your Jell-O." She pressed a kiss to Grams's cheek, waved at a glaring Jack, and hurried down the hall.

At the nurse's station at the far end of the hall stood Braden Martinez—looking solemn and impatient—gauze pressed against his forehead. Before she took the time to consider her actions, she headed straight for him. She hadn't thanked him for helping her get to the hospital that night. And, right now, he looked like he could use a thank-you or kind word. His heavy-lidded gaze slid her way and briefly widened before he stared straight ahead.

"Well, hi there, Sheriff," she said, leaning in front of him and forcing him to acknowledge her. "Thanks for the police escort the other night."

He nodded. "Part of the job." His gaze shifted her way again. "It was either escort you or arrest you for running a red light."

She grinned. "Oh, well, now I appreciate it even more." He didn't grin back—if anything, he seemed to be intentionally *not* looking at her. Which made her linger. "What happened to your head?" she asked, wishing he'd look her way. The eyes said so much.

"Domestic dispute," he murmured.

"The wife got mad at you?" she asked, knowing full well he wasn't married or her mother, Grams, and the widows' group would stop mentioning how available and handsome and what a catch he'd be for her.

That got his attention. One brow arched, and those heavy-lidded eyes locked with hers. "Not my wife."

"Well, that explains why it turned into a domestic dispute." She smiled at him. "Honestly, Sheriff, I'm surprised at you. Messing around with someone else's wife."

He sighed, no sign of a smile in sight. Instead, his posture went rigid and his expression hardened.

She'd have to confer with the widows, but something told her the super-hot, super-broody sheriff might have been cheated on. And she'd just stuck her foot in it. Not that she was into gossip but…if she was going to stay put, she might as well drink the Kool-Aid and get the scoop on the citizens of her home sweet home. And since the baby in her belly—and her belly—were only getting bigger, she was staying put.

And it would be okay. Not at all upsetting. Not a bit nausea-inducing.

"I got caught in the crossfire of a domestic dispute. One I was there to break up. One I had nothing to do with." His brows rose, and he waited.

"Oh, well." She wrinkled her nose, eyeing the gauze pad pressed against his forehead. "Crossfire of what? A knife? A gun?" Pecan Valley had become downright dangerous since she'd left.

"A shoe."

"A shoe?" She laughed, making the churning in her stomach more pronounced.

"Some chunky-heeled thing." He held the gauze away and looked at it.

"Oh my God, you're *really* bleeding." Her smile disappeared, her stomach tightening. "That was some shoe." Was she going to throw up? *Yes. Soon.*

"Solid aim," he finished.

She pressed her eyes shut and crossed her arms over her stomach. Happy thoughts. Bubble baths.

Cookies. Ice cream. Why did most of her happy thoughts revolve around food? Oh, right, because she was pregnant. And nauseous. And he was bleeding. Ugh. No. No blood. She sucked in a deep breath.

"You're looking a little green. The blood?"

She nodded. "So let's not talk about it." Another deep breath. "On your way to get stitches?"

"No. I need to see my father." His tone was curt.

The only thing she remembered about Braden's father was what a bastard he was. He'd show up drunk to all their football games, pick a fight, and get kicked out—humiliating Braden and stealing the limelight from his talented son. "He's sick?"

He nodded.

"I'm sorry." It was the right thing to say.

He looked at her, a small smile on his face. "Thanks."

She would have smiled back but the gauze slipped from his fingers and the gash on his forehead, still bleeding, did her in. Running was her only option. She did, dodging orderlies and gurneys and ignoring the stares. Thankfully, she made it to the restroom before she added public humiliation to the day's accomplishments.

• • •

"That's all I know at this point." Rob-the-lawyer Klein nodded at the waiter refilling his tea glass.

Felicity poked at her cobb salad, not in the least bit hungry. She'd hoped for very different news when he'd called. News in general. Instead, she'd wound up having lunch with Rob, in a very busy café, more deflated than ever.

"I'm sorry it's not good news." His voice was low. "I'm not giving up."

"And I appreciate that." She did, truly. But learning Amber had been a ward of the state since she was twelve would make tracking down relatives a challenge. Even if they managed to locate someone, how would that work? The person would be more of a stranger to Jack than her family.

"No good?" he asked, using his fork to point at her plate.

"It's delicious." She forced a smile and stabbed part of a hard-boiled egg.

"This is nice." Rob sat back in his chair, his gaze sweeping the lunch crowd—enough of a crowd that her lunch would be noticed and *that* news likely shared before she was back home. "It's rare I get out of the office for lunch." He smiled, his teeth drawing her full attention. "The company is nice, too."

Felicity did her best not to stare, but her sister's comments about the man's teeth had her smiling.

Robert Klein's eyebrows rose, and his smile grew.

That was the sort of male smile she hadn't received in a long time. And while it was flattering, she was not prepared for that sort of attention from Matt's lawyer.

Be honest. You're not prepared for that sort of attention from any man. Period. Especially while front and center for all of Pecan Valley to see and speculate upon. She stared at her salad, nervously pushing around the lettuce and ham.

"When does Honor leave for college?" he asked.

Good. Neutral territory. "Too soon." Which was true. This was not the summer she'd wanted. This summer was supposed to be heavy on sunshine, beaches, and laughter.

"Matt was very proud of Honor." He nodded as two men in suits walked past them. "He was always bragging on her. And Nick."

"He did?" She hadn't meant to ask out loud.

"Yes." Rob's gaze returned to her, and his smile dimmed. "I guess talking about him is hard. I apologize."

"No, it's fine." She shrugged. "He... That's nice. Knowing that."

He cleared his throat. "Talking about the ex probably isn't the best way to spend our first date."

Felicity's fork froze inches from her mouth. This was a date? No, this was not a date. This was a meeting—wasn't it? Yes. That's exactly what this was. Or, rather, what she thought it was.

"Felicity?"

She turned, spying Graham a few feet away. Seeing him provided instant relief. "Graham." It was a squeak.

Rob was on his feet, extending his hand. "Graham, good to see you."

"You, too, Robert. Felicity. Let me introduce you to Dr. Veronica Luna. She's just joined the practice." He stepped aside so Dr. Luna could shake hands.

Veronica Luna was breathtaking. Tall and curvy, a dimple peeking out of her cheek, and a solid fall of thick black hair. "Very nice to meet you both."

"Congratulations. Are you new to the area?" Felicity asked, seeing Graham and Dr. Luna as the perfect buffer between her and Rob. "Why don't you join us?"

If Rob was bothered by her suggestion, he didn't let it show. "Yes, please."

"Are you sure?" Veronica asked.

"Yes. Absolutely certain." *Please.* For a split second, she thought she'd actually said the please out loud. The other three were looking at her wearing a variety of expressions. Robert Klein looked confused. Veronica looked startled. And Graham?

He was trying not to laugh.

They pulled up chairs, and conversation turned to Veronica. Where she'd moved from. Her single, no-kid status. The best neighborhoods for house hunting. And what single, kid-less adults did in Pecan Valley. She and Graham were no help, but Rob was full of suggestions.

Graham's whispered, "Didn't mean to interrupt your first date," made her choke on her ice water. He was enjoying this far too much.

"You okay?" Rob asked.

She nodded, pressing her napkin to her mouth and stepping firmly on Graham's toes. He was having a hell of a time covering his laugh. "Fine. Water."

"What's the house specialty?" Veronica asked, scanning the menu.

"How hungry are you?" Rob asked, leaning closer to Dr. Luna.

"Starving." She smothered her yawn. "Dr. Mur-phy didn't take a lunch—"

"Which is common for me, and the nurses give

me grief about it," Graham argued, shaking his head. "So, save yourself the nagging and headaches and take a lunch."

There were dark shadows under his brown eyes. *You should be taking better care of yourself.*

"I'll remember that. If the nurses aren't happy, the office isn't happy." Veronica Luna smiled. "I'm guessing the Cobb salad is a no?"

Felicity stared down at her barely touched salad. "No, it's really good. I'm just not that hungry." She'd been planning on meeting Robert Klein at his office, but he'd called shortly before their meeting to change the location. Food hadn't been part of the equation—she had a roast slow cooking for a family dinner. And the word "date" had never, ever been mentioned. If it had, she wouldn't have come.

Hopefully, Rob was joking. But a quick glance at the white-teethed lawyer had her shifting in her seat. His smile was back—all male appreciation. And, in case that wasn't enough, he added a wink.

• • •

There was nothing more awkward than two adults trying to one-up each other. But Veronica and Rob Klein were going toe to toe. And it was exhausting. While he made his way through his burger and fries, the two of them plowed through their academic career, academic accomplishments, and who was youngest upon graduation. Over dessert, they moved on to their favorite travel destinations and why.

Graham noticed how quickly Felicity drained her

glass of wine. She seemed to relax—a little. Not enough to look like she was truly enjoying herself, but he could tell she was trying.

When Rob excused himself to take a phone call, Veronica blew out a deep breath and said, "He's super competitive. That has to be exhausting. How long have you been going out?"

Graham watched as Felicity went from pseudo-relaxed to ramrod stiff.

"We're not." Felicity's tone was firm. "This…is a meeting. *Only* a meeting."

"Oh?" Veronica grinned. "Does he know that?"

"Absolutely." But she was chewing on her lower lip.

"Good to know." Veronica's gaze bounced between Felicity and Robert, who was animatedly talking on his phone across the restaurant. "Excuse me." She pushed back her chair and headed toward the restrooms.

When Felicity's green eyes met Graham's, he couldn't stop the laughter.

"Hush," she hissed, shoving his shoulder. "It's not funny."

"It sort of is," he argued.

"Nope, not in the least." Her hands toyed with the paper straw wrapper on the table. "We were meeting to talk about Jack, the whole guardianship thing. Period."

"Well, that's good. He's located someone for Jack?" It would make life ten times easier for Felicity and her kids.

But she was shaking her head. "No. That's the problem. There's now a question about whether or not Amber has any family. Finding someone to take Jack might be more difficult than expected." She went back to chewing her lower lip.

"Seems like the sort of thing he could have shared over the phone?"

She nodded. "I know."

But he knew exactly why Rob hadn't left her a voicemail. He wanted time with Felicity. Not exactly an ethical or professional way to go about it but definitely effective. But the tension bracketing her mouth made him think laughter might be in order. "I thought I heard him say something about a date?"

"*This* is *not* a date." The *drop dead* look she shot him faded when she realized he was teasing. "Seriously, Graham, it's been a while, but I think you have to ask someone out for it to be considered a date." She waited, a crease forming between her brows. "It still works that way, doesn't it? Or have I been in mom survival-mode so long the rules have changed?"

"You're asking me? I'm pretty sure that's still the way it works." He shrugged. "I've played enough golf with Rob Klein to know how he works. He wants something, he goes for it. Like a human bull-dozer." He shook his head. "In a charming, nonthreatening way, of course." From the proprietary smiles Rob had been sending her way through the entire meal, there was no misunderstanding the man's interest. And why not? She was…Felicity. She deserved a man who'd see her for the incredible woman she was.

But Rob Klein? Graham didn't like it. At all.

She blinked, those emerald green eyes going

wider. "I'm sorry. Was that supposed to be helpful?"

He wasn't sure. Was he trying to warn her away? Why? Rob wasn't a bad guy.

But Rob returned before Graham could say anything else. "As much as I'd like to stay and have coffee, there's been a hiccup in a deposition I'm working on. I'll see you in a few days, both of you, to finalize as much of the paperwork as possible."

"Sounds good." Graham nodded.

Veronica joined them. "You leaving?" she asked Rob. "I should go, too. It's been a long day. You can walk me out."

"I can do that," Rob agreed—while looking at Felicity.

Graham was always fascinated by human nature. Sometimes it was amusing; sometimes not so much. At the moment, it was a toss-up. Now that Veronica knew Rob was available, she was turning on the charm. But Rob only had eyes for Felicity. And Felicity... She looked ready to crawl under the table.

"See you tomorrow, Graham." Veronica waved, collecting her purse. "It was nice to meet you, Felicity."

"You, too. I'm sure I'll see you around. Pecan Valley isn't that big a town." Felicity smiled.

"Sorry to run out on you, Felicity." Rob edged around the table to stand by her chair.

Either the man was clueless about Felicity's level of interest or he was determined to win her over, Graham wasn't sure. But if she leaned any farther away from Rob Klein, she would end up on the restaurant floor.

"No problem." She held her hand out. "I

appreciate you taking the time to meet with me."
She swallowed. "To discuss my…Matt's…the case. I
appreciate the work you're doing."

"I appreciate you having dinner with me. Let's do
it again soon." Rob cradled her hand in his. "I'll call
you."

Once Rob and Veronica were out of earshot,
Graham said, "That was awkward."

Felicity nodded. "Yes. It was."

"No second date?" he asked, smiling.

Her brows rose. "You think you're funny, don't
you?"

"Maybe." He chuckled. "A little."

"You're not. Not in the least." She sighed,
propping herself on her elbow and smiling at him.
"Do I smell an office romance in the works?"

He frowned.

"Graham, she's gorgeous." Her gaze searched his.
"Veronica. Don't tell me you hadn't noticed."

"She was by far the most qualified." His frown
grew.

"Yes, I heard all about her credentials over
dinner tonight." Her nose wrinkled. "Qualified and
gorgeous."

He shrugged. Whether or not his new hire was
attractive hadn't factored into his decision to hire
her. "Her résumé was all that mattered. And her
references. Besides, my only competition in town is
an all-female clinic. Hiring a woman was a smart
move."

"Graham." Felicity sighed. "What is wrong with
us?"

"What do you mean? There's nothing wrong with

us." He paused. "With me, anyway."

"Ha ha." She glanced at the door. "Rob's a nice guy. Let's face it, there aren't a lot of men to choose from for a woman my age. So what's wrong with him? Rather, what's wrong with me?"

You have standards? Shit. She was right. Rob might be a little pushy and not in the least bit intuitive, but he was decent. "If it makes you feel any better, the same thing happened to me."

She burst out laughing. "Rob Klein tricked you into going on a date with him?"

"Now who's the comedian?" He grinned. "Two words: Widow Rainey."

"Ooh." She leaned forward, waiting. "I can't wait to hear this."

He snorted. "She gave my cell number to Romi Takahashi—told her I was too nervous to call and ask her out for coffee." He leaned back in his chair, stretching his legs out under the table.

"Are you?" Felicity studied him.

"No." He met her gaze. "I've never thought about getting coffee with her." To be completely honest, he hadn't thought about going out with any woman. And, until now, he hadn't stopped to ask himself why.

"Is there something wrong with this Romi Takahashi?"

"Aside from the fact that she expelled Diana from St. Thomas?" Not that she had a choice. When a student was caught with marijuana at school, action was required. But, besides her name, he didn't remember a thing about her. Maybe he'd been too preoccupied with Diana. Or maybe he wasn't interested in the woman.

Hell, in dating. How could he be when every one of Adelaide Keanon's warnings were burned into his brain. His daughter was a danger to herself. She needed help.

"Maybe… Maybe we should go." She wrinkled her nose again, looking young and uncertain. "You take Romi for coffee, and I'll, maybe, try this date thing with Rob. If he calls."

Oh, he'll call. And it bothered him. That she was considering officially dating Rob bothered him. He swallowed. "Why?"

"Because I don't want to be alone for the rest of my life. And I don't think you do, either. I'm not saying you'll wind up with Romi or I'll elope with Rob—it doesn't even have to be Romi. What about Dr. Luna? Or ask Widow Rainey, she'd love to help. I'm just saying we have to start somewhere. We have to put ourselves out there, right?"

From first dates to eloping? Where the hell had that come from? That was some leap. One he wasn't ready to contemplate.

"Right?" she pushed.

"Right." What the hell was the question?

CHAPTER EIGHT

Charity sat on the front porch, sipping her peppermint tea. Felicity was all about the peppermint tea being great for nausea and indigestion. Charity was more than happy to give it a try, since she had serious "indigestion"—an assumption Felicity had come up with that Charity saw no reason to correct. For the time being, anyway. From her seat on the porch swing, she could see the large inflatable being set up at the end of the street. Tonight was the annual Welcome Summer Nights for their neighborhood— Old Town. Cake walks, dunking booths, face painting, karaoke, and a whole slew of other booths and activities the whole family could enjoy.

In true Otto family fashion, her mother had signed them each up for volunteer hours.

Honor helped with face painting.

Nick worked the karaoke machine.

Felicity had been baking most of the day but, knowing Felicity, she'd flit from booth to booth helping out.

Grams was the lucky one. She'd complained of a stiff knee and gotten off easy—sitting at Jack's bedside.

Charity was supposed to man the fishing booth. It was a thrilling activity. Each fishing rod had a magnet attached. If you got lucky, you'd catch a duck with a number on its belly and win a prize. News flash, all the ducks had numbers—so the odds were definitely in the fisherman's or fisherwoman's favor.

The festivities had kicked off when the fire truck showed up to drive around the neighborhood, sirens blaring. The kids loved it. The dogs of the neighborhood? Not so much.

"You ready?" Felicity asked, her trusty wagon piled high with baked goods for the cake walk.

"Am I ever." She finished off her tea and stood. "I can't believe they're still doing this."

"Small towns love their traditions." Felicity smiled. "How's your stomach?"

Charity nodded. "Fine. Much better. I think it's allergies or something. All the pollen or ragweed, you know?"

Felicity was staring at her in open disbelief.

"Well, something," she went on. There were really only two ways to successfully lie. Option A, keep it as close to the truth as possible. Which, in her situation, was pretty impossible. Or Option B, keep it minimal. The more details, the easier to slip up. Ragweed? Allergies? Really? "Fine, I snuck in and ate a bunch of cookies."

Felicity grinned. "You always were a cookie monster."

Charity helped her lift the wagon down the steps to the sidewalk. They walked, arm in arm, down the street to the designated cake-walk area. Numbered sheets of bright cardstock paper had been laminated and duct taped to the street in a circle. The table was covered with plastic bunting, the same bright colors as the numbers on the ground. An iPod docking station sat on the table, to start and stop the music each turn.

Easy, timeless, and familiar... It had been years since she'd been to Summer Nights, years since she'd been home, but these were the times when her memories came rushing back, vivid and strong.

"This was Zach's favorite." Charity smiled, helping her sister arrange the yummy-looking treats on the table. "Mom would get so mad at him for winning everything."

"Because she made most of it." Her sister laughed. "To her, she was taking treats from other kids. To him, he won it fair and square."

They both adored their brother, from his quick laughter and warm smile, to his love of mischief and hypercompetitive nature. No matter how much they might drive each other crazy—and they did—they would always, always have each other's backs.

Charity stared up into the wide summer sky. The sun was halfway down, casting enough shadows for the crickets to start their evening serenade. In so many ways, everything was the same. In others, it was completely different.

"I miss him," Felicity said, sliding an arm around her waist. "Sometimes, I wake up needing to know where he is, right then and there. It eats away at me until I can't think straight."

Charity nodded. It was easier for her. It wasn't that she tried to forget her brother, but travel, away from the places full of memories of him, made it easier to hold that sort of panic at bay. Most of the time. "I know. But we know Zach. He's tough. He'll be fine." He had to be. Their family had been through enough, dammit.

"What are we staring at?" Diana asked, breathless. "Hi."

"Hi." Charity smiled. "The pretty sky."

"Oh." Diana glanced up, but she didn't look impressed.

"You and your dad here?" Felicity turned, glancing in the direction Diana had come from.

"Yeah. We are totally crashing your neighborhood party," Diana whispered. "We're not supposed to be here, since, you know, we don't actually live in this neighborhood."

"Who knew Graham was such a rebel?" she teased, nudging Filly.

"My dad?" Diana shook her head and laughed. "Please. What can I do to help?"

The next fifteen minutes were a blur. Honor and another girl were across the way, their face-painting booth strung with lights, a couple of mirrors, and pictures of past years' face-painting handiwork. They were excited; she could see it from here. Hadn't she been when she was their age?

Once Nick had the karaoke machine set up and the speakers tuned, he and Diana offered to fill the pool she'd use for the rubber-ducky fishing. Which would have been fine if the two of them hadn't gotten a little too carried away and ended up spraying each other—and her. Soaking wet. Considering the Texas heat, she didn't mind too much. Until she got blasted in the face.

"Nickie," she groaned.

"Sorry, Aunt Charity," Nick said. "Gotta go."

The blare of the fire truck sounded about the time she was wiping the water from her eyes.

"Here." Braden Martinez, in his full sheriff uniform, was offering her a bandanna. As usual, his expression revealed nothing.

She plucked her sopping wet shirt away from her stomach and wrung the fabric out. She glanced down at her T-shirt, relieved it was gray and not white. That, by Pecan Valley standards, would have been downright scandalous. "I don't suppose you have a towel tucked into one of your pockets?" she asked, taking the bandanna.

"In my other pants," he said.

She froze, stepping closer. Had he really said that? "Was that a joke, Sheriff Martinez?" she whispered.

The corner of his mouth cocked up for less than a second. It was progress. He still wasn't big on making eye contact, but he'd smiled—sort of. What she didn't understand was why? The Braden Martinez she'd hung around with was full of jokes and smiles, more easygoing than poker-faced. She understood the job required a certain amount of decorum, but this much?

"You used to smile more." All the time. She'd always been able to make him smile. And laugh. He'd laughed, too, once upon a time. "And, if I recall correctly, you had a great smile."

Where is your smile now, Sheriff?

He was staring down at the puddle she was standing in. "Your shoes are wet."

"And squishing." She wriggled her toes, studying him. He'd changed so much. As big and manly as he was, there was something restrained—almost stifled—about him. "But I'll survive. The shoes,

however—well, I might not be able to save them."
Her ancient pair of canvas tennis shoes had served
her well.

His gaze darted to her face like he was on the
verge of saying something.

Maybe she could draw him out? "How's your
dad?"

His gaze narrowed as he turned to assess the
street. "Fine."

Not the best topic. *Fine*. She tried again. "And
your head? Glad to see that whole bleeding thing
stopped," she added. "Anything broken?"

"No." His gaze returned. "My head isn't broken."

"That's a relief." Hands on hips, she smiled at
him.

And, right there, she saw the beginning of what
promised to be an honest-to-goodness smile—

"Charity Ann." Her mother stopped in front of
her booth, squashing any hope of smiles or
conversation. "Why aren't the ducks in the pool?
Why is there water dripping off the canopy?" She
sighed. "And, for goodness' sake, why are you
standing in a puddle?"

"I'll lend a hand, Mrs. Otto." Braden touched the
brim of his hat, stooped to open the large clear
plastic tub full of ducks, and started placing them in
the water.

"Thank you, Sheriff Martinez." Her mother was
all smiles for Braden.

"It's fine, Mom." She waved, then joined Braden,
plopping each rubber duck into the pool. Once it
was crowded with multicolored ducks and the
fishing rods were out and ready to go, she held a rod

to Braden. "You want to go fishing, Sheriff Braden? You never know; you might win a prize."

He stared at the rod, then her. "Never had much luck with that." With a stiff nod, he walked on down the street, leaving Charity to ponder what, exactly, he'd meant.

• • •

Honor was finishing a full tiger face on a squirming five-year-old when Owen made an appearance. She knew the minute he arrived because Emily, the girl who was face painting with her, freaked out. Completely. Because that's what girls did when *the* Owen Nelson was around. Something about his freakishly big muscles, dazzling smile, and all that sent girls into a tailspin.

She sighed, refusing to acknowledge his presence and focusing all of her attention on her work.

"There." She held up the hand mirror. "Good?"

The little boy had no interest in looking at his reflection. He nodded, jumped out of his chair, and ran across the street to Aunt Charity's booth. Not that Honor could blame the kid. Aunt Charity had cool prizes.

"I heard him say thank you." Owen nodded. "And something about how talented you are. And that no one else can paint tiger faces like you."

She rolled her eyes. "Uh-huh. Sure you did."

There was the smile. "Hi."

She nodded, wishing his smile didn't render her momentarily speechless.

"Hi, Owen." Emily waved, her voice all nervous

and pitchy and awkward.

"Hey, Emily." He turned that smile on Emily.

Which was mean because Emily already looked like she was going to fall off her stool. Now, with the knock-the-air-from-your-lungs smile, it was only a matter of time before she fainted—face-first—onto the asphalt at their feet.

"We have a line," Honor snapped, earning a soft gasp from Emily.

"I've been waiting in it." His smile never wavered. "I'm next."

She'd thought the toddler who wouldn't stop screaming was going to be the hardest of the night. Now she knew better. This was. Definitely. Honor held her breath as he sat in her chair and waited. "What do you want?"

"My face painted." He was grinning now.

She sat on her stool and leveled what she hoped was a good, solid glare his way. Had her stool always been this close to the chair? She was practically in his lap. "What do you want painted on your face?"

"Whatever you want." His gaze fell to her lips.

She fought the urge to stick her tongue out. Really? Why was he doing this? He didn't have to. Her family was too preoccupied to notice what he was or wasn't doing. He could drag Emily into the bushes and make out with her and no one would be the wiser. Except for her. She would be. And she wouldn't like it. At all.

Oh my God, what is wrong with me?

"What's wrong?" His voice was soft. "You look pissed off."

"Nothing." She stirred her brush with more force

than necessary, sloshing water onto the table. *Nothing at all*. She wasn't upset about him having a fantasy make-out session with Emily. *Not in the least. Because that would be ridiculous*. "Seriously, Owen, what am I painting?"

"Whatever you're best at." He turned to wink at the toddler in line. "I trust you."

Honor was momentarily distracted by the sharp angle of his jaw and thick column of his neck. He smelled incredible. He had a mole high on his cheek and the thickest lashes—

He was staring back at her now, unflinching. So much so, it was hard to breathe.

Too close. Way, way too close.

"Owen." She cleared her throat.

"Honor." He tilted his head, those hazel eyes flashing.

"Fine." He wanted to tease her. To make her... squirm? She'd do exactly what he said. She was best at butterflies. And Owen Nelson deserved the best and brightest butterfly ever. She was tempted to do a full face, but that would keep him in her chair, up close and far too personal, for longer than she was prepared to handle.

"Let's do this."

In order to paint a person's face, she had to lean in. Sometimes, on an adult, she'd stand to get a better angle. Owen was tall, so she was standing. But that put things in awkward places. Every time she leaned in, he took a sharp little breath. She hadn't touched him, wouldn't touch him, but something was definitely bothering him because he was sitting, eyes closed, hands gripping the arms of her chair.

The butterfly was beautiful.

With long, black antennae, massive wings in brilliant rainbow hues, and—because it was a girl butterfly—she had to have rosy cheeks and long eyelashes. It was so pretty, she decided to add a flower on the side of his nose. And, just to make it perfect, sprinkled the whole thing with iridescent glitter.

"Um, Honor." Emily was horrified.

Looking at it now, on his gorgeous face, she was a little horrified, too. She'd gone too far. It was too late to wipe it off. Everyone had seen it.

"Done?" he asked, his eyes popping open.

She stared down at him. "I guess so." But she didn't offer him the mirror. In fact, she hid it behind her back and stepped away. "I should probably apologize."

His brows shot up. "Does it look bad?"

"It's pretty," one of the little girls in line reassured him.

"Pretty, huh?" He stepped forward. "Let me see, Honor."

She shook her head, stepping back.

He was an athlete. She was not. He was fast. She was not. And she was ridiculously ticklish—something he discovered immediately. It took five minutes for him to free the mirror. In those five minutes she was laughing so hard, tears streamed down her face. Until he looked at his reflection, then she winced, ready to run. What was wrong with her? Why had she done this to him? "Owen…"

"Honor." He lowered the mirror. "How did you know butterflies are my favorite?" He reached around her, no space or air or relief between them, to place the mirror on the table. She couldn't breathe without breathing him in. So she did. Big, deep breaths that flooded her lungs with Owen. His hands settled on her upper arms, and he smiled down at her. "Thank you."

Speechless. Absolutely. She nodded. *It's not fair.*

He pressed the lightest kiss right in the middle of her forehead, waved at Emily, and disappeared down the street.

"You two are together?" Emily asked, in shock. "Like together, together?"

She answered without the slightest hesitation. "We are. Owen Nelson is my boyfriend." She was grinning like an idiot for the rest of the night.

• • •

Graham watched Hank Otto and his wife dance to the smooth tunes of Patsy Cline. The older man moved in perfect time with the rhythm of the music spilling out of the karaoke machine. The booths, tables, and all remnants of the evening's festivities had been cleared away, but the music played on. And a small crowd of lingering volunteers and residents was making the most of it.

"Graham?" Felicity joined him, her wagon loaded with decorations and leftover baked goods. "Still here?"

"I seem to have misplaced my daughter." Not that he was worried. The last time he'd seen Diana, she was with Nick and Honor. "Figured I could help clean up a little, anyway."

"That's very nice of you."

"It was very nice of you to invite us." He shook his head as Herb Otto spun his wife—with flare.

"They do this every year. I think it's their favorite part."

"I'm impressed," he said, nodding at her parents. "Hank is light on his feet."

"He loves to dance. Says it's a good excuse to keep my mom in his arms." She shook her head. "You know how Mom is, all over the place, all the time."

He nodded. He did know. Mimi Otto liked to be involved—at the very center of things, if possible. Sometimes that was a good thing, while other times, not so much. Tonight, he'd learned how worried she was about her daughters, and how she wondered, since he was a doctor, if he had any advice.

Not that she needed or wanted actual advice from him. He figured that out pretty quick. Mimi's worries were an excuse to showcase her daughters, hoping to gain his interest in one or the other. And while he was flattered that she thought he was good enough for either of them, it didn't make her maneuverings any less irritating.

"They make it look easy, don't they?" Felicity asked.

He wasn't sure if she meant dancing or marriage or living life, but he had to give it to them—Mimi and Herb Otto seemed to have it figured out. "They do."

"Felicity," her father called out to them, waving them over. "Put on your dancing shoes."

"Dad," she answered, waving off his suggestion.

"You dance?" he asked.

"No, not really." She shrugged. "But…"

"Do you want to?" He held his hand out. "I'll warn you now, it's been a long time."

"Ditto, Dr. Murphy. Let's have some fun breaking each other's toes." She took his hand and headed toward the designated dancing spot—a wide illuminated circle beneath the corner streetlamp.

The Ottos weren't the only ones dancing, and few of them had the finesse of Herb Otto. But hours of cardio and weights did nothing for grace or coordination, and next to the Ottos, Graham felt clunky and awkward as he botched spinning Felicity into his arms.

"We can just sway," Felicity offered when they bounced off each other, smiling broadly.

"That's swaying. We are dancing." He studied Herb a little longer and tried again, resting one hand at the base of Felicity's spine and holding her hand with the other. "Like this?"

Felicity was watching her parents, too. "I think so."

They weren't very good, but they were determined. When he spun her away, then pulled her in, she tripped on his foot and slammed into his chest. He caught her, laughing and breathless and having more fun than he'd had in a hell of a long time.

"That move was called 'falling with finesse,'" Felicity said between giggles.

"Well done." He winked, righting her onto her feet before trying it all over again.

When the music stopped, the sound of applause startled them. They had an audience. Honor,

Honor's boyfriend, Diana, Nick, and Charity all sat on the lawn, sharing popcorn and sipping soda.

"Make your arm more rigid, Graham," Charity offered, holding out her arm. "Like this, not so loosey-goosey."

"Loosey-goosey?" Diana giggled. "But I see what you mean."

"Mom, he needs to lead." Nick leaned across Diana for a handful of popcorn. "The dude always leads."

"I thought they did great," Owen, the boyfriend, said.

"I like him," Graham murmured, his attention fixing on the large teenager wrapped around Honor. "Smart kid." He paused, his gaze narrowing. "The one with the butterfly painted on his face?"

Felicity laughed.

"Dad, kind of, I don't know, stand between her legs—not right in front of her," Diana said around a mouthful of popcorn. "Your steps aren't syncing up."

"Here I thought we weren't half bad," Felicity said, still slightly breathless—and startlingly beautiful—in his arms.

Now was not the time to notice that. To notice *her*. Or that he liked the feel of her in his arms. Not now. When their kids were watching and criticizing. "Don't listen to them." He smiled.

"No," Mimi Otto said. "You really should. Diana's right." She hauled Herb closer. "See. It really is about how strongly you lead. You follow, Filly."

Felicity shot him a look. "I'm so sorry," she said, not bothering to keep her voice down.

"For what?"

"All the opinionated people in my life." She sighed. "Nothing like trying to have some fun and hearing, basically, you're doing it wrong."

"Were you having fun?" he asked.

She nodded.

"Then we weren't doing it wrong." He winked.

"Well, except, you sort of are," Nick said.

Charity clapped her hands. "Try again. We believe in you."

"Some of us believe in you." Nick said. "Some of us are just laughing at you."

"Nickie." Honor pushed her brother over.

Maybe he should be bothered by all the criticism, but he wasn't. They were all here, together, doing something. Granted, it was criticizing the shit out of his dancing, but he could live with that if this peace could last. "No pressure." Graham sighed. "You game?"

"Is there a choice?" she asked.

"Of course there's a choice." Herb Otto chuckled, an apologetic smile on his face as his gaze met Graham's.

"No," Nick called out. "Come on."

"One more try," Diana added.

"I say you guys go straight for the tango." Charity laughed. "I'll find you a rose to hold in your teeth, Filly."

"Charity Ann," Mimi Otto snapped.

All five of their audience dissolved into laughter. "I told you," Charity whispered, earning more laughter.

"My sister lives to make my mother crazy," Felicity

whispered, laughter in her voice.

Graham couldn't help but chuckle then.

"You look so happy, Mom," Honor said. "You, too, Dr. Murphy. It's nice to see you laugh."

If Graham had been looking for a reason to keep Felicity in his hold, that was it. Honor was right. Laughter was good—therapeutic, even. "Why not?"

"You're a glutton for punishment." But she was smiling up at him.

"Find a good song, Nickie." Honor pushed her brother up. "Something easy to dance to."

"Are you sure about this?" Felicity whispered, soft enough that he had to stoop to hear her. "This could turn into some all-night dance-lesson torture."

Nat King Cole's soothing voice flooded the dark street. "When I Fall in Love."

"I'm willing to risk it. Besides, it's too good a song not to dance to." He ignored everything everyone said, holding her closer, gently, moving with her, not the beat. She was right there with him, step for step. Spinning, turning, trusting him to guide her.

Honor was right. It had been a long time since he'd felt this happy. Too long. How could he hold on to this feeling once the song came to an end?

CHAPTER NINE

Felicity ran her fingers over the neatly stacked papers on the shiny mahogany tabletop. The room smelled of lemon wood polish, cologne, and coffee. The gold-rimmed bone china coffee cup in front of her sat untouched. It would be too cold to drink now—not that she had any interest in it. Her stomach was too knotted. And the words on the paper, the words coming out of Robert Klein's mouth, weren't helping.

"Do you have any questions?" Robert asked. "I know it's a lot to take in."

She had questions. So many questions. But one stood out more than the rest. *How could you do this to our daughter?* Not that she'd say it out loud. No, not say it, scream it—the way she wanted to. Matt wasn't here anyway. There was never going to be an answer.

"The search for Amber's family was a dead end?" Graham asked.

"Yes. We knew it was a shot in the dark. Amber was in foster care most of her life. No relatives to be found. I wish I had a different answer for you. Graham said Matt spoke to you both before he…his surgery." He glanced between the two of them. "I'm taking it you didn't know about the other stipulation?"

"No." The word was hard. "No." Her voice softened.

Robert nodded. "Matt and Amber were clear about what they wanted."

How nice for them. Her hands slipped into her lap, smoothing over her gray skirt again and again. Anger now was pointless but inescapable. Neither Matt nor Amber could have anticipated this might happen, but the simple fact that this condition existed was...beyond Felicity's comprehension.

The only biological family Jack had in this world were Honor and Nick. But that didn't make this okay. While Matt and Amber had no problem leaving Jack in Honor's care, Felicity was dumbfounded. Honor was a child. Eighteen, yes, but still a *child*. How could he? She had her whole life ahead of her.

She knew. Deep down, she knew. Matt had counted on her to do what was right for their daughter and his son.

"I'm assuming you need time to think about this?" Robert asked.

"No." Her answer was quick.

Robert sighed. "Felicity, there's no need to rush."

"No need? Robert..." She swallowed down the arguments that bubbled up. "I'm not rushing into anything. Unless I missed something, there isn't a choice. Jack's mine, end of story. You think I'd let Honor give up her scholarship, her future, to raise her little brother? I could never do that. Matt knew it, too."

Graham shook his head, running a hand along the back of his neck. She'd seen him do it enough to know he was upset—this time, for her.

"I know it's hard to see it this way, but this is a compliment, I think. You're a good mother,

Felicity—one they wanted for Jack." Robert's laugh was quick. "And one of the sweetest women in Pecan Valley. Everyone knows that."

She wasn't feeling very sweet. Outraged was more like it. She signed the document and pushed the papers across the table to Robert. The sooner this was over, the sooner they could move on. Honor didn't need to know about any of this, ever. If she did, she'd feel duty bound to help raise Jack when she was not done growing up herself.

Robert nodded, scanning the pages and saying, "Financially, you and the children have been well provided for. Amber's life insurance policy—"

Felicity held up her hand. "We'll set up some sort of savings account for Jack's college."

"That will be Graham's decision, since he's been assigned as the financial custodian for Jack." Robert's smile was tight.

Graham was staring at the ceiling. "Whatever you want, Felicity."

She swallowed. "I want a drink."

Graham looked at her then, nodding in agreement.

"I'd be happy to take you out for a drink, Felicity," Robert offered. "In a nonlawyer capacity, that is." He smiled. "Dinner? If you're free tonight?"

For the last three days, her decision to "put herself out there" had wavered. Robert's flowers, texts, and freshly baked cookies were thoughtful, but they didn't change the way she felt about the man. She stared at him, too shaken to form a gentle, coherent refusal. After all, it wasn't every day your ex-husband left his toddler from his second marriage to his eighteen-year-old daughter from his first marriage.

Matt. How could you?

By now she should be used to this. Disappointment. Astonishment. Anger. And pain. So much. *Dammit*. It hurt to breathe.

"I should go," Graham said, making a show of checking his watch and phone.

"You're my ride." Thank God she had an escape. "Thank you, Robert."

Robert stood, clearly disappointed. "I know today wasn't what you expected."

"No, it wasn't," she agreed. "Not that I had any expectations." She'd anticipated Matt would leave everything to the kids. Things like property and investments and money, not a toddler. But Matt continued to throw her curveballs.

Bone-deep exhaustion had become a way of life.

Rob walked them to the conference room door, shaking Graham's hand then hers. But he held on to her for a second to say, "If you need anything, Felicity, you know you can call me." He gently squeezed her hands in his. "Anything. I'd like to be here for you."

"Thank you, Rob." She pulled her hands free. He meant well, he did, but all she could think of was putting space between them. Soon. With a shaky nod, she followed Graham, her mind spinning from the last hour.

They climbed into the elevator, the doors closing behind them with a *ding*.

Graham faced her. "Are you okay?"

"No. No. I'm not," she finished. "How can I be?

That was…wrong. *So wrong.*" She broke off. "How… I mean… I was married to him for so long. But I never thought he'd do something like this." The words kept coming. "She's a child, Graham. Falling in love for the first time, playing video games, figuring out who she is—leaving for college. Dammit. That's what she's supposed to do at eighteen, you know? This isn't her mess." She stared at Graham, looking for answers he couldn't possibly have. "How could he do this to her?"

Graham faced her, his brow creasing. "I don't know."

She shook her head, fighting the sting of tears and the roar of blood in her ears. "Dammit." She sniffed. "It's not fair, Graham. None of this is fair." She was spiraling and she knew it. "Jack hates me… And Nick?" Could Nick handle this? How could she make this work?

She welcomed the solid weight of his arms around her, the way he held her against him, the support he offered.

"It's going to be all right," he whispered against her temple.

Eyes closed, she focused on the rapid beat of his heart beneath her ear. "I want to believe that. Tell me how?" she asked, gripping his shirtfront and holding on.

His hands tightened on her back, drawing her closer. "Because you're you, Felicity. Strong and fierce, nurturing and resilient. I've never known anyone as capable of facing something head-on and making the best of it. No, more than that—making it right."

"I'm tired of making it right," she murmured against his chest.

"I wish I could help." His voice rumbled beneath her ear.

He was. Being here. Everything about Graham Murphy was comforting. And, right now, that's what *she* needed. Would he be opposed to staying this way for a little bit longer? At least until she could hold her head up without the threat of public ugly crying?

The elevator dinged.

She sighed, digging deep for strength.

But he didn't move. His arms stayed wrapped around her, holding her tight. It almost opened the floodgates. Almost. Instead, she relaxed, sliding her arms around his waist and leaning into him. Who got on or off the elevator, however many stops they made, she had no idea. All that mattered was the thump of his heart and the support of him—all of him—being there for her.

It had been so long since she'd had someone to lean on.

Of course it would be Graham. Solid. Quiet. Constant.

His hand splayed, smoothing up between her shoulders, then back to her waist. Over and over. Gentle yet firm.

Touch.

She'd missed that.

And scent. No cologne or scented deodorant. Just Graham. A warm and familiar and welcoming scent that drew her in.

Through his starched cotton dress shirt, she could feel his warmth. It was hard to miss the rest. A muscled chest. Broad shoulders. An impressive physique. All man. Beneath her hands. Pressed tightly against her. His heart against hers. His breath against her ear. The weight of his arms around her. She missed that—missed all of this. Of being a woman aware of a man and embracing the flash of heat and flush of want that could spark and burn.

"Felicity?" Graham's voice was low.

Her eyes popped open, and pure mortification washed over her. She'd turned to him for comfort, but a switch had flipped, and a more basic instinct kicked in. Her nose was pressed against the bare patch of skin at the V of his collar. Her hands were twisted in the fabric, gripping the back of his shirt and tugging it free from his pants. And she was aching, arching, into him.

"I'm sorry." She pulled away and stepped back. "Oh Graham, I'm so sorry." Looking at him wasn't an option. The tears were back—with a heaping dose of humiliation.

"It's okay."

If it were, he wouldn't sound so tense. It wasn't okay. Not at all.

She gripped the rail that ran around the inside of the elevator and glanced his way, searching for something to say.

He was flustered, having a friend go from needy to way *needy* was pretty good reason. His dark hair was mussed, like he'd run his fingers through it, and he stood stiffly with his hands shoved into his pockets and his jaw muscle bulging as he watched the floor numbers tick down.

She chewed on the inside of her lip. The *ding* of

the elevator made her jump. He gave her a tight smile and waited for her to lead the way out of the building. The sun beat down, but it didn't stop a fit of shivering that continued even after she huddled in his SUV.

First finding Honor with Owen, finding out *about* Owen and Honor. Then the will. Honor and Jack. And Matt. And now Graham. Rather, her attacking Graham. If her reactions were skewed, it was because everything had flipped upside down. Everything she thought she knew—she was wrong.

They were almost to her house when he finally broke the silence. "Are you going to go out with him?"

She glanced his way. "What? Who?"

"Are you going to date Rob?" He ran his hands along the steering wheel at the red light.

"Oh." She frowned. Robert Klein was the last person on her mind right now. "No."

"Something changed?" he pushed, the muscle in his jaw tightening.

Maybe. Maybe she'd just been fooling herself. Besides, Robert had stayed good friends with Matt until the end. Right now, that was a strike against him. As was his timing. "Who asks someone out at a reading of the will?"

He burst into laughter then.

"It's sort of unprofessional, isn't it?" She kept going. "And, even though we're divorced, the will we were reading was my husband's."

Graham was still laughing.

Laughter was good—a stress reducer that didn't involve her making a pass at one of her oldest and dearest friends. Did it scare her a little to realize she'd started relying on him? Yes. But she liked having him back in her life, so hopefully her earlier unhinged behavior wouldn't chase him away. "Good guy or not, I think I'll pass on his offer."

"Maybe he saw an opportunity," Graham said, those brown eyes smiling again.

She shook her head.

"Can't blame a guy for trying." He turned the corner and pulled onto her street.

"Graham." She waited for him to park. "What happened in the elevator—"

He shook his head, his hands gripping the steering wheel. "It's fine."

"I was…I am an emotional mess." She rushed on, breathless. How could she explain? Because she really wanted to explain. The problem was, she didn't really understand what happened. "I fell apart, which I've been trying very hard not to do. And you—" She broke off. He what? "You're easy to hold on to." Which was true. Holding on to him had been good. "The support and hugging. The touching. You." And all the odd sensations the hugging and touching stirred…

Trying again. "I didn't think. It was all…feeling." A pure, exquisite ache she'd thought was gone forever.

He looked at her then. "What were you feeling?"

His question caught her off guard. Chances are, telling him he'd woken up her libido was going to make him tense all over again. Friends didn't typically affect each other's sex drive. But somehow, he had. "It… You felt good."

He stared at her so long and hard that she wasn't sure what to do. "If I asked you to have a drink with me, what would you say?"

It was her turn to stare at him. "A drink?" As in a date? Or a drink? But she wasn't sure she wanted to know, so she didn't ask.

He nodded.

Both of them were still battle weary from their first broken hearts. They had more than their fair share of worry and responsibility to shoulder. But they deserved a break.

Graham's brown gaze swept slowly over her face as if he were seeing her for the very first time. There was something undeniably appealing about this gentle, wounded man. What that meant, exactly, had yet to be determined, but she very definitely wanted to find out.

"What time will you pick me up?" she asked.

He let out a long, slow breath. "Eight?" he asked.

She opened the car door and slid from the seat. "I'll see you at eight." With a smile and a wave, she made her way to her front door. For the first time in over twenty years, Felicity Otto-Buchanan had butterflies.

• • •

"The blue tie," Diana said, leaning against the doorway. "Or, here's an idea, *no* tie."

Graham wove the blue tie beneath his collar and worked a French knot, relieved by her interest in his date. Diana didn't like many people, but Felicity was a rare exception. Which was good. It had been a hell of a long time since he'd been excited by something. Tonight—he was excited—until he saw his daughter staring back at him in the mirror. She looked pale. Really pale.

"What?" she asked, pushing off the doorframe.

He had to tread carefully. By now, he could recognize when something was off with his daughter. And, there was no denying it, something was off.

"Stop with the look." She flopped onto his bed. "I haven't done anything."

If only he could believe that. He stared at his reflection, focusing all his energy on tying his tie.

"Mrs. Buchanan is a babe. Some of the guys call her a MILF. I'm sure you'd agree."

"Do I want to know what that means?" he asked.

She laughed. "Mother I'd like to f—"

"I don't want to know," he cut her off.

"You're such a prude."

Prude, no. Out of practice, hell yes. He'd come home and taken the world's longest cold shower, but it hadn't erased the feel of her breath on his chest. When her hands tugged his shirt from his pants, he'd been frozen with anticipation. Her sudden urgency had held him a willing captive. Need and hunger had rolled over him until he was shaking with it. If he hadn't stopped her, he wouldn't have been able to keep his hands to himself.

"Dad?" Diana's voice was high and thin, like she was barely keeping it together. "I know you're excited about getting laid and all but I'm sort of wondering when you were going to tell me."

He wasn't going to let her get to him, not tonight. "Tell you what?"

She dug into her pocket and pulled out a wad-ded-up piece of paper. "This. You know, the whole committing me to six weeks of group therapy and tiny paper cups holding colored pills at breakfast, lunch, and dinner."

Sonofabitch. He went back to tying his tie. "I'm not sending you there." *Stay calm, stay cool.*

"Bullshit." She sat up, throwing the paper at him. "You're such a liar."

He glanced at her in the mirror. "We are taking a vacation. Going to the beach house." He'd been biding his time to mention their vacation—on the off chance some unforeseen hiccup derailed his plans. But, as of next Monday, he was taking a leave of absence. This was not how he'd envisioned telling her.

"The beach house?" She laughed, a hard, grating laugh. "Right. Sure. Whatever. We don't like each other. You can't stand being in the same room with me, but I'm supposed to believe you?" She stared up at the ceiling. "Guess you'll be making a stop along the way—to drop me off at this Serenity Heights place. First you get rid of Mom. Now you're trying to get rid of me."

His fingers fell from his tie. She didn't really believe that. Lashing out was her thing. And she was very good at it. But that didn't stop the razor-blade effect of her words, slicing deep and letting the blood flow.

Diana grabbed their family picture from his nightstand, her black-smeared eyes narrowing as she stared at the happy image. He'd memorized it, down to every detail. It was like another life. And Julia, his

Julia and her wonderful smile. They'd been happy then—all of them. There were times he wondered if he'd ever be happy again.

He tugged off his tie. What the hell was he thinking? "I don't want to get rid of you, Diana."

She crossed her bony arms over her chest. "You're saying this is all Doc Adelaide's idea?"

He ran a hand along the back of his neck. "She's worried about you. We're both worried about you." *Every second of every day, I worry about you.* Every time he went to work, every time she went out, he wondered if he'd ever see her again. Why couldn't she understand that?

"You don't need to worry about me. You can't stop me from doing anything, don't you get that? You're not in control." She rolled her eyes. "I'm *not* going to that place. You can't make me. But, if you want, we can *talk* about this? *After* you get laid? You'll be way less tense then."

He stared at her, stunned. "Diana."

"Dad," she mimicked and walked out of his room. "I'm not going to the Buchanans' or Natalie's or Angie's tonight! Just go and enjoy your night." Her door slammed, followed by the angry screaming music she blasted to make sure he knew she wasn't happy.

He stared after her, all the excitement and anticipation he'd felt evaporating. Leaving her alone wasn't an option. When she got like this, she was capable of dangerous things. And, even if he managed to convince her to go with him to the Buchanans' to hang out with Nick and Honor, she'd be sullen and hateful—two things Felicity's kids didn't deserve.

He picked up his phone and dialed. It rang three times before Felicity answered.

"Graham, hi. I'm almost ready."

"Felicity." Why did she have to sound excited? He didn't want to think that she wanted this as much as he did. That would make it worse. "I need to take a rain check." A lie.

"Oh." There was a pause. "Of course. You're a doctor. Things come up. It's the job."

He wished he'd been called in to the hospital. Delivering babies—even an emergency C-section— was less stressful than dealing with his daughter. The words were there. The truth. He knew she'd listen. And he wanted to tell her. But after the day she'd had… What sort of asshole would he be to do that? To add to her burden, knowing she'd want to help. His daughter and their battles were his responsibility—not hers. "I'm sorry about this."

"No, Graham, I understand." She tried to sound cheery, but he heard her disappointment. Hell, he felt it. He'd wanted this, wanted her. Maybe that was the problem. What he wanted wasn't important. Diana was.

"I hope the delivery is easy and mother and baby are healthy." Her voice was soft.

"Thanks." He hesitated.

"Night, Graham."

"Night, Felicity," he murmured.

He set his phone on the dresser and headed to Diana's room.

Last night, when she'd been in the shower, he'd done a quick check. No drugs, no razors, no alcohol. But he knew just how resourceful she could be.

When she was fired up, like now, she was twice as capable of mayhem. It was going to be a long night. He knocked, hard, so she could hear him over her music. Nothing.

Her door was locked.

It took him a few minutes to find an Allen wrench that would fit the door lock, but once he did, the door was open in a matter of seconds.

Her window was open, too, and her room was empty.

CHAPTER TEN

"You're here." Honor hovered in the doorway. Finding Owen on her doorstep, holding flowers for crying out loud, made her flushed and awkward. What was he doing here? And why? And what was up with the flowers?

He smiled down at her. "Your mom said I was welcome anytime."

The smile caught her off guard. That smile *always* caught her off guard. She'd need to work on that. Smiles, flowers, and overall gorgeousness aside, she needed to put Mr. Charming in his place. "She also said to let her know." She waited.

He laughed. "Not so welcome, then." He paused. "Here I thought we were making progress."

She didn't know what to say to that. Yes, they'd texted and talked on the phone a few times, but she was prepared to come up with an excuse. Like, she felt obligated to him, the stress of the situation, or something. She'd say whatever was necessary to send him on his way—far, far away. Admitting she'd been ready to accept any kiss he'd been planning prior to her mother's arrival would be the worst possible idea.

Owen's eyes narrowed a little, like he was trying to figure her out. "And I thought I'd check on Nick, since his job has kept him from working out. He was in bad shape the other morning." One eyebrow cocked. "The morning I basically carried him here—to safety."

Honor couldn't stop herself from laughing. He was persistent, and here, and she was too scattered to think of a witty or scathing comeback.

"Fine." She stepped back and held the door wide. He could see Nick. That was fine. That made sense. "He's plugged into his gaming console."

"Doing better?" he asked, following her.

She nodded. "I guess. He's been pretty quiet." Partly because he felt terrible for what he'd done, or so she liked to believe, and partly because he wasn't okay with their mother going on a date. But it was Dr. Murphy, not some random sleazy dude. That, to Honor, made all the difference. Nick didn't see it that way.

"Nickie." Honor waved her hand in front of his face.

Nick held his headset away. "Yeah?"

"Owen's here." She pointed. "He brought you flowers." She ignored Owen's chuckle and the miles of goose bumps it caused.

"The flowers are for you." He deposited the massive arrangement in her arms.

Nick was up. "Hey, man."

"*Black Ops*?" Owen asked, eyeing the television screen. "You any good?"

"Hell, yeah." Nick grinned.

Considering how much time he spent on the thing, he should be. But Honor kept her opinion to herself. With any luck, she could leave Owen with Nick and retreat to her room. Alone. Far away from Owen.

"I owe you, man." Nick's gaze shifted between them. "I mean, if you hadn't brought me home, I don't know if I'd have made it."

Owen looked at her. "You were in pretty rough shape."

She got it, already. He was the hero. And she should be nice to him. It was hard not to smile at his ego—but she did her best.

"And covering with my mom like that? You and Honor? I can't believe she bought that." Nick grinned at her. "And the other night, at the festival, too."

"It was her idea," Owen said, nudging her. "I just went along with it."

For some reason, Honor had the urge to snap at both of them. Did they not see how offensive that whole exchange was? Owen's smile, the whole nudge thing, had her bristling. To be fair, everything about Owen seemed to set her on edge. Like the way he was looking at her—standing too close to her—being hot.

"Maybe we'll get lucky and she'll buy our break-up, too?" she snapped, shooting daggers at her brother and ignoring Owen.

"She's still mad at me," Nick explained.

"And I'll stay mad until you stop acting like an ass. But since you seem to be on some sort of streak, guess you're out of luck." She turned away and stomped into the kitchen for a vase.

"Ooh…" Aunt Charity sat at the table, a box of Froot Loops in front of her. "Who are those from?"

"Owen." She all but growled his name. Stupid boys.

"The boyfriend?" Charity asked, filling her bowl.

Lying wasn't something that came easy to her, but saying nothing worked. She dug through the lower cabinet until she found a crystal vase.

"What's up?" Charity pushed. "Nick's the wound-up and irritable one. You're the optimistic Zen kid."

She pulled scissors from the drawer and snipped away the flower stems. "I'm Zen. I'm totally Zen." With a sigh, she filled the vase with water and arranged the white lilies, roses, and baby's breath. "They are pretty."

"And expensive," Charity sounded off. "What did he do?"

"Owen's here." Her mother pushed through the kitchen door. Her face had been washed clean, the pretty blue dress she'd been wearing for her date had been replaced with yoga pants and a sweatshirt, and her hair was smoothed back into a ponytail.

"You changed." Charity frowned. "What happened?"

Her mom smiled. "Babies come when they feel like it."

"That sucks." Her aunt rinsed her bowl out and put the cereal away. "Did you see what Owen brought Honor? Maybe Graham should take lessons from the kid."

"Have you seen the *kid*?" her mother asked. "There's nothing kid-like about him." She glanced at Honor then, clearly worried.

"Mom." She sighed, further exasperated. "Please stop. I'm not going to...to sleep with him, okay? I get that he's hot. It's sort of hard to miss. But we're not even that serious."

Her mother and aunt stared pointedly at the flowers.

"Fancy flowers like that mean one of two things," Aunt Charity said. "One: he's really, really sorry. Or two: he's really, really head over heels in love." She winked. "Which is it?"

Honor might not like Owen Nelson—or at least that's what she kept telling herself—but he had nothing to apologize for. She shook her head, immediately dismissing the other option. He wasn't the sort of guy who would love anyone more than he loved himself. At least, that's how he'd always acted in school. He'd charmed his way out of everything—projects and classes and relationships. And, somehow, everyone had continued to love him. So this, *all* of this, was completely unexpected. Enough so that she couldn't help but be suspicious. Why on earth had he brought her flowers? "I have no idea," she answered.

But her mother and aunt weren't looking at the flowers or her. Both of them were smiling at something over her shoulder. And Honor knew, she just knew, he was behind her. She was not going to turn around.

"Came for drinks," Nick mumbled. "Should I just start knocking from now on? On, like, every door, so I don't walk in on women-talk or something likely to scar me for life?"

Charity laughed. "Whatever. You must be the boyfriend with the great taste in flowers. I'm the fun-loving aunt with a mile-wide overprotective streak." She smiled brightly, making Honor smile, too.

"Guilty." Owen stepped forward to shake her hand. "Nice to meet you."

Nick pulled two cans of soda from the fridge.

"We're going now. Before things get awkward again." He left, balancing sodas, chips, and a package of cookies.

Honor did her best not to look at Owen. Had he heard her? Could today get any worse?

"Glad you came over, Owen," her mother said. "Popcorn?"

"Thanks for having me, Mrs. Buchanan. Sounds great."

Honor held her breath and hoped he'd follow Nick out. Instead, he crossed the kitchen to stand a few inches from her. He waited, silently, until she looked up at him. "Without a doubt, option two." He was staring at her like she was all that mattered, like her mother and aunt weren't watching and listening to everything—like he meant all the weird and wonderful things that started coming out of his mouth, "Freshman year. Mr. Hamm's class. You had this black shirt with blue birds stitched on it. Made your eyes so blue." He shook his head. "First time you ever smiled at me, we were reading Othello out loud. You didn't want to smile at me—but I earned it. That was it for me. Every smile, it's the same thing all over again."

Honor stood there, staring at him, beyond stunned.

"Game's ready," Nick yelled from the living room. "Coming?"

"Yep." Owen's gaze lingered a moment longer, then he left—taking all the air in the kitchen with him.

"Oh my God," Aunt Charity said. "Honor, honey. Wow."

"You see?" her mother whispered. "How can I not worry?"

"Oh, no, you should totally be worried," Aunt Charity agreed.

Honor stared blindly at the door, heart echoing in her ears. What had just happened? If he'd been trying to cement their cover for Nick's recklessness, he'd taken things a little too far. He didn't need to say he was head over heels in love with her. And the other stuff? He remembered the shirt she'd been wearing? The first time she'd smiled at him? He didn't need to say any of that—he shouldn't have. So why had he?

• • •

Felicity pulled the bag of popcorn from the microwave and dumped it into a brightly painted bowl. Honor, who'd been red-faced and nervous since Owen Nelson had made his heart-stopping public declaration, stood distracted and shifting from foot to foot.

"Think that's enough?" she asked her daughter.

Honor stared into the bowl.

"Honor?" she asked.

Honor picked it up. "It's great. It's good. Thanks." She headed slowly toward the door, hesitated, straightened her shoulders, and walked out.

"That was impressive. He totally rocked her world. Hell, he totally rocked my world." Charity sighed. "How are you holding up?"

"Honestly?" Felicity asked, sitting in the chair opposite her sister.

"I'm thinking that having a boy be that into Honor might be freaking you out?" Charity shrugged. "I could be wrong, not being a mom."

"No, no, you totally nailed it on the head." She sighed. But… Maybe if Owen weren't so manlike, it'd be easier. Her little girl was still her little girl. "You get it, though, right?"

Charity nodded. "He's super intense. If we're being honest—if I were Honor, I would totally jump him. Totally."

She glared at her sister.

"Come on, Filly." Charity rolled her eyes. "Did you see the way he looked at her? Do you remember being young and in love? All the passion and heat." She grinned. "Having a guy more fascinated with you and your body than his own wants and needs." She sighed, rubbing her arms. "Let's not forget the all-important endurance."

"Charity," she groaned, resting her head on the table. Yes, she remembered. She and Matt had always been crazy about each other. In the beginning, they couldn't keep their hands off each other. One kiss was all it took to get them naked. Which was why Felicity had walked the graduation stage barely able to conceal her pregnancy—with Honor. She and Matt married that summer, right before they left for college.

"How do you think Doc Murphy's going to stack up?" Charity asked. "Something tells me he's going to be good with his hands."

"Do not go there," she said.

"Why not?" Charity asked. "How long has it been?"

Felicity peeked up at her sister. "For what?"

"Since you had sex?" Charity asked, bobbing her eyebrows.

"Since before the divorce." Matt was her one and only.

"But that's like…years." Charity shook her head. "That's depressing."

She sat up. "I guess so. But he was all I know. It's not like I can hop into bed with someone just for sex. That would be…weird."

Charity snorted. "Or super hot and exciting."

Would it be? She didn't know how to do that or if she wanted to. Yes, she was single, but that didn't mean she was going to suddenly set aside her kids for one-night stands—even if the sex might be exciting.

It was the wrong time to remember just how warm and strong Graham Murphy's hold had been. Better to steer the line of conversation into more neutral territory. "How'd your visit with Maudie go?"

"She's so old." Charity frowned. "Her wrinkles have wrinkles."

Felicity laughed. "That's mean."

"But true. Not that it matters. I need a job, and she's eager to give me one." She shrugged. "Since I need to stay here, I don't want to be a mooch."

"I appreciate that." Not that finances were a problem. Her father had retired and left her the family business shortly after her divorce was finalized. The Otto Family Drugstore pretty much ran itself, but Felicity put in a few hours each day to keep it that way. It was her job to stay on top of day-to-day operations, close out the registers and deposits, and handle the occasional troubleshooting. She was content. But Charity in a nine-to-five job in Pecan Valley was hard to imagine. "You don't have to settle for something, Charity. You could even work at the store if you want."

Charity wrinkled her nose. "I don't. Though, I do appreciate the offer. Travel is where my heart is. If I can't travel, I might as well help other people take their dream vacation."

This was the first time the two of them had had five minutes alone without some crisis to handle. Flare for storytelling aside, Charity was a private person. Still, Felicity didn't know what had happened to bring her home for more than a whirlwind visit. "Can I ask what happened? All your emails and postcards were so happy. Don't get me wrong, I love that you're here. But, well, why are you giving up your dream?"

Charity's big blue eyes met hers. "I've sort of been waiting to tell you because I knew you were going to flip, and things have been so stressful and crazy since I got home that I didn't want to add to it."

Her gut tightened. "Something bad?"

"Well… I'm trying not to think about it that way." Charity laid her arms on the table and tapped her fingers against the wooden top. "I met this guy in Italy. He was a dream, Filly, the deluxe model. Charm, money, education, *and* he was gifted with a massive d—"

She held up her hand. "I get it."

"I thought I was in love—we were in love." She

sighed. "Until his wife showed up."

"Oh, Charity," she murmured. She knew firsthand how devastating it was to have your heart torn to bits. "Take it from me, a broken heart doesn't last forever." She took her sister's hand in hers and gave it a squeeze.

"My heart is fine." Charity smiled. "Really. I've dealt with that. But there's another, bigger, likely-to-stick-around problem that I'm not dealing with so well."

Every STD ad Felicity had ever heard of scrolled through her head. Oh God, was Charity sick? Had the Italian bastard given her something horrible? "What is it?" she asked, her grip tightening. "Whatever I can do, I will. You know that, right?"

Charity nodded. "That's just it. You can't do anything. This is all me. I mean, your support and guidance would be great but… I'm going to have to figure out this whole motherhood thing." She smiled. "Your turn to be the cool aunt, Filly."

By now, Felicity hoped she'd learned how to keep breathing and blinking without revealing any internal struggle. But she was failing. She loved Charity, adored her, but her little sister's habit of living in the moment had led to real consequences this time. Consequences Felicity could not carry for her.

"Surprise, right?" Charity asked. "Good surprise?" Her voice broke, just enough to force Felicity to her feet to hug her sister.

"The best surprise," she murmured, holding her close. "You're going to be great."

"And I can stay, right?" Charity's arms wound

around her. "I know this is bad timing and the house is going to be that much crazier if Jack moves in, but I can honestly say this is the most terrifying thing that's ever happened to me." She sniffed. "How many goldfish did I kill? Even plants? Now I'm supposed to keep a human being alive?"

Felicity held her tighter, aching for her sister. Learning she was pregnant with Honor had been a surprise, but she and Matt had been so in love and excited that fear had never entered into it. The same with Nick. Felicity immersed herself in mother-hood—made cookies for parties, costumes for plays, and never missed a game or concert or field trip. Putting the kids first was one of the reasons Matt cited on their divorce papers. But she and Charity were wired differently.

"Don't worry, Charity," Felicity said, stroking her sister's hair. "You and your baby will be surrounded by people who love you. You're not doing this alone, okay?"

Charity nodded.

They stayed that way, locked together, until Charity said, "Okay, okay, enough. I'm not liking this emotional junk, so let's move on to eating ice cream or something." She smiled at her, already rummaging through the pantry. "Hey, maybe my pregnancy will stop Honor from jumping Owen. You know, I'm a walking poster for premarital sex prevention."

Felicity sat, hard, in her chair. "Really?" She was still coming to terms with Honor and Owen.

"She's eighteen, Filly." Like that said it all. "And, hello, did you see that kid?"

Yes, she'd seen him. And heard him.

And now, after the day she'd survived, she really needed that drink.

. . .

Nick kept checking the clock. It was after eight. Dr. Murphy was late.

Maybe he wouldn't show.

Or he'd changed his mind.

If he was lucky—yeah, right—his mother had snapped out of this whole weird dating Dr. Murphy thing and called it off.

His phone vibrated for the eighty-seventh time in, like, two hours and his patience snapped. Eugene and half the JV football team had decided to harass the crap out of him about tomorrow's big lake party. And Fran, his wannabe girlfriend, was making it extra hard to say no by sending him bikini pics. No other junior was stacked the way Fran Mendoza was. Thing was, she was super sweet, too. Too sweet to drag into his mental breakdown.

And now Diana was blowing up his phone with rapid-fire texts—things were getting better and better. Done. He turned the phone off and tossed it onto the recliner behind him, texts unread.

He didn't want to deal with Diana, not tonight. If she said how cool it would be for her dad to hook up with his mom one more time, he would lose his shit. His mom had enough to deal with. She needed to stay as far away from Dr. Murphy and Diana as possible.

His mom deserved the best.

And the best man, the best father, would never let his daughter get mixed up with drugs, sneak out, and screw around with some loser who didn't give a rat's ass about her. Dr. Murphy being clueless made it hard to respect the man.

Besides, Dr. Murphy was linked to his dad, had been best friends with his dad—that was a big fat strike against him.

Now he needed to make his mom understand. Dating Graham could never work. Ever. Since no one else got that, it was his job to point it out.

"Nick," Honor gasped, leaning into him as a zombie charged the screen.

He shifted his direction and avoided being killed with ease. "Chill." He finished the round and picked up his soda can. "I'm empty. Want anything?" he asked Owen.

Owen shook his head. "I'm good, man."

With a nod, he pushed through the kitchen door. His mother was at the table, propped on her elbow, reading a book. She glanced up when he came in, instantly smiling.

"Need anything?" she asked, already standing.

"I can get it." He tossed the can in the recycling bin and opened the fridge. "Plans change?" he asked, doing his best to sound noncommittal.

She nodded. "Babies. They're on their own schedule."

Nick had vague recollections of his father running out of T-ball games, family dinners, and movies when his patients went into labor. Part of the job.

"You okay with that?" He popped the tab on his soda and waited. Her smile wavered and pressure crashed down on his chest. He didn't know what was worse: seeing her dating or seeing her unhappy.

She shrugged. "I was looking forward to going out."

"Because of Dr. Murphy?" he asked, clearing his throat. "Or going out?"

She looked at him with that look—the mom-look. "What's up, Nickie?"

He cleared his throat again. "Mom, you can't date him. I know he's cool, and you think he's cute or whatever but, you know, Diana. And Mrs. Murphy. And *Dad*."

His mom frowned. "What about Diana and Julia and your dad?" She leaned against the counter, crossed her arms over her chest, and waited.

"Diana is a fricking nightmare, Mom. Like, you have no idea. How does he not know how screwed up she is?" He held his hands up in front of him. "You don't need that. You don't want that. *I* don't want her in *my* life."

Her eyes widened. "Nick—"

"No, Mom, I'm serious." His attempt at persuasion sounded more like desperation. "You don't think it's weird to date your best friend's husband? I get Mrs. Murphy is dead, but still, isn't that sort of really, *really* wrong?"

She blinked.

"And he was Dad's best friend. Which means he can't be all that great, you know?" He swallowed, the grainy nanny-cam video he'd walked in on too fresh. Whether or not his dad regretted leaving his family was beside the point. He'd left them, period. Even if he had come back, even if he wanted his real family again, it wouldn't change what he'd done in the first place. Besides, the fight was the night before Honor's graduation, meaning sometime between their arguing and Honor's ceremony, they'd made up and were coming together. If they hadn't, Amber would still be alive and taking care of her kid in the hospital. Bitterness tightened his throat. He didn't want to think about his dad anymore, period, or anyone linked to him. As far as he was concerned, that part of his life was over.

His mother was staring at him—looking way worried. He smiled, sipped his soda, and tried to calm down. "You can do better."

"I can?" she asked.

He nodded. "When you're ready, yeah."

"But I'm not ready?"

"No." He sighed. "Are you? I mean, is there someone you're interested in?"

Don't freak out. Stay chill. It wasn't working.

And she saw it.

"No." She shook her head slowly. "No one."

"You and Dr. Murphy were just hanging out? As friends?" He'd been freaking out over nothing? Come to think of it, his mom was the only one who hadn't geeked out over Dr. Murphy's butt or how cute he was.

"Does that bother you?" She waited, looking anxious.

Did it? No. Hell no. As a friend, Dr. Murphy was awesome. She needed someone to hang out with who she wasn't related to. "Nah." He shook his head, breathing easier. "Okay, cool." He paused. "Sooo, we're good. You and Dr. Murphy aren't dating and…

everything's cool."

"Totally cool," she repeated, smiling.

Wrong or not, Nick pretended he didn't notice the effort behind her smile or the disappointment in her voice. Now that he and Honor were basically adults, it was his job to look out for his mom. He was okay with her and Dr. Murphy being friends. And Diana was fine to hang out with now and then—he just didn't want her around all the time. Or living here. Besides, his mom didn't need to be saddled with someone else's kid.

CHAPTER ELEVEN

Graham held the embroidered throw pillow on his lap, his fingers running along the piped edge over and over. The simple repetitive act was oddly soothing. Not enough to shake the sense of impending doom that kicked in once he'd pried open Diana's bedroom door. Just soothing enough to keep him from yelling. Or throwing things. Or sobbing uncontrollably. None of those things would help, and he needed help, desperately.

Adelaide waited, pen poised, glancing back and forth between them. The room seemed smaller than when they'd arrived. The couch creaked loudly every time he shifted. He sat, rigid, fingers worrying the stupid pillow. Only the soft recording of rhythmic waves and the regular tick of the second hand of the wall clock broke the silence.

"Diana?" Adelaide's voice was neutral.

Diana continued to peel the black polish from her nails, sweeping the bits from her shredded tights onto the polished concrete floor.

She had her nail polish. He had the stupid pillow. Neither of them was talking but they both had so much to say.

"After your father's call this morning, I thought you might want to talk," Adelaide prompted. "Is there anything in particular you'd like to discuss?"

Diana didn't look up or say a word—just kept picking away. He shoved the pillow between his side and the arm of the love seat, pressing his hands flat against his thighs.

"He mentioned you spent the night away from home?" Adelaide continued.

Diana's left hand was now polish-free, so she set to work on her right hand.

"We're both concerned about that. Where did you go, Diana? Were you safe?"

Worried, yes. And pissed as hell. Last night had been the worst of his life. Nothing compared to not knowing where she was or what might be happening to her. Did she need help? Was she hurt? Hurting herself? Lost? Alone? Every nightmare scenario imaginable played through his mind until he was frantic.

But beyond the worry and pain and helplessness, he was furious. So furious he'd put his fist through the drywall. After driving the streets of Pecan Valley most of the night, he'd prayed he'd come home and find her waiting. Instead, he'd come home to an empty house. The handful of her friends he knew of had no idea where she was, or that was what they told him. When he'd exhausted all of his options, he'd called the police, his bloodied fist submerged in a sink full of ice, when she'd walked in the front door.

She hadn't stopped, even when he'd called to her. She'd headed up the stairs and into her bathroom—no door slamming or screaming, tears or hostility. Her silence had broken him. While she was in the shower, he slumped over in relief—doing his best not to cry like a baby.

She still hadn't said a word. And he'd been so

uncertain of what to do next, he'd called for backup. He'd expected her to push back when he told her they were going to see Adelaide. She hadn't. The drive had been as silent as the session so far.

"You're angry," Adelaide continued, "over the brochure I gave to your father."

He didn't look at her. He couldn't. Not yet. He wasn't in control.

"Did he tell you I gave him the brochure?" She sat up. "He didn't want it. He said sending you there would be deserting you and he wouldn't do that."

For a second, Diana stopped chipping.

"It's my professional opinion that you're a risk to yourself." Adelaide paused. "Last night only affirms my belief that Serenity Heights is the best option for—"

Screw control. "She's not going," he cut in—but he didn't sound like himself. The words were hard and clipped and raw.

Diana jerked back, her bloodshot, kohl-lined eyes locking with his.

"I need you to listen." He swallowed, the jagged wedge shoved in his throat making it hard to say what needed to be said. "I didn't want to let your mother go, Diana. You know, I hope you know, how much I loved her. But she was so tired, baby girl. And she'd been hurting for too long." He stopped, the horrible pain on his daughter's face silencing him. There was no way to do this without pain.

"Losing your mother was hell—for both of us. You needed me, and I wasn't there. You lost your mom and you lost me, too…" He broke off, his voice wobbling and his eyes burning furiously. "I screwed up, and I'm so sorry, Di. I let you down, over and over. I get it, why you hate me, I do." It hurt to suck in the air to keep going. "I won't send you away, but I won't let you keep me out, either. Whatever I need to do to fix us, I'll do it. But you have to give me a chance."

Big tears streaked down Diana's pale face, tracking mascara in their wake.

"I love you, Di. And last night—" He closed his eyes, his voice breaking roughly. "Last night was the worst of my life." He took her hand in his then. "You can't do that, Di. Get mad at me, yell at me, but running away—I can't lose you."

She pressed her hand to her mouth, fighting tears.

"I wasn't lying to you about a vacation, a real vacation. We can go to the beach house, me and you. You like it there; you used to love it there. Maybe?" He swallowed. "I'm not saying it'll be easy, or that I have answers or know what the hell I'm doing, but we have to try."

Diana was crying hard, wiping tears away with the back of her other hand. "You promise?"

"What?" he asked, aching to hug her. "Promise what, Di?"

"You're n-not s-sending me away from you?" Her sobs were hard and angry.

The question split his heart wide open. "I promise," he whispered, cradling her hand against his chest.

But she was shaking her head.

"You don't believe me?" he asked. "How do I make you believe me?"

She kept shaking her head, looking so young and lost underneath her smeared makeup.

"You don't trust your father?" Adelaide was calm—this was her job, after all. "Who do you trust?"

Diana sniffed, tugging her hand from his and pulling a tissue from a nearby box to wipe her face. She blew her nose and curled up in the far corner of the loveseat, looking almost as exhausted as he felt. "You think you know me. Why don't *you* tell me?" Eyebrows raised, arms crossed, she stared at Adelaide.

Adelaide clicked the end of her pen and laid it across her tablet. She glanced his way, then focused on his daughter. "Well, only one person comes to mind. As far as I can recall, she's the only person you both respect and like. I'm assuming that means you trust her as well."

Diana frowned.

Adelaide knew.

And Graham had no idea who it was. How had he let things get this bad? His daughter was a handful; there was no denying that. But, dammit, he was the parent—he needed to start acting like one.

"Felicity Buchanan," Adelaide said, instantly dinging Graham's newfound determination to focus solely on his daughter. The therapist flipped through her notes. "You've mentioned her, many times, as a decent person who lives to love her kids." She flipped a few more pages, reading, "She would do anything to make her kids happy. And she makes you feel safe."

"Because she gets it," Diana bit back.

He wasn't sure what that meant, but he wanted to know. "You need Felicity to talk to you?" Graham asked, confused. How was Felicity supposed to help? He didn't relish the idea of dragging her into this— especially knowing the amount of crap she was already shouldering.

"What, so she can say whatever you tell her to say?" Diana rested her head on her knees.

"Felicity won't lie to you, Diana—even if I asked her to. Which I would never do." He sighed, irritation returning. "I'm not sure how Felicity can help," he told Adelaide.

"I think Diana's insecurity stems from being alone with you for a long period of time—feeling pressure—not just the possibility you're taking her to Serenity Heights." Adelaide crossed her ankles, watching him.

Nothing she said was comforting. How the hell did he fix that? "I need help here," he murmured, glancing at Diana. "What, exactly, do you want Felicity to do?"

Diana didn't even bother to look up. "Go with us. Maybe?"

Adelaide made an approving noise. "Perhaps the Buchanans would be willing to accompany you?"

"On vacation?" Because asking Felicity to drop her responsibilities for his kid's abandonment issues was the fair thing to do. He shot Adelaide a look of desperation, but the therapist remained cool and detached, no expression at all. At the moment, her professionalism felt more like betrayal, and considering how alone he was in this, it didn't help with the anger simmering right beneath the surface.

"Yeah." Diana turned her head to look at him. "Like we used to?" A hint of interest crept into her voice. "Felicity and her kids need a break, too."

True or not, that wasn't his first priority. His daughter was. This was about reconnecting with her—trying to bridge the chasm that he'd let widen in the time since Julia's death. Their family of two was held together by threads so fragile, it wasn't a matter of if they broke but when. He hoped time together in a place full of good memories would change that.

Now Di, through Adelaide, was saying she didn't want to be alone with him and had managed to turn this thing on its head.

On one hand, having Felicity with him would be…amazing. When it came to parenting, he could use her guidance. And her calming presence would work wonders on Di. But there was that new thing he'd been grappling with since the elevator and after. She wasn't just a friend or fellow single parent. She was a caring, passionate woman with needs and wants, a woman he deeply cared for— possibly more than he or Diana were prepared for.

"There has to be another way to do this, Di. You know what her family is dealing with." It wasn't a small request; she had to see that. That was before the household learned about Jack's imminent arrival. Her kids were going to be, understandably, emotional minefields. Injecting that sort of hostility into his and Diana's already polluted dynamic wasn't good for any of them.

"You're not even going to ask her, are you?" That hardness was back, her fingers shredding her tissue. "I wasn't expecting your whole 'whatever it takes' bullshit to fall apart that fast." Her air quotes only made it worse.

He ran a hand along the back of his neck and stared at the pattern on the carpet at his feet. Losing it now wouldn't go over well. "I wasn't expecting the two of us to need a moderator, Di. Can you give me a second to metabolize what you're saying? Can't we work out some sort of compromise?"

Diana stared at him for a long time, tearing the shredded tissue into tiny pieces. "Like I go to Serenity Heights for a few weeks and then we go to the beach house?"

Graham was up, pacing the length of the small office. "No. Serenity Heights doesn't figure into this equation, Di. Not at all."

"You asked me what I wanted." She shook her head. "What you want is for me to do what *you* want."

"What I want is for you to trust me. For you to accept that I'm not giving up on you. That I want to be your dad again." He stopped, shoving his hands into his pockets so she wouldn't see him tremble. "I'll call her."

"When?" Diana pushed.

The panic from last night lingered, keeping him off balance and grasping. "Today." The sooner the better.

"We should take them donuts." Diana stood up. "Honor loves Boston cream ones, and Nick likes apple fritters. You know, butter them up."

How could this pretty young girl be capable of so much damage? His daughter was a human tornado, swallowing up everything and leaving a path of destruction in her wake.

And he was going to put Felicity and her family directly in Di's path. With donuts, apparently. "I can't guarantee they'll agree, Di," he murmured, watching her instant withdrawal. "But I'll try to convince them, okay? You're right. I'm pretty sure we could all use a break."

Diana smiled. "Okay."

Graham memorized that smile, hoping it was the first of many to come. He wanted his daughter to smile at him, to talk to him—to trust him. First, he had to earn it. To do that he had to swallow his pride, shoulder a ton of guilt, and beg Felicity to help him save his daughter.

• • •

"I think that's it." Honor's gaze traveled over the list she'd made when she and her mother had gone to the new-student orientation last spring. It was a "recommended" supply list—for decorating her dorm room as well as suggested items for her classes.

"No other tech?" Charity asked, stirring her slushee with a long red straw. "No discs or flash drives or whatever?"

"She's not going to spy school from the

nineteen-eighties," Nick teased.

"Nick." Their mother was laughing.

"Are you implying I'm not tech savvy?" Charity asked. "Because I'm not."

Honor was laughing, too.

"Your lips are purple. Both of you." Nick shook his head, nodding at their drinks. "Like, bright purple."

Her aunt smiled widely, making sure they all saw just how purple her lips were.

Honor covered her mouth. "Really?" She dug around in her purse for a compact mirror. One look had her groaning. She rubbed her teeth with her fingers, bared her teeth, then frowned. "Awesome." The color wasn't budging.

"Really." Nick nodded.

"It's a good color, right?" Charity teased.

"You wear it well," Honor agreed. How could her aunt make it look adorable when she looked like she was recovering from some seventeenth-century plague?

Nick shook his head. "I'm not sure anyone can wear that color well."

Her mother nudged him and held out her hand for Honor's list. "May I?"

Honor slid her phone across the table as a shout from the other side of the shopping center food court drew her attention. Gaming Central was crowded, kids of all ages pouring in and out of the arcade. Nick had spent most of the time they'd been shopping there—escaping the boring stuff, as he put it.

"Is the computer bag going to work?" Her

mother smothered a yawn.

"It's perfect, Mom." Honor nodded. Considering her grandparents had bought her a way too expensive computer for her graduation present, she needed something to keep it safe. "I have everything I need. Thanks for today." It had been Charity's suggestion. She needed her college stuff, and everyone was on edge, so they'd hoped a day trip outside of Pecan Valley might be the distraction they all needed.

Her mom probably should have stayed home and napped, but knowing her mom, napping wouldn't happen.

Nick was still a little tense and snappy, but he was trying—and she appreciated the effort.

"I'm getting some coffee." Her mother stood. "Anybody want anything?"

"Ooh." Charity peered around Nick. "They have those big molasses cookies, don't they?"

Nick started laughing. "I'm a fan of sugar and all, but I'm thinking the cookie sandwich, bag of gummy fish, and your purple slushee have to meet some sort of quota."

Charity's eyes went round. "Oh my God, I did eat all of that, didn't I?"

Nick leaned closer to their aunt. "And the double cheeseburger meal—"

Charity covered Nick's mouth. "I've got it, Nick. No, thanks, Filly, I'm good."

Honor laughed. It was true. Aunt Charity had been eating the entire time they'd shopped. For someone as tiny as she was, her appetite was impressive. Okay, for a three-hundred-pound rear tackle, her appetite was impressive.

"I feel like a bear on the verge of hibernation."
Charity shook her head.

Nick opened his mouth, but Honor kicked him
under the table.

"Not a word from you." Charity pointed at Nick.
"Here, take my money and go play your games."
She shoved some ones his way.

"Paying for my silence?" Nick asked, standing.
"I'm not going to argue. Let me know when you're
ready to leave." He headed off, blond curls
bouncing.

"I'm glad you made him come, Aunt Charity."
Honor watched her brother. "He needed a break
from reality."

"I'm not sure gaming on his couch at home versus gaming in an arcade is really all that different,
but I'm glad he came, too." Charity sighed, her gaze
narrowing as she peered over Honor's shoulder.
"Um, isn't that very tall man-boy with the dark hair
talking to your mom your boyfriend?"

Honor froze.

"He's got a whole crew of equally large, muscular
friends with him." Charity shook her head. "Is it a
club or something?"

"Football." This was bad. This was very bad.
How was she supposed to act? How was he going
to act? It wasn't like they were in the confines of
her home. No. They were out. In public. With his
friends watching. There was no way he was going to
pretend—

"Hey." He pulled out the chair next to hers, dark
hair spiked up, hazel eyes fixed on her, and his

hand reaching out to take hers. "Hope you don't mind me crashing. Nick said you guys were out shopping."

She stared at him. Like, stared. Hard. Confused. "What are you doing here?"

"Nick said you'd be here?" he repeated, his fingers threading with hers. "I had to do some paperwork on base this morning, so I figured I'd try to meet up with you guys."

On base. A hard, jagged knot stuck in her throat. "What about your friends?" she asked. "Aren't you here with…people?"

"I told them I wanted to spend time with you." He shrugged. "They get it."

They got it, but she didn't. As amazing and mind-blowing as his declaration in the kitchen had been, it just didn't make sense. She was… And he was… And they just didn't make sense. So why was he here, smiling at her, holding her hand, making her insides tighten with pure anticipation?

"You guys are too cute." Charity stood. "I'm grabbing your mother for some old-lady shopping. I'll text you in a bit. If you think you guys can occupy yourselves…?"

There was no reason to panic. They were less alone than they were at her house most of the time. But his sudden appearance had thrown her for a loop. Because… Owen.

Now Aunt Charity was gone, and she was still staring like an idiot.

"Your teeth are purple."

She covered her mouth, horrified.

"Grape slushee?" He peered into her cup. "My

favorite." He took a long sip, then smiled.

She laughed.

"We match?" he asked, taking another long drink from her straw.

She was staring at him again. This time it was because he was without a doubt one of the most beautiful man-boys she'd ever seen. He was. He knocked her heart around and made her all light-headed and flustered. Whether or not it was a good thing had yet to be determined.

"You're mad?" he asked, staring at their hands.

Was she? Mad? That he'd surprised her. Had he seriously come here for her? *Like, seriously?* "I'm not sure I understand why you're here. I mean, it's weird, isn't it?"

His eyes locked with hers. "That I want to be with you?"

She swallowed hard, searching for a coherent response. He had a way of saying things that prevented her from forming meaningful sentences. "But my mom and aunt Charity aren't here."

He smiled, his free hand toying with one of her curls. "That morning…" He broke off. "Your mom catching us was the best thing that ever happened to me. If she hadn't turned on that light, you'd still be ignoring my texts and phone calls. All I want is a chance here." His gaze swept over her face. "For you to give us a chance."

Us. The two-letter word had her reeling. "Owen." *What?* Her mind went blank. *Say something.* This wasn't happening. He wasn't serious. And she was absolutely not falling…absolutely *not* in love with him. *No way.*

"Honor." He was smiling that grin that made her insides melt.

"I—I'm not mad." Her words were breathless and wavering, and she was holding on to his hand, leaning into him.

"I'm glad." He nodded, his fingers tracing along her jaw. Unsteady fingers. He was shaking. Because of her? One look at his face, the warmth in his eyes, and her heart gave up the fight.

"Okay," she whispered.

He shook his head. "Okay?"

"I'll give you a chance, Owen Nel—"

Then he was kissing her, and finishing her sentence wasn't important. He was kissing her, and nothing else mattered.

. . .

Charity pocketed her change and headed toward her sister. Her sister who was standing in front of a lingerie shop—staring at a rather racy bit of lacy naughtiness. *Way to go, Filly.* "I approve. You'd look good in that."

Her sister jumped. *Busted.* She held out her soft pretzel, willing to share—a little.

"No, thank you." Filly eyed her pretzel. "I thought you were going to the bathroom."

"I did." She grinned. "But these things smell *so* good. Now stop changing the subject. I bet Graham would be more than happy to play doctor with you in that getup."

Felicity shook her head. "Charity."

"What? Look at you getting all flustered and

red. Why else would you be thinking about buying something like that?" Because, eventually, when they both woke up and realized how crazy they were about each other, her sister was going to rock Graham Murphy's world. Or he was going to rock Filly's. Either way—rocking of worlds was in their future.

"I was looking," Filly argued. "Not buying."

"Why does it have so many straps?" Charity asked, tilting her head. "Talk about impractical." With a built-in push-up bra and intricate straps and hooks, sleeping was not its intent. It was meant to be worn—and removed. And, hopefully, the remover wouldn't get trapped in all the intricate straps and hooks. "I'm not sure getting out of that would be…sexy. It's sort of like a pretty bear trap. You might have to gnaw off a limb to get out of it."

Felicity laughed. "Bear trap?"

Charity shrugged. "When in doubt, nakedness works. I'm not sure guys are as into this sort of stuff as we women think they are. Besides, something tells me Graham is just as hard up as you are, so this won't be necessary." Seeing Filly all sexified in something like this might just be too much for the good doctor.

"Would you stop." Felicity was beyond flustered now. "Graham and I… That's not going to happen."

Charity loved her sister. She didn't always understand her, but she loved her. Why Filly would choose to pass up an incredibly sweet and sexy man was beyond her. He ticked all the boxes. Single. Employed. Devoted. Handsome. And, as Di had pointed out, wealthy to boot. Unless her sister had found *the* perfect man, there was no excuse for not jumping on Graham Murphy. Immediately. Like, drive back to Pecan Valley and tackle him now.

Then it happened. A horrible thought. She said it wasn't going to happen with *Graham*… Was there someone else? "Wait. No, please don't tell me you're thinking about Rob, white-teeth-lawyer guy. You're not, are you?" She winced. "Hold my pretzel; I feel nauseous." She was only partly kidding.

Felicity rolled her eyes. "Oh, stop. He's not unattractive."

"Felicity, please tell me you're joking." Charity squished her pretzel and stared at her sister in horror.

"I'm not joking." She paused, lowering her voice. "Rob Klein *is* attractive."

Charity couldn't care less what the moms with school-age kids who were already wishing summer was over thought or what the elderly power walkers overheard. As for the teens staring mindlessly at their phones—they wouldn't care. But she did. Her sister could not wind up with Rob Klein. She couldn't. He wasn't any better than Matt had been. His ridiculous teeth made him highly suspect.

"But no, I'm not interested in him—not to date or anything else." With a final look at the nightgown, Filly hooked arms with her and added, "I'm not planning on sleeping with *anyone*. So let's change the subject."

She could breathe again—and mourn the mangling of her pretzel. "Why? What is stopping you? I know this may come as a shock to you, but I know you've had sex. And, if I recall, you enjoyed sex.

Because you told me you did. So why would you give it up?" Charity dodged a stroller. "I mean, there will be no judging if you decide to seduce the good doctor."

Filly was chewing on the inside of her bottom lip.

"Spill," Charity pushed. "Come on, Filly. No secrets. I mean it about no judgment—you know that. I get that it must be hard to be attracted to someone who's not your husband—sort of. In theory anyway. But it's totally normal. You shouldn't feel weird about it."

"But I do. It's not like I haven't dreamed about it." Filly's whisper was almost funny. Almost. "Not that I can control my dreams—they just happen."

Charity nodded. "But those dreams have got you thinking?"

"But dreaming about something and doing it are very different things. And—" She broke off, looking around them. "I've never seduced someone. Ever. I mean, Matt's the only man who's ever seen me naked."

Charity wasn't sure what to say. Her poor sister's sex life consisted of Matt "Dickwad" Buchanan. She'd never pegged the guy as incredibly imaginative, so how great could Filly's experience be? "Then you should give it a try. Maybe it's your calling. I can think of a man who would probably be more than willing to see you naked. And to let you seduce him." The look on her sister's face had her dialing it back. "And it would be wrong to try because…?"

Felicity shook her head. "We're not talking

about this anymore."

Because her big sister was freaking out. Over sex and lingerie and Graham and all the things that should be fun — not stressful.

"What do you want to talk about?" Charity asked.

"Baby stuff." Felicity sighed. "We're here. There's a maternity store."

Charity froze. "Um, no, thank you."

"You said your pants are tight. You're only going to keep getting bigger, Charity. Might as well get one or two pairs of pants. Maybe a shirt or two."

She couldn't live in her yoga pants much longer. Her mother was likely to burn them if she tried. Still, standing in front of a full-length mirror was something she now dreaded. She liked her body. It wasn't perfect, but it suited her. Now, with the basketball swell more obvious every day, it didn't. She didn't look like herself. "Just tell me I'll get my body back."

Felicity hugged her. "Is that what's worrying you?"

"That I'm inflating like a balloon? It's sort of worrisome."

"You're pregnant. It would be more worrisome if you weren't growing. You're growing because your baby is growing." Felicity hugged her again. "Worrying isn't good for you, you know that?"

"Says you." She took her sister's hand.

"I'm trying, okay? It's just, there's been so much to worry about recently. Every time I think things are evening out, they fall apart."

"No one has fallen apart, Filly. You've made sure of that. You're always so good about taking care of everyone else, you know? I mean, I get it, the whole mom-nurturer thing. But it's like you've removed yourself from that."

"I take care of myself."

Charity rolled her eyes. "You eat well and exercise, yes, I know. Mom reminds me of that every single time she sees me. I mean here." She pointed at her sister's chest—her heart.

Filly's gaze fell from hers, and she went back to nibbling the inside of her lip.

And just like that, Charity was struck with inspiration. "I'll make you a deal."

Filly's brows rose. "I can't wait to hear this."

She laughed. "Just hear me out, will you?"

Her sister nodded.

"I'll buy fat-lady maternity clothes, whatever you think I need. But then we go back to that lingerie store and—"

"No. Absolutely not." Felicity crossed her arms over her chest. "I'm too...too—"

"Scared to see that you've still got a rocking bod that deserves the loving of a good man? Whose initials might be—and probably are—GM. Who comes with a lot of baggage but is totally worth it?" She paused, making a big production out of taking a deep breath. "Who lights up when you walk into a room and clearly cares about your kids and, when you weren't looking, has totally checked out your butt—"

"Charity." Felicity cut her off.

"Was that a yes?" Charity poked. "I'm pretty

sure you said yes, you'll buy lingerie and I'll buy maternity clothes. You have no idea how depressing that was to say."

Her sister laughed. "I love you."

"I love you, too." She paused. "And I want you to be happy. That's all I'm getting at, okay?"

Felicity nodded. "Okay."

"Good." Charity smiled. "Let's start with the lingerie and then get the maternity clothes."

Felicity sighed. "Really?"

"Yes, really."

They were halfway to the boutique when Felicity asked, "He really checked out my butt?"

You are so hot for the good doctor. "Yes, he did. And he definitely liked what he saw."

CHAPTER TWELVE

Felicity sliced another orange and placed one half in the juicer. The methodical slice, juice, repeat offered her a chance to think through what, exactly, she needed to say this morning. Now that Honor had everything she needed for college, Charity had some proper maternity clothes, and she'd been coerced into purchasing something silky that would probably reside in the back of her underwear drawer, it was time to get back to reality. Jack was forever family and he'd be coming home, to their home, tomorrow. That was reality.

Honor would take it in stride.

Nick. Nick was going to have a hard time.

Her parents had taken a regular time slot at Jack's bedside and, once their replacements arrived, they were heading from the hospital to the house for support. Now that Jack had been cleared to come home tomorrow, she had some work to do. Every night for the last week she'd been packing up boxes and putting them in the attic. After careful consideration, she'd decided to turn her craft room into a nursery. Having it on the third floor, next door to her room, would spare Honor and Nick some of Jack's late-night tantrums. She hoped.

It would be an adjustment. For all of them.

"Oh my God, that smells incredible." Charity opened the oven door and peeked inside. "Breakfast casserole and orange sticky buns?"

SASHA SUMMERS   203

"Mom and Dad are joining us." Felicity smiled at her sister.

"Thanks for the warning." She shot her a look, tugging her oversize T-shirt and running a hand over her sloppy bun.

"You look fine, Charity." Felicity's quick inspection of her sister showed no signs of her secret pregnancy. Which was good. Selfishly, she wasn't ready for that information to come out.

Not today anyway. Today was about Jack.

"Says you," Charity groaned. "You know Mom."

Felicity smiled. She did indeed. And chances were, their mother would say something about Charity's choice of attire. And her hair. And her lack of makeup. Their mother was old-school, meaning "faces on," presentable hair, and "real" clothes on before eight every day—no exceptions. That way they were ready for unexpected company or the need to go on some surprise outing.

"You have time to go change." Felicity laughed, the distress on her sister's face pathetic but comical.

"Oh right, then she'll say something about me not helping out in the kitchen."

Felicity shot her a look.

"Well, I know I didn't do anything. And you know I didn't do anything. But if she knows…" Charity wrinkled up her face.

"Who knows?" Honor asked as she entered the kitchen. "Mmm," she said, sniffing. "Orange sticky rolls? Mimi and Grandad coming over?"

Felicity nodded.

"Cool. It's been a while since we've done the family breakfast thing." Honor slipped her arms around her mother and rested her head on her shoulder. "And you know I'll never pass up your orange sticky rolls. You're going to have to send them in care packages next fall."

Felicity's hold tightened for a second. She'd miss her sweet daughter's spontaneous hugs, the happy swing of her strawberry-blond ponytail, and her laughter. All too soon, Honor would be moving into her dorm and starting an exciting new chapter. Until then, Felicity needed to collect as many moments with her daughter as possible.

"Love you, Mom." Honor squeezed her back.

She pressed a kiss against Honor's temple and let her go. "I love you, too."

The doorbell rang.

"Since when do they ring the doorbell?" Charity asked, tugging at her shirt again.

"Is the door locked?" Felicity asked. She'd gone for her morning power walk at sunrise, but she didn't remember locking it when she got back. Locks weren't necessary in Pecan Valley.

"I'll get it," Nick called, his footfalls beating a trail to the front door. "Oh, hey, come on in." Then he added, "The Murphys are here."

"They are?" Charity grinned at her. "I wonder what sort of flowers he brings to your mom?" she mock whispered to Honor.

Honor grinned.

Felicity rolled her eyes. "Oh, please," she protested for good measure. And yet, she was happy Graham was here. Happy and blushing because an image of the silky thing she'd purchased sprang to mind.

Seconds later, Nick, Graham, and Diana were in the kitchen—and Honor and Charity were all smiles. Not only did Graham have an incredible bouquet of flowers, Diana carried a pastry box loaded with the kids' favorites and some fresh croissants.

"We're crashing breakfast," Diana said, offering the pastries to Honor.

Graham looked like hell. Like he hadn't slept for a week and was on autopilot. When those light brown eyes met hers, he shied away. "Always room at the table," she answered, accepting Diana's hug. He was here, looking like that—she wasn't about to turn them away. If anything, she felt bad. They had no idea what this morning's topic of conversation would be.

"You look rough, Graham." Charity frowned. "Long nights in the delivery room?"

She saw the way Diana glanced at her father, the slight defiant tilt of her head, and instantly understood. Diana was the reason he'd canceled. From the looks of it, she'd put him through the wringer. Her heart hurt for them.

"Kids. The ultimate adventure," he answered, his smile exhausted.

The oven timer dinged, and a flurry of activity followed. Felicity moved the orange sticky rolls to a platter while Honor and Diana loaded the pastries onto a tiered cupcake plate—Nick stole an apple fritter and dodged his sister's playful swat, laughing. Charity made a fresh pot of coffee for their father. Poor Graham sort of propped himself against the counter, watching the easy chaos with red-rimmed eyes.

She poured him a cup of coffee and pressed the mug into his hands. "Black, right?"

He nodded. "Thank you."

She gave his hand a pat. "I'm here, you know," she murmured. "If you need to talk?"

He nodded, those soft-brown eyes sweeping her face before he focused on his coffee. "I'd like that. Not now, of course." His fingers tightened around the mug. "Sorry we invaded."

"You're always welcome." She paused, fighting the urge to smooth his tousled hair. Graham Murphy needed a hug. And she ached to give him one.

He tore his gaze from her, turning to watch Diana, his jaw muscle working.

"Thank you for the flowers."

"I felt bad about canceling. It wasn't by choice." Which was oh so sweet to hear. "Maybe we can try again?" He smiled. He should smile more often.

She nodded. Absolutely not thinking about the silky thing. Or his reaction to the silky thing. *Stop thinking about it. And him. Now.* "Thanks for the donuts."

"They were Di's idea." He shook his head, watching as Nick shoved an entire donut into his mouth.

"And there won't be any left if Nick keeps eating them," Charity interrupted them. "At least save me one. A chocolate one."

Nick held the tiered tray up. "I don't know, Aunt Charity. You said you wanted to start eating better. Chocolate donuts?"

Charity pouted, instantly deflating.

"One isn't bad." Diana jumped to Charity's

defense. "They're fresh donuts. Technically *better* than packaged ones. So, you know, *better* for her."

"Good one." Felicity laughed. "Give her a donut, Nickie."

Once her parents arrived, the volume kicked up—as did the chaos. Her mother had a gift for turning even a simple conversation into a production. Felicity didn't mind. She knew the laughter wasn't going to last once she found the courage to do what needed to be done.

"Jack's doing better," she started. "He'll be able to leave the hospital tomorrow."

"Man, it's got to suck for him." Diana served herself more breakfast casserole as she spoke. "No mom and no dad. Being in that cast."

"He's frustrated," her father agreed. "And, for a little guy, he's developed a pretty good aim to help pass the time."

"If it's not bolted down, it's airborne," her mother agreed, glancing her way.

Nick sighed loudly and slumped back in his chair.

"They found someone to take him?" Honor asked, blue eyes concerned.

Felicity spared Graham a look, taking confidence from his nod. He was right; she could do this. Now, surrounded by people who loved her and her children, was the best time to put it out there.

"Yes. And no." She set her napkin on the plate. "Amber has no family and, as you know, your father's parents died a long time ago."

"Aunts? Cousins?" Nick poked the half-eaten orange sticky bun with the tines of his fork. "A neighbor?" His smile was strained.

"There is no one." Felicity cleared her throat. "He's going to come live with us." She paused, watching Honor nod and Nick's face turn beet red.

"Are you shitting me?" Diana asked, her food falling from her fork to the table. "How is that fair? Seriously?"

Felicity ignored her parents' reaction to Diana's outburst. "It's not. None of this is." She shook her head. "I know it. It's going to be a big adjustment — for all of us. But it's the right thing to do." And the only other option — unless she was okay saddling her eighteen-year-old with a toddler.

"For the baby, yeah." Diana stopped, turning to look at Nick. "You okay?"

Nick didn't answer — he couldn't. His jaw was so tight, Felicity feared he'd crack a tooth.

"If we didn't bring him home, then what, Jack would wind up in foster care? Right? An orphan?" Honor shook her head, those blue eyes filling with tears. "And he's not an orphan. We're his family. He's our brother."

"No, he's not," Nick snapped. "He took Dad. He broke our family." The accusation in his eyes was razor sharp. "And you're bringing him home? My home. So now he gets you, too?" His voice broke.

She was up, heading around the table — but Nick was faster. He shot out of the kitchen, stomped up the stairs, and slammed his bedroom door with enough force to rattle the china in the hutch.

"What else can you do, Filly?" Her father's hand descended on her shoulder, turning her to face him. "He's upset. He has every right to be upset — you all do, if we're being honest here. But he'll come around. Nick's got a good head on his shoulders and a tender heart." He pulled her into his arms and hugged her gently, patting her back.

Felicity wanted to believe that, she did. But Diana was right there—the living, breathing representation of what she worried Nick would become. Angry, volatile, twisted, and manipulative. And while she didn't want to think he'd ever be a danger to himself, there were times she didn't know what he'd do— what he was capable of.

And right now, he needed her. Even if he didn't want her. There was nothing she could do or say to make this better. Chances were, she was the last person he wanted to see right now. He wouldn't listen to Honor, her parents, or Charity. The last person she wanted him talking to right now was Diana.

Still wrapped in her father's embrace, Graham sat—staring after Nick. When their eyes locked, he stood. "I'll go," Graham said, not waiting for an answer before he followed Nick upstairs.

• • •

Charity wasn't surprised. She'd known, without Filly saying so, that Jack was coming home. Where else could the little monster go? He was all alone in the world. Still, Nick's reaction was heart-wrenching. These kids had been through too much—and the hits just kept on coming.

But she'd spied a silver lining. A really big, really beautiful silver lining. Graham Murphy was crushing on her sister—seriously crushing. Not just an "I want to take you to bed tonight" but the "I want to wake up to you every morning" sort of thing. The potential for something big and real and lasting. The sort of thing she had no experience with but recognized when she saw it. Years ago, her sister had looked that way at Matt. Her parents still looked like that, most of the time. It was a warm, unspoken connection that communicated volumes.

This morning, Graham Murphy had looked at her sister that way. And when he realized Charity had seen it—he turned an adorable shade of red.

With any luck, things were going to be extra crowded here at the family homestead.

Honor and Nick.

Jack.

She and the stranger in her belly.

And, eventually, Graham and Diana.

All of them—one big happily family. Good thing it was a big house.

"We'll get the dishes," her mother offered. "Why don't you and your father take your coffee onto the deck? Breathe a bit?"

Charity started clearing the table, needing something to do. Luckily, Honor and Diana followed her lead, the loaded silence turning unbearable. Best way to diffuse tension? Laughter. She did her best to ease the tension in the air, launching into the time one of her tour members tried to shoplift a replica of the Coliseum under his shirt.

Over and over, her gaze returned to the porch. Felicity was up and pacing while her father sat rocking. There wasn't a thing she could do—except distract.

"What happened?" Diana asked, pulling her attention back to their kitchen cleanup.

"I talked his way out of a fine." She shook her head. "My Italian's not that great but..." She shrugged.

"You were always good at talking your way out of things." Her mother wasn't necessarily praising her.

"You'll have to teach me." Diana was all smiles.

Honor lingered by the back door, drying the same bowl she'd been drying for a good five minutes, watching her mother and grandfather.

"Honor?" She took the bowl and stored it in one of the upper cabinets. Another story—this time about her train breaking down on the tracks and the impromptu concert that sprang up among the passengers. Sitting there, surrounded by instruments and people from all over the world, all connected through music, had been a magical thing.

Diana was all ears. Honor tried. But the tension was still there, tainting the air. Her mother was agitated, glancing back and forth between Filly and her dad on the back porch and tidying up the kitchen with a vengeance.

"You can go out, too, Mom," Charity volunteered. The less time they spent together, the better. The woman had an uncanny sixth-sense when it came to her youngest daughter. If she found out about the baby in her belly... Yeah, her mother would have a cow. No one needed more drama right now. "Dad could probably use more coffee." Her mother was all about taking care of Dad.

"No, no. I can't sit still right now." Her mother

put on one of Felicity's aprons, tying the ribbons behind her. "Want one?" she asked, then frowned when she did a head-to-toe once-over of Charity's ensemble. "Charity Ann, *what* are you wearing?" Her disapproving headshake, tongue click followed. "Even if you'd gone to the gym this morning, you still should have showered and dressed for breakfast. After all the effort your sister put into breakfast and all."

Charity smiled and nodded. "You're right." Easier to agree with her than point out that 80 percent of the population didn't wear makeup for a *family* brunch. At least she was wearing a bra. That was something.

"I know I'm right." Her mother turned on the faucet and squeezed a stream of blue-green soap into the farm-style sink.

"Mimi, we can load the dishwasher," Honor offered.

Her mother waved the suggestion aside. "They never get things as clean as a good hand-scrubbing."

The look of horror on Diana's young face almost made her laugh—almost. Instead, she rolled her eyes and continued scraping plates into the trash.

"Maudie said you stopped by?" Her mother scrubbed the sticky-roll pan with surprising vigor. "Finally."

Not responding to her dig. "Yes, ma'am."

Her mother shot her a narrow-eyed look full of reproof. "You don't sound grateful, Charity Ann. That woman's giving you one of the most successful businesses in Pecan Valley. I'd think you'd be grateful." She went back to scrubbing, with extra oomph.

"I am," she argued. And she was. "I'm still in shock." Her delivery needed work—big time. No one in the kitchen believed her. She didn't believe herself.

"I thought you lived in Europe," Diana said, continuing to stack plates.

"I did." A sudden craving for gelato hit her.

"What happened with your job, Charity Ann? You seemed so happy. And so determined to stay away from Pecan Valley." Her mother stopped scrubbing the pan long enough to look at her.

There it was—*the look*. The one she'd been trying to avoid. "Downsizing." Charity shrugged, acting as if the storage of the leftovers was a top priority.

But her mother stared at her for a second longer than was necessary; Charity could feel it. Her mother was deliberating whether or not to believe her.

"That bites," Diana said. "To live there and have to come back *here*."

Charity did laugh that time. Pecan Valley wasn't her favorite place, but there were many, many things about this quiet, sleepy town that she was fond of. Which was a surprise, really. But she was pregnant and that, she was learning, wreaked havoc on one's emotional state.

"Do you want to go to Europe, Diana?" Honor asked. "I do. I'm going to take a semester abroad. Italy or Greece or France. Maybe Germany. Somewhere."

"You should," Charity agreed. "Travel is never a waste of time or money."

"If you have both to spare," her mother interrupted. "But I suppose it is best to get that all out of your system while you're young."

"Aunt Charity is still young, Mimi." Honor laughed.

"And gorgeous," Diana added, smiling. "You could be a movie star. Seriously."

Except she was a terrible actress. Standing here, lying to her mother, was horrible. She was close to cracking just so her mother would stop giving her *the look*.

"She is young and pretty." Her mother smiled at them. "But something tells me her adventuring days are over and she's home. Everything happens for a reason." That smile made Charity nervous.

Her mother was right. There was definitely a reason she was back in Pecan Valley, but neither Graham nor Felicity would have ratted her out. In the beginning it had been this baby—and losing her job. Now she knew it was more than that.

Felicity needed her. Her sister had always believed in her, supporting her dreams even when they seemed impossible and illogical. Now it was her turn to be there for her sister—for Honor and Nick. She didn't know how or what to do but, whatever it was, Charity would do her best to be there for them.

CHAPTER THIRTEEN

"Wine?" Felicity offered a nearly full extra-large wineglass.

Graham looked up from the crib he was assembling and took the glass. "Thanks."

"You really don't have to do that," she said for the fiftieth time.

He nodded. "I know."

She sat on the floor beside him, humming along to the radio broadcast—a tribute to Glenn Miller. Between the upbeat swing music and the sweet sangria they were sipping, her spirits were lifting. Her gaze wandered around the room. She and Graham had made a lot of progress this evening. Now that Jack's toys and books had replaced her crafting bins and cabinet, the room looked like a nursery. A happy, cheerful nursery. With color. "Think he'll like it?" she asked.

Graham leaned against the wall, his long legs stretched out in front of him and the crib instructions on the floor beside him. Those brown eyes surveyed the changes they'd made before he nodded. "I think so." He glanced at her. "Eventually."

"Meaning a nice room and familiar toys aren't going to make tomorrow easy?" She nodded, slowly spinning her glass. "Yeah, I know. Not by a long shot."

One brow rose and the corner of his mouth kicked up. "Maybe not in the beginning, but I have no doubt you'll figure things out."

"That makes one of us." She lifted her glass in a mock toast. "What a day." Her smile fell flat; she could tell by the look on his face. *Right. Enough wallowing.* "Have plans for tomorrow?" As soon as the question was out, she regretted it. He'd already done so much for her. Asking him to be there was too much.

"Tomorrow?" His confusion was almost comical. "I thought I'd lend a hand here with Jack, if that's okay." He sipped his wine.

"Okay? It's more than okay." Her laugh was nervous. "I feel pretty guilty asking."

"You didn't." He turned back to the instructions. "I'm offering."

And it was a huge relief. Like it or not, he had a calming effect that was missing in her boisterous, well-meaning family. Calm, right now, went a long way. "Well, I appreciate it. Having the backup, I mean."

He nodded, setting his wineglass on a large farm animal picture book, and went back to screwing the side onto the crib. The old house creaked and popped, settling in the evening wind. That's what old houses did. But tonight, with Nick at her parents' cabin and Charity treating Honor and Diana to mani-pedis and a double feature at the newly restored drive-in movie theater, she realized this—quiet—would soon be a rarity. Toddlers, especially out-of-sorts, cast-ridden toddlers, were vocal. Every visit to the hospital was proof of that. She might as well enjoy this chance at peace and quiet—together.

"Okay. This should do it." He stood, snapping in a plastic bracket and standing back to inspect his work. The screwdriver and wrench sticking out of his business dress pants had her smiling. "Done."

"Thank you, Graham. And not just for the crib. For today, everything. All of it."

Brown eyes met hers. "You don't have to thank me."

"I do," she argued. "Nick wasn't going to talk to any of us. We might be family but, to him, we've all turned against him." It hurt so much. "I hope, in time, he realizes I'll never, ever turn my back on him."

"He will, Felicity." His smile was sad. "I didn't really do anything. He talked, and I listened."

"Exactly. Thank you." She glanced into her drink, watching the deep-red wine as she spun her glass. "He's upset. And he has every reason to be."

"You do, too, you know?" His voice lowered.

"Maybe." She glanced at him.

"No *maybe*, Felicity." A bone-weary sigh tore from his chest. "I admit we weren't close these last few years—Matt and I, I mean—but we used to be. I knew him. I thought I knew him. And the shit he's pulled, the depths of his selfishness, are..." He dragged his fingers through his thick, dark hair, leaving it standing on end. "What he did—I don't know *that* guy. Or understand him."

The urge to smooth his hair had her hand itching. "That's a good thing." She finished off her wine. "If you did understand him, I'd have to kick your butt out."

He laughed, flooding her with warmth.

But the sparkle in his dark eyes and the dimple in his right cheek caught her off guard. Graham, happy, was devastating. In a good way. That startling flicker of heat she'd first experienced in the elevator returned with a vengeance. What she was feeling now had nothing to do with security. And the tripping rate of her pulse was anything *but* calm. She swallowed down the knot in her throat and forced herself to breathe. "But since you don't, you can stay and drink wine and…" And what? That was the question. Her skin tingled. "Stay. If you want."

He was staring at her now, his smile almost inviting.

No. Graham was being Graham. She was seeing exactly what she wanted to see. Wait. Is that what she wanted to see? She hadn't had enough wine to answer that honestly.

"Have you noticed that we always seem to end up talking about our kids?" she asked, placing her empty glass on the dresser, shooing the cats out of the crib so she could put freshly laundered sheets on the mattress. *Surreal. That's what this is. All of it.* Honor had just graduated from high school and now she was setting up a nursery?

His chuckle earned her full attention. "You're right."

"Let's try something new. So, Graham, what are *you* up to? Anything particularly interesting? Read any good books? Watched any noteworthy movies?"

He paused, considering, then nodded. "I was watching a documentary on the expected life span of the planet." He did his best not to smile—and failed.

The sheet popped off the mattress when she spun to stare at him. "Really?" It was her turn to laugh. Hard. "Because you thought it would cheer you up?"

He was laughing again, full-bodied, rich and warm. She loved everything about the sound of it—and the way he looked right now. At ease. Happy. And oh so appealing.

"I'm not good at downtime," he confessed, collecting his glass from the floor and putting it on the dresser next to hers.

"Cheers to that." She clinked her empty glass against his, smiling.

His gaze slipped to her mouth.

The flicker of heat turned into a burning throb.

He cleared his throat, the muscles of his neck working. His gaze fell from her mouth and he took a long sip of wine.

Silence followed, a crushing, inescapable silence that grew until Felicity had a choice to make. The first choice—close the distance between them and carry out any one of the incredible scenarios her brain was sifting through.

The other option? Divert and distract.

There were times she wished she had a little more of Charity's brash and daring. Sadly, she didn't, so divert and distract it was. "What happened with Di? It was Diana, the night we were supposed to go out? Not work?"

His smile disappeared and he took another drink of his wine. Almost draining his glass.

"That bad?" Clearly it was. *Way to stick your foot in it, Felicity.*

His smile was hard.

"We don't have to talk about it." She shrugged, eager to change the subject. "We can talk about… the expected life span of the planet? Honor's boyfriend? The latest proposals before the school board—riveting stuff, let me tell you."

He paced the nursery, stepping over the cats, to adjust one of the toy bins on the shelf. "She found the Serenity Heights brochure and ran off."

Her insides knotted. "Oh God." She followed him.

"I spent last night driving around looking for her. Came back, alone, so frustrated I put my fist through the drywall." He shook his head. "A great example, right?"

"Graham," she whispered, taking his hands. The knuckles on the right hand were discolored and swollen. "It looks painful."

"I'm fine." He flexed—and winced. "She walked in when I was on the phone with the police. Didn't say a thing. Not a single word. No explanation. No apology." His voice hitched. "We went to her therapist and I…*lost* it." He rubbed the back of his neck.

Because he loved his daughter more than anything. For Nick to disappear? God, she couldn't imagine it. The panic and fear and anger and loss… Seeing Diana today, she never would have thought Graham's funny, too-skinny, quirky daughter was capable of that sort of behavior. If anything, Diana had seemed happy today. Really happy. "Is she going to Serenity Heights?" She suspected she already knew the answer.

"No. I can't do that to her." He shook his head. "We are going on vacation, though. To the beach house, hopefully." His gaze bounced from her to his glass and back again. "If I can get her to believe me—about the vacation. She thinks I'm lying, that I'm going to dump her at Serenity Heights."

Felicity blew out a long, slow breath. "Ouch."

"She's very good at striking out. I'm not saying I don't deserve it, but it's exhausting." He finished his glass and set it on the shelf.

"You don't deserve it, Graham." She hated how defeated he looked. "We, parents, screw up. Sometimes badly. Beating yourself up, over and over, for something we can't change isn't healthy."

"Diana and I don't have what you'd call a healthy relationship." His gaze searched hers. "But, dammit, I want to change that if I can. Somehow. I've taken six weeks off and hoped, maybe, she and I could figure out how to be a family."

"Good." It sounded like a good way to start.

"I thought so. Until she mentioned her… stipulation." He ran his fingers through his hair, agitated. "She wants you to go, too." Those brown eyes were fixed on her then.

Felicity stared right back. "What?" It didn't make any sense. At all.

"She thinks my promise of a vacation is a way to get her on the road, then I'll detour to Serenity Heights and leave her."

She hurt for Graham. And Diana. The two of them were in a place so loaded with anger and pain, she didn't know how they'd make it through. But they had to—that was the only choice. That's what families do—stick together. No matter what. "Oh, Graham."

He sighed. "I don't know if she thinks having you along will prevent me from dropping her there, or if she thinks you, your family, would make things easier for us. A buffer."

"That's her condition?" She walked to the window seat and sat, crossing her arms over her chest. Pecan and Praline jumped up, rubbing against her until she was absentmindedly stroking their soft golden fur.

"I told her I'd ask. I also told her you'd say no." He shrugged, but she heard the hint of desperation in his voice. "I've done what I said I'd do."

He was asking for her help. No, not just Graham. Diana, too.

His phone vibrated, immediately earning his full attention. "Excuse me," he murmured and left the nursery, phone in hand. "Dr. Murphy—"

She sat, reeling but frozen. As much as she wanted to help Graham and Diana, the idea of bearing that sort of responsibility was terrifying. She couldn't. Not with Nick... Jack's arrival... Charity's baby. The likely fallout when Pecan Valley, and her parents, found out about Charity's baby. And Honor—she'd be off to college in no time.

"It's too much," she whispered to the cats, both of whom seemed to be intently listening—as long as she continued to pet them. "It is too much, right?"

Pecan mewed.

"Too bad I don't speak cat," she answered.

She glanced around the room. After the divorce, she'd spent hours making this house hers, from her dream kitchen to a tranquil bedroom retreat. But it was more than stone and brick, pretty decorations, and family mementos. This was a sanctuary—and not just for her. Her children, their friends, family, and more. Everyone was welcome. Her home was loud and chaotic and frequently messy because it was always full of people and conversation, laughter and companionship. And she was thankful for it.

Diana and Graham didn't have that.

"They barely have each other," she continued to her feline companions.

If Diana wanted Felicity's family and all their noise and pandemonium in her life, it made sense. She'd had none of those things since her mother died. Graham was quiet and thoughtful. It wasn't that he didn't want to give his daughter what she needed. It was that he didn't know how.

"No, six weeks. Yes. I'm looking forward to it." Graham was still talking when he walked back into the nursery. "Thank you. You, too. And good luck with Mrs. Campos." He smiled, hung up, and placed his phone on the dresser. When he looked at her, he was uneasy.

She tried to smile but failed.

"I'm sorry."

"Don't be." She held up her hand. "I get it, Graham. I would do anything for my kids. Anything."

His brow cocked. "I tear Matt apart for being

selfish, then ask you to be responsible for my family. The irony isn't lost." The edge in his voice was razor sharp.

"If things were different, I would say yes. I would. But, right now, I can't." She stood, hugging herself. "You're trying to save the relationship you have with your daughter. Matt didn't do that. Don't compare yourself with him, Graham." Her temper flared, just enough to add snap to her words. Graham Murphy was not Matt. He was hardworking. Loyal. Kind. A man who wanted to do the best for his child. A good man. A handsome one. A man who set a fire inside her and made her ache to remember what it felt like to be a woman. A man she'd bought lingerie for, for goodness' sake.

None of which was relevant to what they were talking about right now…

"You okay?" He moved to her side. His concern—those big brown eyes searching hers—only added to her irritation.

She nodded. "Yes."

Was she? If she were, she'd still be worrying about Diana. Not Graham, right here beside her, standing so close like he was. And his velvet brown gaze fused with hers—warm and alive. All she could think about was how incredible he smelled. How his rumpled, dark hair needed smoothing. The longer he looked at her, the harder it was to fight the urge to touch him. She knew how it felt to be in his arms. And how much she wanted that again now.

Right now.

She blew out a long, slow breath, determined

not to launch herself at him.

"I can head out." He cleared his throat. "Since things are done here."

What was he asking? He should definitely go.

Yes. Go. The sooner, the better.

But she said, "No." *Don't leave.*

"No?" he whispered, one step closer to her.

"Stay." One word, and she'd changed everything.

The realization that she was now cradling Graham's face, that her lips were clinging hungrily to his, hit a good thirty seconds *after* the fact.

But then his hands were sliding up her back, and his lips sealed more firmly to hers. Heaven help her, the tip of his tongue traced the seam of her lips, and she was swaying into him. Want outweighed everything. And, oh, she wanted this. She wanted him.

• • •

He'd imagined kissing her. When it came to Felicity, he'd imagined a lot of things.

But it was nothing like this.

She was in his arms. A living, burning flame he couldn't control—he didn't want to control. The sweep of her lips. The slide of her fingers through his hair. The brush of her breath on his cheek. The taste of her mouth. She was assaulting every one of his senses. Again. Since the elevator, things had changed for him. He was in trouble. Thoughts of physical intimacy, things like desire and cravings, had been dormant.

Until now. Yearning made his blood sing and

instincts kick in with a vengeance.

His hands ran up her back, pulling her closer. Her curves, against him, knocked the air from his lungs. It didn't help that she was moving, impatient, her hands sliding down his chest and tugging the tail of his shirt from his pants.

"Felicity..." His hands caught hers, firm but gentle. If he didn't stop this now, stopping would no longer be an option. And, dammit, he knew this was too much, too soon. For both of them. But the fire in her green eyes shook his resolve. It had been so long since he'd felt this way, needy and raw. He ached to touch and taste and explore every inch of her.

He blew out a long, slow breath, wishing she'd stop looking at him that way.

But what worried him more? That she *would* stop looking at him that way.

The featherlight stroke of her fingers against his bare stomach triggered a head-to-toe quiver.

"Dammit," he whispered. Right or wrong, his senses were invaded, submerged—happily—in the woman in his arms. At the moment, she was all that mattered. Had he ever been so aware of another person?

The spot behind her ear smelled of cinnamon and berries. No...orange, from baking this morning. He drew her scent deep, his restraint melting away as she leaned in to him. He ran his nose along the shell of her ear, his lips nipping at her earlobe until her breath hitched.

He did that to her. And knowing that was powerful. A surge of exhilaration and hunger rolled over him—kissing her was all he could do. And, damn, he liked kissing her.

She was so soft. The dip in the middle of her lower lip demanded extra attention. A hint of wine clung to her mouth, making the too-sweet red his new favorite flavor. And when her lips parted, his hands were tangling in her hair to pull her closer. The touch of her tongue was a jolt to the system, one he'd forgotten existed but didn't want to forget again.

He took his time exploring the warmth of her mouth, tasting her, breathing her in and leaving them both gasping for air.

When her fingers unbuttoned his shirt, pushing it wide to stare at his chest, he tilted her chin up—forcing their eyes to meet. All his want and hunger, passion and need blazed back at him from her green eyes.

Ignoring the rational arguments for why this was a mistake wasn't easy, but her touch helped, short-circuiting the rational side of his brain.

When his phone started vibrating, he was willing to ignore that, too. But one of the cats decided to swat it off the dresser. It landed with a thud and a crack—instantly severing the connection between them.

"Oh no." She knelt. "Praline, what did you do?"

He was breathing hard, doing his best to rein in the craving thrumming through his veins.

"Graham, I'm so sorry." Her nose wrinkled as she held up the phone. The glass face was lined with hundreds of tiny, spiderweb cracks.

He was sorry, too. But not over his stupid phone.

"Nothing that can't be fixed."

The cat meowed, flopping over and rolling onto her back.

"She's sorry." Felicity glanced his way, her cheeks flushing red.

He looked at the cat and ran a hand along the back of his neck. What was he doing? He wasn't sixteen years old. He knew how to control himself. He jerked his shirt into place and began buttoning, missing a button.

"I'll replace it," she offered.

"It's fine, Felicity." Then why was he snapping at her? *Don't be an asshole.*

"You're mad?"

"No." But he still sounded mad. He sucked in a deep breath. "I'm not mad at you."

"At the cat?" She was trying to tease him, but she looked, and sounded, nervous.

"I should thank the cat." He tucked his shirt into his pants.

"Oh." Her brows shot up, and she chewed on the inside of her lower lip. "Because he stopped... us." Her nose wrinkled up, and she hugged herself.

I am now officially an asshole. Talking about emotions didn't come easily—as was evidenced by his daughter's need for therapy. Even though he didn't know what the hell to say or what exactly he was feeling, he couldn't walk away from this. Uncomfortable or not, he had to try talking to Felicity.

"When I'm with you, everything gets...scrambled up." He swallowed. "I forget things. Important things. Like control. Cause and effect. Being responsible."

She was frowning at him now.

"I don't want to risk ruining what we have." He swallowed again. "Or losing you."

Her mouth opened, but she didn't say a word. She stood there, flushed and bright-eyed, staring at him. What the hell did that mean? Was he making it worse? He was pretty sure he was.

But now that he'd started, he couldn't seem to stop talking. "What was happening here tonight—"

"M-me throwing myself at you, you mean?" Her words ran together, and she covered her face with her hands.

Dammit. He *was* making this worse. He stepped forward, pulling her hands away, but she continued to stare at his shirtfront. "I'm not complaining."

Her head popped up, those green eyes fixed on his face.

"But if we do this, I don't want to rush into things. Or mess it up." His voice lowered. "You're important. And *this*"—he took her hand in his—"scares the shit out of me."

Her gaze fell from his to their hands. Her thumb traced along the top of his hand before her fingers threaded with his. She took a deep breath. "We're on the same page, then." When she looked at him, he could breathe again. "What do we do now?"

He had plenty of ideas. *Things to look forward to.* For now, he'd be content to hold her hand and savor her smile. "A dance?" he asked, the radio playing Nat King Cole's version of "As Time Goes By."

"Yes, please."

Would he ever get used to that smile?

He wasn't sure what he liked more—her smile or the feel of her in his arms. They swayed more than anything, his arms around her waist, her head resting against his chest. With any luck, the song was on repeat.

Praline meowed loudly, leaping from the dresser to weave between his legs.

"I'll deal with you later," he murmured, loving the way Felicity laughed.

CHAPTER FOURTEEN

"Thanks," Nick called out, tapping the side of the beat-up truck he'd hitched a ride in. The old man waved and pulled away from the curb, the one working taillight disappearing around the corner and fading into the dark of night.

He was here. No backing out now.

Crickets chirped. A few tree frogs croaked. The single streetlight on the corner flickered and hummed. The wind whipped through the pecan trees lining the fence of Pecan Valley Cemetery. Not that he was ready to acknowledge the fence—not yet. One thing at a time.

Sneaking out of Granddad and Mimi's had been easy. Wait for the snoring. He knew which boards squeaked, which door stuck, and how long it would take him to walk back into town. He'd been prepared to walk all night if he had to. No one would mess with him. And, if they did, he had a sledge-hammer and a serious case of repressed rage to help defend himself.

He got lucky with the ride.

Now he was here. Staring down at the duffel bag with his grandfather's sledgehammer in it, a bottle of water, a flashlight, and a bottle of vodka. He wasn't sure if the vodka was for before or after, but he was sure he was going to need it. Once he was face-to-face with Matthew Buchanan's headstone, he'd know.

Screw it. He pulled the half-empty bottle from the bag and gulped, wincing and gagging until it was gone. "Fuck," he spit out, throwing the bottle across the street to smash against the uneven asphalt.

He tucked the flashlight into his pocket and hefted the bag onto his back before walking the perimeter of the fence. When he found a tree sturdy enough to climb, he was up and over and in. He landed, the sledgehammer in the bag slamming into his back with enough force to knock him breathless and onto his knees.

Cut grass, dirt, and musty flowers.

A cemetery.

He pushed himself up, dizzy and unsteady, and turned on his flashlight. Maybe it was the vodka, maybe it was the dark, but it took him a hell of a lot longer to find his dad's headstone than he'd anticipated. Long enough for him to feel buzzed.

Once he found it, he stood staring, gulping in air. His father wasn't alone. Even in death, *she* was here. Right beside his dad.

Amber Strauss. Not Buchanan.

That was something, wasn't it? He'd never married her.

Not that it made him feel better. Something about seeing Amber's name on that stone only reminded him of everything she'd taken. His family. Happiness. His dad… It didn't matter that she had no one else in the world. She didn't deserve it, not after what she'd done.

He didn't understand why.

"What did she have, Dad?" His voice was high

and broken like a kid. A whiny, pathetic kid. He cleared his throat, refusing to look at her headstone—refusing to think about her. Not anymore. He balanced the flashlight there, the beam making the dirt black, like a hole. A massive, gaping, bottomless hole.

Nick stepped back, momentary panic setting in.

"Fuck you," he ground out, stomping on the very solid dirt beneath his feet. He knelt, unzipping the duffel bag and pulling out the sledgehammer.

"You picked her." His eyes burned. "You left us. You deserved to be unhappy." He stood, wiping at the tears. "You deserved it." He hefted the sledgehammer up and onto his shoulder, the tears making the words on the tombstone blur and dance. "You deserved this!" He screamed the words—and kept on screaming—as he swung the sledgehammer with all his weight. It landed hard, the impact radiating up his arms and into his chest, wrenching it free from his hands to fall on the ground.

The corner of the headstone was gone—no more than a chip—but a deep crack splintered down a good two inches into the marble.

And his heart twisted at the sight of it.

He wouldn't cry. Not for his father. Never again. He wouldn't remember the way his father laughed. Or how strong his hugs were. Or the scent of his cologne. Or how broad his shoulders had been, how many times he'd fallen asleep on one.

You can't hurt me anymore. I won't miss you.

He sniffed, a lump lodging in his throat.

"I hate you," he ground out. "I hate what you did to us." Because he couldn't miss him—couldn't love him. He wouldn't.

When he'd fallen on his knees, Nick didn't know. The dewy, freshly turned earth soaked through his jeans. Dirt from his father's grave. He pushed away, crawling back to wipe it away, only vaguely aware that the ground beneath him was brighter now— the face of the broken headstone illuminated by something behind him.

I'm glad you're dead. But he couldn't get the words out, no matter how badly he wanted to mean them.

The tears dripping off his cheeks only pissed him off more. But he couldn't stop them.

All he could do was cry. And cry.

"Nick?" The word was soft. Low. Calm. "Nick Buchanan?"

The vodka put everything in slow motion. Spinning around. Jumping up. Running. None of that was going to happen. Instead he looked over his shoulder, holding up a hand to stop the blinding spotlight.

"It's Sheriff Martinez," the voice said, still calm. "You okay?"

He nodded.

The light cut off. A car door slammed. Followed by the jingle of keys.

He was going to be arrested now. For drinking and breaking in and vandalizing his father's headstone… *Because, like Diana, I'm a fuckup*. "Fucking great," he bit out as he fell, face-first, into the dirt and passed out.

* * *

Charity finished her box of Junior Mints and eyed the bucket of popcorn. If she was smart, she'd stop while she was ahead. Her night promised heartburn as it was; no point adding to it. Especially since the first movie was still wrapping up. But it was the movie's fault she was eating her feelings. Nothing like sitting through a happily-ever-after chick flick to remind her of her situation—pregnant by a married man, living at home, keeping secrets from, well, everyone, and going to the drive-in movie theater with two teenage girls for entertainment. *Who even knew drive-in movie theaters still existed? Whatever.*

Bottom line? Her life was way more disaster flick than rom-com.

Bitter much, Charity? She took a bite of a red licorice twist and a handful of popcorn.

Her phone vibrated, and since it had to be Felicity or her folks, she answered it without bothering to check. "Hello?"

"Charity?" The deep rumble on the other end of the line had her sitting up in her seat.

She knew that voice. Braden Martinez, their brooding, hot sheriff. If she wasn't pregnant and eating her body weight in junk food, she would happily show the man how fun being bad could be. She sighed.

"Shhh," Diana hushed her from the back seat of the SUV.

"It's Sheriff Martinez." He paused, then added, "Braden Martinez."

Like she didn't know who Sheriff Martinez was. "Hi."

"I'm sorry to interrupt your evening, but I have your nephew with me."

Nick. Considering he was supposed to be spending the night with her parents, this couldn't be good. She slipped from her car, ignoring Honor's and Diana's hushing, and slammed the door behind her. "What's happened?"

He sighed. "He's drunk."

"Shit," she bit out. Not that getting drunk was the worst thing a teenager could do. "Where?"

He cleared his throat. "He was at the cemetery."

She ran a hand over her face. "Is he okay?" *Really?* She knew the answer to that question. If he were okay, he wouldn't be drunk at the cemetery. Unless that was something kids did for fun these days.

"Passed out." There was a hint of amusement. "Some vandalism, though. He took a sledgehammer to his father's headstone."

"Oh God," she moaned, her chest tightening.

"I thought, if you could come get him, maybe..." He broke off. "I'd be willing to let him off with a warning this time. Considering."

She blinked. Was he serious? "But... Will you get in trouble?" she whispered.

"Only if you tell on me." No denying the amusement this time.

"Thank you. Seriously, Braden... I mean, Sheriff Martinez. I'll be there as quick as I can." She hung up without waiting for a response. A glance at the massive screen told her they had a good fifteen minutes left in the movie. She yanked the car door open. "We're leaving," she said, returning the tinny speakers to the stands outside the windows and starting the car.

"What's wrong?" Honor asked.

Diana leaned forward between the seat, listening.

"Nick," Charity said, refusing to say more.

She tried not to speed—too much—as they headed to the other side of town, taking the farm-to-market road that circled it. The drive was mostly silent except for Honor asking if he was okay and Diana asking where they were going. Once they knew that, it was pretty easy to figure out the gist of it.

Still, pulling into the cemetery to find Braden Martinez leaning against the trunk of his black-and-white police car was unnerving.

"Stay put," she said, climbing out of the car before either girl could argue.

Braden wasn't smiling. This Braden Martinez was nothing like the easy-going, quick-to-smile guy she'd had a major crush on in high school. This guy was… different. He had that blank expression down to an art. She wasn't a fan. As a woman who prided herself on reading people, the poker-face thing was beyond irritating. So was the way he watched her. What was he thinking? Was he judging her? Her family? Her nephew? There was no way he could understand what Nick had been through—what they'd all been through. By the time she was standing toe to toe with the six-four sheriff, she was irritated and extra emotional.

"Sheriff Martinez," she snapped—for no reason. Pregnancy sucked.

His brows rose. "Evening."

Chill. He had called her to come get Nick. And he was offering to let him off with a warning, which was huge. *Be nice*. She sighed. "Sorry. Where is he?"

"In the car. Out cold." He jerked his head to the car he was still leaning against. "Honor with you?"

"And Diana Murphy."

His brow furrowed, everything about him stiffening. "Oh." His gaze swept hers quickly, then away.

That look. "Graham is, hopefully, with my sister." Why was she explaining why Diana was with her?

Because she didn't want him to think she was involved with Graham. She couldn't have been more surprised by that revelation.

His brows rose. His posture eased. "Oh."

Was that almost a smile? Almost? Did she care? She'd figure that out—later.

"Guess I should get him home?"

He nodded, pushing off the car to tower over her. "I'll get him."

Her hand shot out, resting on his forearm. "Why are you doing this, Braden?"

He stared at her hand, the muscle in his jaw tightening. "He's a kid." His gaze swiveled to her. "He's been through enough. We all do stupid things when we're hurting. He's hurting." Braden had been a lot like Nick at this age. Unlike Nick, Braden's father hadn't left. Unlike Nick, Braden had wished his father would leave. Mr. Martinez senior wasn't a good man.

Of course he got it. He was hot and sweet and…

Oh my God, pregnancy sucks. She nodded, squeezing his arm lightly. "Thank you." Which wasn't enough. But how could she repay his above-and-beyond awesomeness?

He opened his mouth, took a step toward her, then stopped. With a stiff nod, he headed to the car and opened the door.

"Nick?" he asked, calm and low—like this was a normal evening for him. She couldn't help but wonder if it was. In Pecan Valley? Unlikely.

"Huh?" Nick groaned. "What?"

"You think you can walk?" he asked.

"Sure," Nick answered, sitting up—and sliding over the other way.

With a sigh, Braden reached in and pulled out her way-drunk nephew. Without complaint or disapproval, he lifted Nick and carried him to her car.

"Hey, Sheriff Martinez," Diana said, scooching across the back seat for Nick. "How's it going? Just another night on the job, huh?"

"Diana." He grunted, depositing Nick.

"I'll buckle him in," Diana offered, leaning across to pull the belt into place.

"You do that," Braden said, closing the door and turning toward Charity. "You need help getting him home?" His gaze bounced from her to his squad car, then the moon overhead.

"I'm not sure I can carry him—"

"You can't." He frowned. "He can sleep it off in the car."

"I was kidding," she offered, oddly touched by his concern.

One brow rose, then settled—unreadable once more.

"Thanks again." She knew how big a break he was giving Nick. She only hoped her nephew understood. When he sobered up, that was.

Until then, she had to figure out what to tell her sister. Because, even with her limited parenting instincts, Charity knew this wasn't the sort of thing you hid. *Crap*.

He nodded. "You be safe getting home." He didn't look at her, just walked back to his car, got inside, and drove off.

• • •

"Oh God." Honor waved her hand in front of her face. "Your breath."

"Sorry." Nick's mumble was thick and slurred.

"Snap out of it—we're home." With a tug, she helped him from the car and waited while he steadied himself. Aunt Charity had yet to reveal what the hell had happened tonight, but it didn't take a rocket scientist to know it was nothing good. Her brother was fall-down drunk. Again. At the cemetery by their dad's grave.

What had he done?

How had he even gotten there? No way Granddad and Mimi had brought him. And the sheriff was there. As far as she could tell, he hadn't arrested him or anything, but still…

It was like he'd mind-melded with Diana recently.

"You look like shit," Diana offered, peering up

at Nick with narrowed eyes. "You and drinking. Not a good combination."

"Thanks," he muttered, swaying back and forth.

"She's right." The edge to their aunt's voice was surprising. Aunt Charity didn't get mad. Ever. One look told Honor she was mad now. Big time. Good. Maybe he'd listen to Aunt Charity. Hopefully he would. What was wrong with him?

"Can you make it to your room without your mom figuring out what's going on?" Aunt Charity asked. "Because, Nick, I'm not sure what to say to her yet. And honestly, I don't know how much more your mom can deal with right now."

His head hung—hopefully with regret but more likely from alcohol.

"Harsh," Diana mumbled.

"Honest," Honor shot back. Sometimes Diana just didn't get it. Like now. They didn't enjoy torturing their mom—they loved and respected her. Well, she did. With Nick's latest stunts, she wasn't sure she knew who her brother was anymore. And it hurt. Deeply.

They'd been a team forever. Now more than ever, she needed her brother. Not some irresponsible, self-absorbed child bent on making decisions that could only lead to bad things, but her brother—and her best friend.

As far as she was concerned, there had been enough bad to last them all for a long time. They were all due some good. Preferably a lot of good.

Like Owen. He'd been popping up in her thoughts often. Now, however, was not the time to get warm fuzzies over him.

At least Dr. Murphy's car was still here. That was good news for her mom. Well, it was until they burst in on them with her drunk son. She sighed.

"What's the story?" Diana asked. "We need to get our stories straight."

"The truth." Honor glanced at Nick, hoping he'd agree. Whatever had happened tonight, Sheriff Martinez knew. Considering the way Pecan Valley worked, word of Nick's antics would probably be common knowledge by morning. If their mother found out about this through gossip... No, it wasn't right.

"I'm thinking it can wait until morning." Aunt Charity was worried.

Honor frowned. "Mom has always been honest with us. She might be disappointed, but she'd rather hear the truth than find out later we lied to her. And we will *all* be lying to her—by keeping this a secret." She saw the guilt on her brother's face and squeezed his hand again.

"Okay," he whispered.

"Okay." Aunt Charity didn't sound remotely okay.

"Well, chances are it would come out anyway." Diana pointed at her father's car. "My dad will know. He's got like this built-in radar for alcohol. Or pills. Or pot. Well, you get it. He's going to know."

"Why is he still here?" Nick snapped, his head popping up—before he groaned.

"Why shouldn't he be here?" Diana snapped back. "Geez, chill out. They're two consenting adults—"

"Would you knock it off already?" He pushed off the car, stalking up the path. "They're friends. Period."

"Sure, *friends*." Diana snorted and ran past him to wait on the front stoop.

"Diana," Aunt Charity called after them. "Nick. Let's all try to keep a cool head. Okay? This is going to be hard enough."

Honor followed them up the path, already bracing herself for whatever would happen. She'd done that a lot over the last month. Just when she thought there was nothing left that could knock her off her feet, she was flat on her back again. Not that she was the only one whose new normal meant a constant state of preparing for the worst. Her family was right there with her. But at times that made things worse. How could she turn to them knowing they were in the same position she was in? She couldn't. Even if she really, *really* needed someone to talk to.

Diana didn't bother knocking on the front door. "Everyone decent?" she called out, smiling sweetly at Nick. "We're back."

Honor shook her head and closed the door behind them. Like her mom and Dr. Murphy would be having sex. She paused. And if they were—well, what was wrong with that? At least someone was enjoying their evening.

Still, she couldn't help but wince at the idea.

"Sit," Charity said to Nick, pointing at one of the overstuffed leather recliners in the living room. "Honor, can you get him some water?" Her eyes narrowed. "And some pain reliever. And I am in serious need of some antacid." Her aunt's sad smile reflected the defeat churning in her own stomach.

"Sure thing," she mumbled, taking another glance at Nick before pushing through the swinging wooden door into the kitchen. "Mom?"

Her mother looked up from the pecan pie she was cutting. She seemed…different. For one thing, she was humming. Her ponytail was off-center and loose. And she was smiling. A really big smile.

She was happy. Really happy. Because she hadn't walked out of the kitchen and seen Nick.

"Having a nice evening?" Honor asked. She didn't want to think about Diana's suggestion, but the seed had been planted. Her mother rarely had a hair out of place. Or creases in her shirt. Or a look like *this*.

"Yes." She smiled. "Graham and I have the nursery done, mostly." She glanced down, her hands running over her shirt, then going up to tackle her messy ponytail. "What happened to the movies?"

"We cut it short," Honor said, a lump taking up residence in her throat.

"What's wrong?" Her mother waited. A deep line formed between her brows, and she gave up on trying to smooth her hair.

Honor sighed. "I need to get some antacid for Aunt Charity." She pulled a glass from the cabinet. "And some pain reliever for Nick."

"Nick? Is he sick? I would have gone to get him so you girls could enjoy your night. Granddad and Mimi didn't call—"

She faced her mother, medicine in hand. "I don't think they know he left, Mom."

Her mother's shoulders slumped, and her expression faltered. "Oh." She took the pills and water from Honor. "I see." Her smile was tight as she pushed through the kitchen door and left Honor alone.

The silence was broken by the ringing of the house phone. Probably Mimi—freaking out over Nick's disappearance.

"Hello?" she answered.

"This is Robert Klein. I'm looking for Felicity Otto-Buchanan?"

Honor rested her forehead against the kitchen cabinet. "I'm sorry, Mr. Klein, she's sort of tied up with something at the moment. Can I take a message for her? This is her daughter, Honor."

"Honor?" He chuckled. "You're the reason I'm calling. I'm your father's lawyer—I'm sure your mother has mentioned me." He paused. "Even though your mother has agreed to adopt Jack, we need to get your signature on two papers transferring your guardianship to her—since you're eighteen and a legal adult. I should have caught that when she was here. It won't take long at all..." He kept talking.

But she didn't hear anything else he said.

Or understand a word he was saying.

"Transferring guardianship" seemed to repeat and grow. Over and over. Louder and louder. Transferring guardianship? *She* was transferring guardianship of Jack? To her mother?

"Excuse me, Mr. Klein, can I just clarify something?" she asked, surprised by the calm in her voice.

"Yes, of course."

"What happens if I don't sign them?" she asked softly, dreading the answer.

There was a long pause. "Well, your father and Amber designated you as Jack's guardian—since you are his next of kin—in the event that your mother was unable or unwilling to adopt Jack. But, as you know, your parents agreed the night of the accident that she'd take Jack. In the hospital." He cleared his throat. "She was quite adamant about it when we met to go over the details of the will."

The night of the accident. The night of the accident? She remembered every single detail, from her father's shattered face to the resignation in his eyes. She remembered his sweet words—and his request for a moment alone with their mother. In some delusional place in her mind, she'd thought he was apologizing to her for all the horrible things he'd done to them.

But he hadn't.

No.

Instead he'd asked her mother to take Jack. He'd asked, knowing she'd never, ever say no. Honor slumped against the counter, torn between defeat and rage. "I see," she murmured.

"Honor." He cleared his throat again. "You were aware of this, right?" An awkward chuckle. "Otherwise, I'll feel terrible—"

She interrupted. "Of course I was. We don't keep secrets."

"No. I didn't think so." Another awkward chuckle. "I'll see you tomorrow?"

Honor wrote down the time and place and hung

up. She didn't know what to do. What to think. What to feel. But the shouting on the other side of the door made up her mind for her.

Her fingers were shaking as she texted, *Can you meet me?* and hit send.

Owen's response was immediate. *Where?*

You tell me. Leaving now. She hit send, took the keys to Amber's shiny convertible—parked and covered in the garage—and left.

CHAPTER FIFTEEN

Felicity almost dropped the glass of water she was carrying when she walked through the kitchen door. Nick was standing, swaying, inches from Graham, the threat in her son's posture making her stomach flip.

"What's going on?"

"I'm pretty sure I know what's been going on." Nick glared at her, shaking his head.

She waited, the charged atmosphere going thick.

"You missed a button," Nick ground out.

Graham's buttons. Once they'd started dancing, fixing his shirt was forgotten. But now, with Nick glaring at the both of them, looking pointedly at Graham's misbuttoned shirt, she realized the conclusion her son was making. He was shaking with rage.

"You said you were just friends." Nick sounded hollow. "You said you weren't ready to date. Sleeping with someone isn't dating?"

It was like a slap to the face.

"Nick—" Graham's voice was razor-sharp.

Nick faced Graham again. "I'm not talking to you."

She was between them, a hand on each chest, restraining Nick, drawing support from Graham. It sickened her. "Enough, Nick. I don't know what happened tonight, but respect isn't optional, no matter how bad you feel." It took effort to stay calm, but she did it.

Until she caught the scent of alcohol on Nick's breath. "You've been drinking?" Panic lodged in her chest. "What happened, Nick?"

Nick's lips pressed flat. His jaw muscle clenched tightly.

"Graham, you and Diana should go." As much as she appreciated his willingness to champion her, having him here would make talking to Nick impossible. And, clearly, her son wasn't okay.

Seeing Graham hesitate said so much—meant so much to her. He wanted to be here. He loved her kids and hated seeing them hurt. He cared about them. All of them. "He needs to stay hydrated," Graham said, slipping into the cool, impartial doctor mode with ease. "Keep a close eye on him."

She nodded.

Graham's light-brown eyes met hers, so warm and tender that it took everything she had not to beg him to stay. She could do this on her own—she knew that. But she didn't want to. "If you need anything—"

"We're good," Nick ground out.

"Thank you." She'd had so much to say before. In his arms, there'd been a glimmer of possibility that things could be good between them. But now, with Nick, all of that would have to wait.

With a nod, Graham headed for the door. "Come on, Di."

"Guess we're not going on that vacation together now, huh? That sucks." Diana had been sitting on the floor, both cats piled in her lap, watching with wide-eyed interest. Now she stood. "Are you guys going to be okay?" she whispered, her too-skinny hand gripping Felicity's forearm. "You will be, right?"

Felicity nodded, patting her hand. "We will. Families fight, Di. It can be a good thing. As long as things don't get mean, that is. You hang in there, work things out, forgive and go forward, stronger than before. That's what *fighting* should be."

Diana shrugged. "If you say so." Her kohl-lined eyes bounced to Nick. "Remember, you and drinking, not a good mix."

"Says you," Nick bit back.

"Hey, I can hold my alcohol." With a cocky shake of her head, she led her father outside. The front door closed, and the room went silent.

"What happened?" she asked. "You said you wanted to go with Granddad."

"People say things all the time. Doesn't mean anything." He was hurt. Angry. And he wasn't going to hold back. "Like you saying you and Dr. Murphy were just friends."

"Nick."

"I don't want to hear it." He shook his head. "You also said sex is supposed to mean something— remember that? It's *special*. Emotional. All that bullshit?" His eyes narrowed. "But I guess being alone and sad makes sleeping around okay, too?"

"Sleeping around?" she snapped. He was going for the jugular. "I didn't lie to you, Nick."

"About you and Dr. Murphy? Or about sex being special?"

"That's not fair, Nick." Charity was up on her feet. "She has every right to be happy."

"Because Graham Murphy would make her

happy? How? By letting Mom raise his fucked-up kid along with Dad's baby?" He stared at the ceiling. "Ever think he's latching on to you because he knows he can't handle Diana alone? She's seriously messed up. A walking nightmare. You want him? Then you get her, too. How can you want that here—all the time?" He rolled his head. "Amber and Dad didn't factor that into their whole let's-give-Jack-to-Felicity master plan."

"Enough, Nick." He'd hurt her deeply, but he'd also pissed her off. How dare he throw Matt and Amber in her face or suggest Graham was using her? She hated this. All of it. "You want to lash out at me? Fine. You've done that." She was shaking. "You've been drinking, clearly. Sit down before you fall down and tell me exactly what happened."

He pressed his lips together but sat.

"Well?" she asked, staring down at him.

Listening to Nick recount his evening hurt her heart. He didn't say much—just the facts, the actions—his voice almost devoid of emotion. And that, his flat tone, made it even worse.

Felicity sifted through the words spinning in her head. This was Nick. Not Diana. Nick. Her son. *Her* son had snuck out of her parents' house, hitchhiked into town, broken into the cemetery, damaged Matt's headstone, and been so inebriated that he passed out. He was having a hard time sitting upright now. Did she yell at him? Did she hug him? "How much did you drink?" she asked. "What did you drink?"

"Vodka," he answered and finished the glass of water. "Not a full bottle, but I emptied it."

"A bottle, Nick?"

"He threw up on the way here," Charity volunteered softly. "A lot." She paused. "A lot—*lot*." There was definite emphasis on the last word.

Hopefully most of the alcohol was out of his system. "Can you get him more water?" She held out his empty glass to Charity, and she hopped up, hurrying into the kitchen.

Nick stared at her, red-faced from vodka and anger.

"Do you know how lucky you were tonight, Nick? You could have…" She didn't want to think about what could have happened. "You could have been hurt. Hurt someone else." Her gaze searched his face. "You're my son, Nickie. No matter what, I'm here for you. I hate that you're hurting like this." She sat on the ottoman in front of him and took his hands. "If there were a way to make it better, I would. You know that, I hope."

His stare was hard. "Prove it."

She did, she tried, every day. It wasn't that easy. Being a parent was never that easy. She stared at her son, aching from the pain and anger in his big eyes. The wounds her son carried were her fault—her and Matt's. All the apologies and hugs in the world couldn't change that. "I don't know how."

"Easy." He shook his head. "Me or him."

"You or Graham?" The clarification was necessary. Jack was still the elephant in the room, looming on the edges of everything. But there was nothing he could do about that—no matter how much he resented it. Which he did, so much that he was going to take all his aggression out on Graham. If she tried to point that out, he'd only dig in harder. His life was spinning out of control. Sending Graham away wouldn't make anything better. He was doing it because he could. If she let him.

He nodded, his nostrils flaring. "You have to think about it?"

"No." Her lungs emptied. "No. You, Nick. Always. If giving up Graham proves that, then I won't see him anymore."

He slumped back into the chair at the same time Charity returned with a full glass of water.

"What do we have to do with Sheriff Martinez? Do I need to sign paperwork? Do you have community service? What?" She glanced at Charity for answers.

"Nothing." Her sister shook her head. "He gave him a warning."

"Seriously?" Nick asked, looking just as stunned as she was.

"That's sort of what I said. No offense, kiddo, but you're getting off easy." Charity shrugged. "If you don't have the world's worst hangover tomorrow, it won't be fair."

"I know," Nick agreed.

Felicity studied her son. Did he know? Really?

"I do," he repeated, barely able to look her in the eye. "I sort of lost it tonight. Dad… Jack…" His jaw tightened hard. "Next time…" He shrugged. "I won't."

"You can be angry, Nickie." Felicity touched his chin, waiting for him to look at her. "You have every right to be angry. It's what you do with it that's important. Lashing out at the world only makes it worse. And, in all likelihood, hurts the ones around you. The ones who love you more than anything."

He wrinkled his nose, his bleary eyes filling with tears.

"Besides, Sheriff Martinez might not be willing to let you off with a warning next time."

"He's a really decent guy," Charity added. "I asked him why he was doing this, and he said he understood."

Felicity knew what Braden Martinez had suffered; the whole town knew. The accident that changed his life forever had been front-page news. Did Charity know about that? About Braden's poor wife? Every time she saw the man, she felt compelled to hug him—an impulse the very private and reserved man wouldn't appreciate.

"I'm hungry," Charity sounded off. "Ice cream, anyone?"

Felicity shook her head. "This guy needs a shower and bed."

Nick nodded. All signs of his previous temper were gone.

She helped Nick up and as far as the stairs. "I should call Mom and Dad so they don't wake up and panic."

He wrapped his arms around her and hugged her for a long time. It was going to be okay. She didn't know how, but she had to believe it. She had to.

"Need anything?" she asked.

He shook his head.

"I'll be up in a few." She watched him make his way up, then she headed back into the kitchen. "Honor?" Not in the laundry room. Or the garage…

But Amber's car was gone. So were her keys. With a frown, she stared around the kitchen. A hastily scribbled note made her heart sink.

Robert Klein, his office address, a meeting time for tomorrow, and his phone number. Felicity picked up the phone and dialed.

. . .

"He's on the verge, Dad." Diana sat, knees drawn up, wide-eyed and upset. "I know what that looks like. And he's so there."

Graham tossed his tie on the back of the sofa and ran a hand along the back of his neck. Did he want to know what she was talking about? Right now, he was still battling the urge to head back to Felicity's. It took a lot to get him upset, but Nick Buchanan had succeeded. Not for himself, but the way he'd spoken to Felicity. Nick was a teenager, volatile and self-absorbed, to boot. But he was a good kid deep down. Today had been a lot—for all of them. Enough to put Nick over his breaking point. "What happened?"

"Tonight?"

"Something happened before tonight?" He flopped onto the couch opposite her, doing his best to act calm. If he overreacted, she shut down. If he acted indifferent, she blew up. Calm and slightly curious seemed to work best.

"Yeah. This isn't his first slip." Her eyes pinned his, like she was evaluating her options. "I took him to hang out with some friends one night. He texted me." She waved away any questions. "He was upset so, you know, I was all come hang out and relax."

"You mean get high?" he asked, trying to keep his calm.

"Yeah, Dad, exactly. It's not like meth or cocaine or something." She smiled. "Anyway, it hit him way hard. But he walked it off."

He swallowed all the questions and reprimands he had. All of them. It was hell. "What happened, then?"

"He saw some video. His dad and Amanda fighting—on some nanny-cam thing his aunt was watching." She leaned forward. "Mr. Buchanan said he'd made a mistake leaving Felicity. Sort of gutted Nick, right?"

Graham shook his head. "Right." He rarely used words like "hate" or "despise," but he'd make an exception when it came to Matt Buchanan. Of course he'd made a mistake. He'd left Honor, Nick, and Felicity. Left them—all the love and laughter and noise. A family, a real, messy, devoted family. How could he ever have believed he'd create something like that with Amber?

"Tonight, we were chilling out and Charity gets a phone call from Sheriff Martinez. Next thing I know, we're missing the last fifteen minutes of the movie, flying to the cemetery. Nick's passed out in the sheriff's car. Word is he broke his dad's headstone."

It hurt to breathe. Whatever anger he felt fizzled out. In its place was an aching hole. "Word from who?" he asked.

"People." Her smile grew. "I know people."

He nodded. "Right." Because his daughter would know the sort of people who participated in or knew about illegal activities taking place in a cemetery at night.

"Cemeteries are good places to party, Dad. No one goes there at night." She sighed. "So, yeah, they saw Nick climb over the fence and break his dad's headstone with a sledgehammer. Then he was screaming. Sheriff Martinez showed up, and then Nick went face-first into the dirt."

Her fingers spun the strands of woven bracelets on her wrist. "I don't get it. I mean, his dad was a freakin' asshole. Why does he still get so worked up over it? Are we surprised Felicity is getting stuck with his kid? Really? I mean, she's Felicity. Like, the perfect mother. Who wouldn't want to give their kid to her?" Her chipped nails flicked a charm. "Why does each new piece of evidence that his dad is, in fact, a world-class sleazebag make Nick lose his shit all over again?"

Graham couldn't help but smile. His daughter had a way with words. He might not always agree with what she said, but sometimes—like now—she was pretty astute. "I guess he keeps hoping something will prove us all wrong."

She blinked, her brows rising. "How is that even possible? You mean, the shithead accidentally cheated on Felicity? He, oops, accidentally knocked up Amber? And then, surprise, he accidentally forgets his real family?" She shook her head. "I don't get that."

"I don't think there's a way to undo any of that— you're right. But Matt wasn't always like that. Once, he was a good dad—and a good husband. I'm sure Nick wants to hold on to that somehow. Still, those memories don't align with the last few years."

"So he can't even trust his own memories? Because of the shit his dad pulled at the end?" Her eyes widened.

"Yes."

"That is the saddest thing ever." She wrapped her arms around herself. "Nothing can mess up what I *know* about Mom."

"She was incredible," Graham agreed.

"Felicity is pretty awesome, too," Diana said, watching him. "I'm sorry we crashed your party tonight."

He was too surprised to stop his chuckle. It was okay, though. She was smiling—a real smile.

"You like her?" she asked. "A lot? 'Cause, you know, Mom would be cool with it, I think." She paused, sniffing. "And I'm cool with it."

"You're sure?" he asked.

"If I wasn't, you wouldn't date her?"

"No," he answered honestly.

"That's stupid." Diana frowned. "I'm sure there will be some days I'm not cool with it. Are you going to break up with her every time I have a mood swing? Jesus, Dad, grow a pair."

He laughed again.

"I mean, if Nick doesn't screw it all up—or that Jack kid—we could be a decent family." Her head cocked. "Messed up, for sure, but isn't every family?" She stood, unfolding and stretching her spindly limbs. "I'm gonna take a shower. Wanna watch a movie or something? I'm sort of wound up."

He blinked. *Calm.* "I'll make the popcorn." *Stay calm.*

"Coolness." She kicked off her boots and slid down the hall in her mismatched socks.

He sat there, processing. It was only nine thirty. He and Diana would watch a movie and eat popcorn, assuming she didn't change her mind. But what was Felicity doing? Was she okay? And Nick?

He pulled his phone from his pocket and headed into the kitchen to make microwave popcorn. He typed in a dozen texts but never hit send. Finally, he asked, *Everything okay?* and sent it.

He was tossing in his bed well after midnight, waiting for a response.

• • •

Charity sat at the small wrought-iron table outside the local Scoops Ice Cream Parlor, a romance novel open in front of her. She knew the dark and brooding hero would woo the virgin maiden into a haystack at any moment, but her stomach was hurting, and she just wasn't feeling it.

"Too much ice cream," she whispered, dropping her spoon in the dish with a sigh.

But the pain only grew, sharp enough that she couldn't ignore it.

"What's up, kid?" Her hand rested on her stomach.

The stranger in her belly didn't offer up an explanation, so she stood, deciding a walk around the small patio might be all she needed. She had been sitting for a while. "A little change is a good thing." She paced, depositing the sundae in the trash and wandering back to her table. But now she was dizzy, too, so she held on to the back of her chair until it passed.

"You know, you're making things difficult." She stared down at her stomach. "I'm not complaining, though."

Driving might not be a good idea.

Calling for a ride. Calling who? Felicity and Honor were a no. Her parents. A hell no. Grams was a terrifying driver during the daytime... Who the hell could she call?

She knew one person. Their on-again-off-again high school relationship was one of the few things she remembered with true fondness. He'd had the patience of a saint and, if she remembered correctly, had been a pretty good kisser. For all his big, silent, manly ways, he'd been a good guy. And since people used words like "reliable" and "solid" when he came up in conversation, it appeared he still was. Not to mention how incredible he'd been with Nick. *Totally a good guy*. He'd probably come. *If* she called.

"Sheriff Martinez?" she asked. "Or we drive." Drive. Definitely. She was all about not needing a big, strong man to come to her rescue anymore. *I got this.* She tucked her book into her bag and headed to her car—where she leaned against the side, her stomach clenching.

Everything is okay. Everything is fine. We're okay. But not fine enough to drive. "Fine." She dialed the cell number on the card he'd given her earlier that night. Then hung up. Did she really need someone to drive her? Really?

Dizziness and cramping were perfectly normal during the first trimester. She knew because she'd read the pregnancy book until the wee hours of the morning. It had been fascinating. And terrifying.

"We can do this," she said. "Just give me a minute."

But her phone rang.

"You called?" Braden's voice was monotone as ever. "Sheriff Martinez here."

"Hey," she mumbled. "I'm really sorry to call you, Braden. Should I call you Sheriff Martinez? Or Braden? You tell me."

"Charity?"

"Forgot that part, didn't I? Yes, hi. It's me. Can you give me a ride?" she asked. "I know that sounds really weird, and you have way more important things to do but—"

"Where are you?"

"Scoops," she answered.

"At one in the morning?" he asked.

"Yep. I like living on the edge like that." She covered her face with her hand. "Sorry if I woke you."

"On patrol. Be there in five." He hung up.

She was sitting on the curb when he got there. Her stomach was killing her now. And her lower back hurt, too. But she wasn't going to cry. Because crying would mean something was wrong, and there was nothing wrong.

"You okay?" he asked as he climbed out of his patrol car.

"Honestly? I'm not sure." She tried to smile up at him. "Maybe I had a little too much cherries jubilee—my favorite."

He squatted in front of her, waiting.

"I'm pregnant, Braden," she whispered, her voice wavering. "And something's not right."

His face twisted, raw with pain and grief. It was so quick, she might have imagined it—probably had. "I got you." He scooped her up and deposited her in the patrol car before she knew what was happening. He turned on the lights, had the siren blaring, and sailed down the empty streets of Pecan Valley until they reached the hospital.

She didn't want to be here. "I don't think—"

He was already out, getting a nurse and a wheelchair and helping her from his car to the chair. "Want me to call someone?"

"No." She grabbed his hand. "No. It's sort of a secret. And everyone who knows has more than enough to worry about. Besides, this is probably nothing. Right?" She looked up to find him staring at their linked hands.

"We've got it from here, Sheriff Martinez." The nurse smiled.

He nodded, his gaze searching Charity's.

Why her hand tightened on his was a mystery. She was a strong, independent woman—a soon-to-be business owner. A mom-to-be. She wasn't a clinger. At all. Except she was—clinging and pathetic and on the verge of tears.

No, no, no. Pull it together, Charity Ann. She let his hand go and forced a smile. "Thanks for the ride."

He nodded again, his gaze never leaving her face.

The nurse wheeled her inside, her shoes squeaking on the linoleum floors as they cruised down the hall. Something about the bright overhead lights had

Charity hugging herself and holding her breath. She hated this place. Everything about it. Hated being questioned and probed and having vials of blood taken and the gowns with the weird pockets and ties in the back. But she went into the bathroom and put it on, leaving a urine sample as requested before heading back to her bed. Her feet were freezing.

Braden Martinez sat at the bedside, spinning his hat in his hands, looking out of place and uncomfortable. But he was here. She was so damn happy he was here.

When he saw her, he stood and helped her into her bed.

"You stayed?" *Obviously, Charity.*

"I figured you'd need a ride after?" He kept spinning the hat. "Maybe."

"Oh, right." She nodded, running her hands along the sheet. "Guess it's obvious I'm a little shaken?"

"Understandable." He cleared his throat. "Scare like this... It's not easy."

She glanced his way, the gruffness in his voice surprising. Sort of like the way he'd looked at her when she'd told him she was pregnant. "No, it's not. Now there are tests and waiting..." Her voice wavered, her eyes burning. *Don't cry.* She sniffed.

His dark brown eyes met hers. "Good?" he asked.

She pulled up the pile of blankets. "My feet are kind of cold."

Without a word, he left her curtained-off partition—returning with a pair of no-slip socks. He slid the socks on her feet quickly, then pulled the blankets down and wrapped them up tight. He wasn't gentle or lingering or anything but matter-of-fact, but it didn't change the impact his kindness had on her. His unflinching gaze regarded her steadily, ready and waiting for whatever needed doing.

"Thank you," she whispered, smiling at him before she burst into tears.

"Miss Otto?" A man, looking way too young to have M.D. after his name, pushed the curtain aside. "We have your results back." He flipped through the pages. "You have a urinary tract infection."

Her heart was thumping, waiting for the rest. "That's all?" she asked, between sobs. Please, please let that be all. She almost choked on the question, "The baby is okay?"

The doctor nodded. "There is nothing abnormal with your bloodwork. Get some rest, drink plenty of water, and follow up with your OBGYN." He glanced at Braden. "You can take her home as soon as we get the release forms ready for her signature." He left minutes later.

"Good news." Braden smiled. He actually smiled.

She grabbed his hand. "I know I said this but thank you—for staying."

He nodded, holding on to her hand until it was time to go.

CHAPTER SIXTEEN

Nick eyed the hospital with dread. He'd spent the night heaving into his toilet until his eyes were going to pop out of his head and his ribs were in danger of cracking. All it would take was one more heave, he knew it.

He'd have done it all again not to be here now.

Not that she'd asked him. She knew better.

He hadn't had a choice. It took a lot to rattle his mother, a lot to threaten the supreme calm she brought to any situation. This morning, she'd spilled her coffee, dropped her purse, and said "shit." With Honor missing in action and Aunt Charity in bed with some urinary tract infection thing, he was her only backup. Calling Granddad and Mimi would only add to the drama—thanks to him sneaking out the night before.

No, he owed her, dammit. What he'd done last night was bad enough. But what he'd said to her... He was ashamed of himself. He'd put her through hell, and she'd given him nothing but love.

To make this morning suck more, he was beginning to think he'd nailed his head with the sledgehammer the night before. Every single sound was magnified. His stomach was making horror-movie noises. And his tongue was too big for his mouth.

Lesson learned. Next time he was on the verge of losing his shit, he'd call Owen. He'd rather have sore muscles from working out than a hangover that made death appealing.

His mother paused in the hallway, catching his hand with hers. "Thank you again for coming, Nick. He doesn't like me—at all." Her smile was forced. "The only woman he doesn't mind is Grams."

Great. He'd heard all about how the kid cried nonstop. Charity said he'd gotten so red a few times that she worried his head would explode. "She can have him."

His mother laughed. "Nick."

"It's an option." He was teasing. Partly.

But part of him, a pretty big part of him, still hoped someone from Amber's family would turn up to take the kid away. Far, far away. Any minute now.

No matter what Honor said, Jack wasn't family. He wasn't supposed to be a permanent fixture in his life. Jack was Dad's. The one time he'd seen the kid, asleep and tiny in the hospital bed, had been hard enough. There were baby pictures of him and Honor all over the house. This kid looked like them. He looked like the pictures of their dad when he was a baby. Seeing him made it hard to deny—somehow—that they were connected.

It had to get to his mom, too. It had to.

That's why he was here. For her.

Not Jack. The kid was going to live with them because it was the right fucking thing to do. And a nightmare. No one wanted this. No one wanted him. It was sad but true. Nick rolled his head, doing his best not to panic when they climbed in the elevator, pressed the button, and waited.

"I'm going to have to take notes on how to care

for his cast. It's a beast." His mother was chewing on her bottom lip. "Poor thing hates it."

"So I've heard," he mumbled.

She sighed. "We're all going to have to be patient with him, Nick. It's not going to be an easy transition. For any of us."

"No? Really?" He closed his eyes—not thinking about the last time he was in this elevator. The last time he saw his father.

She shook her head.

"Sounds like he's a happy-go-lucky kinda kid." He rocked on his feet, anxious to get this over with. Not that it was going to be over. They were taking the kid home with them. Forever. His head pounded.

"Maybe he is. Right now, he's scared and hurt and lonely. With limited vocabulary." She shook her head. "His mother and his father disappeared, Nick. Can you imagine?"

He'd lived it. Older, maybe—but he was pretty sure knowing your father willingly deserted you was worse than what the kid was going through. "Sort of, yeah," he reminded her.

"You do. Of course you do. I didn't mean it like that." She took his hand and squeezed. "Besides, you're stuck with me."

"He's got you now, too." He tried hard to sound like it didn't bother him. But it did.

Her hand squeezed again.

The elevator doors opened, and Nick winced at the screams coming from somewhere on the floor. "Please tell me that's not him."

"That's him." With a deep breath, she set off down the hall, head held high, determination in each step. His mother was a woman on a mission. A real-life fricking superhero.

He was a suck-tastic sidekick, hanging back and useless. When they got to the door, his mother went right in. He stood outside, where he could see everything that was happening but no one inside could see him.

He didn't give the old lady knitting a second look.

But the little boy—Jack—he couldn't look away.

His chest hurt, instant pressure clamping down on his lungs and heart.

Jack wasn't a kid.

He was a baby, pudgy and pathetic. Tears streamed down his red cheeks, making the pressure harder to bear. His white-blond curls shook with his hiccups. And he wiggled, trying to get away from the large blue cast swallowing him up at the waist. It covered his entire right leg, part of his left leg, and had some handle-looking bar running between his legs. A major pain in the ass. Jack turned away from his mother when she smiled at him, closing his eyes and sobbing into the blanket he gripped tight in both fists.

Maybe Nick was wrong. Maybe he was lucky.

He understood his father was gone and wasn't coming back. Jack didn't. He'd had a mom and a dad. Now they were…missing. He was too little to ask questions or understand what was happening.

Jack was…alone. Completely alone.

It hurt to breathe now, physically hurt.

Mrs. Baker left, smiling at him, then waddled down the hallway to the elevator. Nick watched, tempted to escort the older woman to her car just to get away. But that was running away, and he wasn't a runner—not when his mother needed him.

"Hey, hey, Jack," his mother crooned, doing her best to soothe the crying kid. "We're getting out of here today. It's going to be okay now."

Jack wasn't listening. He covered his face with the corner of his blanket and fought the cast to turn away.

Nick couldn't take it. He walked into the hospital room and stood there, watching.

"Is he in pain?" he asked.

"What?" she asked, patting Jack's hand.

"Is he in pain?" he asked, louder this time.

Jack stopped crying. He turned and stared, straight at Nick.

Nick swallowed, eaten up with all the horrible things he'd thought and said. None of this was Jack's fault. He was a baby. Just a baby—with no one and nothing.

Jack tried to sit up, but the cast wouldn't let him. With a grunt, he flopped back, still staring at Nick. "Da," he said, reaching toward him with both hands. "Da," he repeated, smiling at him like he was the best thing in the whole fucking world.

Nick swallowed hard, his eyes burning and his chest hurting. How could he explain that their dad was gone? He wasn't coming back.

"Da." Jack stretched, his little fingers wiggling.

He didn't remember moving. Didn't remember crossing the room or sitting on the bed or leaning over him. He did remember hugging him. He felt the cling of Jack's little arms around his neck and the softest brush of Jack's curls against his cheek.

"Da." It was a sigh.

"I got you, little bro." He forced the words around the knot crushing his windpipe. "You hear me?"

• • •

Honor rolled over and stared at the sliver of light creeping through the blinds. Daylight. Not a streetlight. She sat up, staring around the dim interior of Owen's bedroom.

"You okay?" Owen lay on top of the blankets beside her.

Oh God. She'd spent the night here. And now... She ran a hand over her tangle of red curls. Bedhead, every morning. More like a rat's nest. "I'm fine."

"You sure?" he asked, sitting up.

She caught sight of the clock. "No. Dammit." She hopped up.

"What time were they going?" he asked, already knowing what she was worried about.

"An hour ago." She tugged on her jeans. "My mother is probably freaking out."

"Promise me you won't get mad," he interrupted.

She paused. "I'm not promising anything."

"I texted Nick and got your mom's cell number. I called her last night." He stood, turning on the light. "I mean, with everything else..."

"She's been through enough without me adding to it?" she asked, not in the least bit angry with him. He was right.

"Pissed?" he asked, his hands hovering by her

shoulders, almost touching.

She shook her head and buried her face against his chest. "No."

"Whew." He chuckled, his hands running up and down her back. "Would kind of suck if you were. Since I love you and all."

Honor laughed, but her heart kicked up to record-speed. It wasn't true. It couldn't be. "You're so full of it." Last night had started out with her raging, dumping everything on him—everything. From her father's betrayal to her brother's rebellion to being Jack's legal guardian to her fear of leaving home. He'd held her close, asking questions but listening more than anything. When she was done and the tears started, he kept on holding her.

She was the one who attacked him.

And he was the one who shut her down—fast.

"Am I? Why do you say that?" he asked, tilting her head back.

"You know why." She shrugged out of his hold. For the first time, she'd taken a risk, tried to shake off her inhibition. And he'd held her away from him. It was humiliating—and painful. She sat on the bed and slipped on her shoes, awash in embarrassment all over again.

"Because I wouldn't sleep with you?" he asked, crouching in front of her as she tied her tennis shoes. "Hey." His hand grabbed hers and held it still. "Honor?"

She tried to laugh it off. It came out like a croak. "I'm not good at this, okay? I'm pretty sure you've figured that out by now." With a slight tug, she broke the contact. When he touched her, she short-circuited. "Let's be honest. I don't know how to do *this*. And last night, I didn't come here thinking we'd... But then..." She stood, shoved her phone into her pocket, and reached for Amber's keys.

"Stop a sec, okay?" He blocked her path. "You came here because you needed someone to listen to you. You picked me." His hand rested along the curve of her cheek, drawing her gaze up to his gorgeous face. "I want to be that guy for you. Not some creep wanting to get into your pants. That's not what I want for us, okay?" He kissed her, a slow, gentle kiss. "I do love you. Since the day you smiled at me in English class, I've loved you."

It would be easier to laugh off if she didn't want to believe what he said. And if he'd stop looking at her like that—like she mattered. Like maybe he did love her. "Are you serious?" *Do I want to know*? Because, no matter how hard she'd been fighting it since that day in the mall—no matter how many times she'd told herself she did not love him—she did. So much.

He nodded, the tenderness on his face kicking up her heart rate. "I'm serious." His forehead rested against hers. "But... I do want to get into your pants."

She laughed, breathless. "Next time, maybe."

"Maybe?" He groaned.

She kissed him, sliding her arms around his neck and giving it all she had. In his arms, it was okay to let go. He'd seen her at her worst, sobbing and dripping and leaving wads of tissue all over his floor. Still, he loved her. And she loved him.

He broke away. "Want me to drive?"

She shook her head. "No."

His smile faded.

"But if you want to show up in thirty minutes or so?"

"Twenty?" he asked, kissing her again. "Fifteen?"

She broke away. "Long enough for me to take a shower. Tame this." She pointed at her red hair.

"Don't tame it. I like it." He opened his door and led her down the stairs. Owen's dad was deployed, and his older brother was rarely home. For all intents and purposes, he lived on his own—and he kept the house immaculate. That had been a surprise. So had learning he took care of his elderly neighbor's yard and her yappy little dog. Or that he'd learned how to work on cars because he didn't have the money to pay someone to fix his. And, of course, his willingness to help her brother deal with everything he was dealing with. Then, last night. Not the cocky jock she'd pegged him for. But, until recently, she hadn't given him the chance to prove otherwise. Why did she have to be so stubborn?

"You got this," he said, so matter-of-factly she almost believed him.

With another kiss and wave, she climbed into Amber's convertible and made the drive across town.

She parked in the garage and headed inside, hoping it wasn't too bad. But there wasn't a temper tantrum taking place. If anything, it was quiet. She found Aunt Charity sitting at the kitchen table flipping through a travel magazine with a massive blueberry muffin in front of her. "Morning."

"Morning. Hungry? Your mom made some

blueberry muffins."

"Are they home?" She shook her head. "Is everything okay?"

"They've been home a while. I think they're in the nursery." Her brows rose. "Go see for yourself."

Honor frowned. "Bad?"

"I'm not saying a thing." She shooed her toward the door and turned back to the magazine she was reading.

Honor headed straight for the nursery, expecting to hear Jack any second. Finding Nick lying beside Jack, reading a book about a poky puppy, was the last thing she'd expected.

"Hi," she said, leaning against the door.

"Hey," Nick said. "Jack, say hi to Honor."

"Hi," Jack said, smiling.

Honor stared back and forth between the two of them, in shock. "What did you *do*?" she asked, dropping to the carpet beside the toddler. "How did you get this little guy to smile? And to stop crying?"

"I look like Dad." His laugh was quick.

"Da," Jack agreed, putting his hand on Nick's arm.

Honor blinked, studying her brothers, her heart in her throat. Except for the eyes, Jack really was a younger version of Nick—and their father. Still, it couldn't be easy for Nick, feeling the way he did about their dad. "You're okay with that?"

"We're good." Nick nodded. "You're interrupting the story."

Jack patted the book, smiling at Nick with pure joy.

Honor stared at the two of them, a comfortable

warmth flooding her chest. Maybe things would be okay. Weird, yes. No denying it. But maybe— eventually—okay. "Sorry." She laughed. "I'm going to take a shower." But they were already reading again.

"Amazing, right?" Her mother was waiting outside.

"Is he really okay?" she asked, watching the two of them.

"I can hear you," Nick called out. "I'm fine. Go away. Make sure Aunt Charity doesn't eat all the muffins."

"I made two dozen," her mother argued.

"Have you seen her eat?" Nick quipped.

"There you go." Her mother shrugged, her gaze a little too penetrating. "What about you?"

"Can we talk in your room?" She led the way, not waiting for an answer. Once the door was closed, she jumped right in. "I'm not mad at you, Mom. I admit I was surprised, maybe even a little hurt that you didn't tell me about the will... But I get it." She hugged herself. "You're my mom. You'll always try to protect me. And Dad did what he thought was best, I guess."

"I'm pretty sure he never thought it would happen, Honor." Her mom reached for her.

Honor wanted to believe her. She wanted to go on thinking the best of her father—especially now that he was gone. "Jack has no idea how lucky he is to have us."

Her mother nodded. "I think—I hope—it's going to be okay."

"It will." She kissed her mother's cheek. "I'm

going to take a shower before Owen comes over."
And this time she wouldn't spend thirty minutes
trying to smooth her curls into submission.

• • •

Felicity rocked, smoothing Jack's curls from his
forehead and humming "All the Pretty Horses." It
had taken five days for him to accept his new
surroundings. Nick was the key. Every day, the two
of them grew closer. When Nick walked in, Jack lit
up. And when Jack called him "Ni," Nick was all
smiles.

Now his tantrums revolved around diaper changes, fatigue, and frustration over his damn cast.
Felicity didn't blame him in the least. But they had a
couple of weeks before it was gone forever. Hopefully the bone had healed and that would be the end
of it.

Jack's thumb slipped from his mouth as he
drifted off to sleep. She stared down at him, tracing
the curve of his cheeks with her fingertips. Honor
was leaving in a few weeks. Nick only had two years
of high school left. Then she'd be a single mom—of a
pre-schooler. "We're going to be okay, Jack. You
know that?"

His little mouth sucked in his sleep. She stood
and carried him to his crib, taking extra-special care
to ease the cast onto the mattress first.

She stood over him, smoothing the blanket up
and turning on his nightlight as she left.

The house was quiet.

Charity was having dinner with Maudie to finalize

the handoff of the travel agency. Nick had gone with friends to a party at the lake and was spending the night at her parents'. This time, he promised, he really was spending the night at her parents'. And Honor was on a date with Owen.

She was alone. And that meant there was nothing to distract her from missing Graham.

Which meant she needed to find something to do. Immediately.

She poured a glass of wine and carried it and the baby monitor into the living room. Charity had given her a book "guaranteed to distract her," but so far it had failed to deliver. With a sigh, she skimmed four pages, then slammed the book down. She stared at her phone, took several sips of wine, and gave in.

The phone rang three times.

"Felicity?" Graham. Graham's voice.

She could breathe. "Hi."

"Everything okay?"

"Yes." She closed her eyes. *I wanted to hear your voice.* "Everything is fine."

"I'm glad. I was going to call but didn't know when would be a good time. How is Jack settling in?" he asked.

"It's been amazing, thanks to Nick." She filled him in on the transformation of both boys. And it felt better, talking to him. "How's Diana?"

"She went to the party at the lake tonight. I'm hoping there is a party at the lake."

"There is. Nick went with some of his friends." Hopefully he'd be nice to Di. They hadn't talked about her or Graham since he'd blown up. And he'd said a lot of things that morning—some of which she was hoping were alcohol- and emotion-fueled, but she was too scared to find out.

The last few days had been relatively calm. As nice as it was, something had been missing. Not something—someone. Graham. And Diana.

"With any luck, she'll have a good time and stay out of trouble."

"Things better?" she asked, hoping so.

"I think so." He chuckled. "But I don't always know what's going on in her head."

It was easy to imagine his smile. But imagining Graham made it impossible to ignore how much she missed him. She opened her eyes, staring around the house. Honor was out with Owen. Jack was asleep. And she wanted him here, now. She wanted to have this conversation with his arms around her. She wanted to bury her nose against his chest—

"How's Charity?" he asked.

She shook her head. How much time had she spent thinking about him over the last five days? Little things like making coffee—he liked it black. Or petting Pecan—she still needed to replace his phone. And lying on her bed—aching. The ache was always there. Like now.

"Felicity?"

I'm here. Mentally torturing myself. And aching. "What?"

"Is Charity feeling better? Dr. Luna said she was pretty shaken when she saw her in the ER."

"Yes, she is. As scared as she was, I think the UTI made her realize she wanted this baby." She shook her head, smiling. "She still believes she's missing the parenting gene, but I'm hoping she'll get over that as her pregnancy progresses."

"And you?" He paused. "How are you?"

I miss you. "Fine. A little tired." *Partly because I'm lying in bed thinking about you instead of sleeping.* But sharing any of that with him would only complicate things. "The whole toddler sleep schedule is taking some getting used to."

"I don't envy you." He chuckled. Oh, how she adored the sound.

"And you? What are you up to? Home alone?" she asked.

"I'm good."

"Then why are you home?" She paused, finishing off her wine. "I might be chained to a toddler, but you are not. You should go out. Turn off whatever sad documentary you're watching and go have fun."

"How do you know I'm watching a documentary?"

"I'm hanging up." She laughed. "You're going out."

"Felicity… It was good to hear your voice." His tone was deeper, gruffer, and her insides turned molten. And his words had her grinning like an idiot.

"You, too," she whispered. Too good. *Enough with phone calls or daydreaming.* "Bye, Graham." She hung up and headed straight into the kitchen to refill her glass. She wasn't going to think about Graham going out and having a good time. It's not that she didn't want that for him—she did. At the same time, she didn't. Widow Rainey might have mentioned something about Graham and pretty Miss Takahashi to Charity when she'd stopped by the travel agency. According to her sister, the old woman was convinced the two of them would click. And she and the widows were developing a plan to get them together.

Felicity had been careful to act like it wasn't a big deal, especially since Charity had been watching her like a hawk. But it sort of was a big deal. Did she want Graham clicking with someone else?

What is wrong with me? I'm a terrible, selfish person.

A terrible, selfish person who was going to turn off all thoughts of her kids, Graham…everything. Wine, a bubble bath, some music—she could relax. It had been a while, but she was going to give it a try.

Right.

It took twenty minutes to locate her stress-relieving bath bomb and another ten minutes for her rarely used oversize claw-foot tub to fill. While the water was rising, she plugged in Jack's baby monitor and put on a playlist with soothing natural sounds like waterfalls, birdcalls, and other ambient noise.

Relaxing. She twisted her hair up and clipped it on the top of her head, stripped, and slipped into the hot water and eucalyptus-scented bubbles with a sigh. *Relaxing.*

"I can do this." She rested her head and took a sip of her wine.

Her mind wasn't cooperating. "No worrying about Nick or Diana at the lake. Or thinking about what Honor and Owen might be up to. Or if Graham is calling Miss Takahashi. Just bubbles and waterfalls. Relaxing." Saying the words out loud helped. For about five minutes. Then images of Nick drinking, Honor and Owen—not going there—and

Graham dancing with Miss Takahashi popped up to derail her plans.

I'm relaxing.

She closed her eyes and focused on the calming sounds of the rain forest—then the doorbell rang. "Oh no." She stood, grabbing a towel and running for the door—dripping water as she went. *Please don't ring it again. Please.* Towel wrapped tightly around her, she ran down the stairs—nearly slipping—and across the foyer. She peeked through the peephole.

"Graham?" *This is bad.* Worse because she'd said his name loud enough for him to hear her.

"Felicity?" He spoke through the door. "I'm sorry for ringing the doorbell. I forgot about Jack."

"It's okay." He had a bouquet of flowers. "This isn't what I had in mind when I told you to go out and do something."

He brought her flowers. She was in a towel. And she ached for him.

This is so bad.

"I did go out. But once I was in the car, I headed this way." He paused. "I can't come in?"

"Oh, sure." Because having a conversation through a door was weird. "I wasn't expecting company," she said, unlocking the door and pulling it—slowly—open.

His head-to-toe inspection did nothing to soothe her nerves. The way his dark hair fell forward onto his forehead—hard not to reach out and smooth it into place. But touching him would be bad.

He smiled, the corners of his warm brown eyes creasing nicely. "I'm interrupting. Bubble bath?" he asked, his gaze lingering on her shoulder.

She wiped the bubbles from her skin. "I was trying to relax. Everyone is out and I'm not good at occupying myself, either."

"I can recommend a couple of documentaries."

She laughed, tugging her towel up and shaking her head. "Maybe for insomnia?" She cleared her throat, her gaze getting tangled up in his. Dripping water and towel aside, she was so happy he was here.

"Trouble sleeping?" He went from adorable Graham to Dr. Murphy in a matter of seconds. Which made him even more adorable.

She shook her head.

Eyebrow cocked, he studied her expression. "I'll send you a list." He smiled.

"Normally, I bake, but Charity asked me not to tempt her anymore." She stepped back. "Coming in?"

He hesitated, his gaze returning to her bare shoulders. "No. I don't think so." He blew out a slow breath and held out the bouquet of daisies, sunflowers, and roses. "I may have made a stop along the way."

"Graham..." She took the flowers. "You can come in. I mean, you came all this way." And it made her happy. *He* made her happy.

"I missed you." His gaze met hers.

Ridiculously happy. So happy that she really wanted to grab his arm and tug him inside. Or at the very least admit the truth, even if her voice wobbled. "I miss you."

But admitting that didn't change how her son felt.

"What's wrong?" he asked.

"Nick." She bit her lower lip, scrambling for a way to say what she needed to say.

"Everything okay?" He came inside and carefully shut the door. "What happened?"

Words clogged her throat. Some she wanted to say, some she didn't.

"Felicity?" he asked. "Hey, you can talk to me."

She could. He would listen—be there for her. She placed the flowers on the foyer table and wrapped her arms around him. An odd, muffled choke-groan caught in his throat before his hands landed on her shoulders. "Is this a good idea?" he murmured gruffly.

No. Not at all. "Hugging?" she asked, knowing good and well what he was asking.

"What's wrong with Nick?" His arms slid around her, loose.

"He was really upset." She swallowed.

"I know." He sighed. "Did you talk to him?"

"I did." Better to rip off the Band-Aid. Still, she tightened her arms around him. If she told him about Nick's ultimatum, he'd leave. That was who Graham was. He'd never do anything to threaten her family—the relationship she cherished with her children.

Just as she cherished her relationship with Graham. She cared about him, deeply.

That's why, right or wrong, she couldn't bring herself to tell him what Nick said. "It didn't go well."

He bent his head, his breath warm against her shoulder. "What can I do?"

She shook her head, too distracted by the brush of his breath on her skin. It started out as hugging, but now that he was this close, she wanted more. Like turning into his chest, burrowing against him, and breathing in his scent. Much better.

Stay. It was selfish but true. She didn't want him to leave. She wanted to stay right here in his arms.

His gaze traveled slowly over her face. Beneath her hand, his heart beat like crazy. Like hers. He cleared his throat. "I should go."

He should. That would be the responsible thing to do. And they were both responsible adults. But, just once, she wanted to do what she wanted to do.

"Felicity?"

"I'm thinking." Her gaze settled on his mouth.

"Thinking? About?"

Honesty is the best policy. At least, that's what she'd been told her whole life. "How nice it would be…if you stayed." She held her breath.

His nostrils flared, the tic in his jaw muscle a clue that he was fighting for control. "You'd regret it."

She shook her head. "No. No, I wouldn't."

He pressed his eyes shut. "You're standing in a towel, asking me to stay. And, believe me, I want to." When he looked at her, those brown eyes were blazing. "But tomorrow—"

"If you leave, I'll spend the rest of the night aching for you, like I have been every night for…too long. I try not to. I bake or take bubble baths or rearrange my kitchen cabinets—anything." *Stop. Stop talking*. The words kept coming. "But then I remember your touch. How it feels to be in your arms." She swallowed. "The taste of your mouth. And I know what I want. More than anything. You."

CHAPTER SEVENTEEN

How the hell was he supposed to leave now?

He was what she wanted. He was what she ached for.

She'd laid it out there—honest and fearless. Now she was waiting on him. All the logical reasons he'd stopped himself, again and again, from calling or dropping by were impossible to remember.

He smoothed the auburn curls slipping from the knot on her head, silky-soft, wrapping around his finger. Her lashes fluttered against her cheek as he slid the clip from her hair, running his fingers through the mass of curls.

She leaned in to his touch, her emerald green eyes locking with his. "Stay," she whispered.

His hand drifted on its own, tangling in her hair and pulling her against him. "I'm not going anywhere." Her lips parted beneath his, welcoming him, hungry for him. There was no way he could deny her. His tongue dipped inside, tracing the velvety softness of her mouth.

Her soft moan ended any hope of sanity returning. She, this, consumed him. One minute they were standing in the middle of the foyer, the next, he had her pressed against the front door. The kiss went on, deepened, and caught fire.

She broke free long enough to tug his shirt loose, her fingers flying down the buttons and pushing the fabric aside. His shirt was gone. Nothing felt better than her touch—except the light kisses she pressed against his throat. While he was bowled over by sensation, she managed to grab his belt and began leading him to the stairs.

But once they reached the steps, her towel slipped to her waist. Her breasts shook in time with her ragged breath. Cheeks flushed. Lips parted. Auburn hair mussed around her shoulders. And those blazing green eyes. He couldn't look away. Or breathe.

"Felicity," he whispered, his hand smoothing the hair from her shoulder. "You are beautiful."

She shook her head, her hair falling forward as she tugged her towel back up.

He leaned closer, grasping her face. "You are." He waited, wanting her to hear him.

A long, slow breath slipped from her lips, and her gaze focused. The doubt there was a kick to the gut. She didn't know? Didn't believe him? Matt had no idea what he'd done to her.

But she was looking at him now, a small smile on her face. "Thank you." Her hands slid up his arms and around his neck, crushing her breasts against his chest.

"Dammit," he hissed, sliding his hands up her bare back. "You feel good."

Her fingers twined in his hair and pulled his head down so she could kiss him. Between the cling of her lips and the brush of her nipples on his skin, how they got to her bedroom was a mystery. There was a lot of bumping into furniture and bouncing off walls before he wound up sitting on the edge of her mattress kissing her as she stood between his legs.

He couldn't get enough.

He kissed his way across her clavicle, his hand sliding up slowly to cradle her breast. She arched into his hand, her fingers raking through his hair. He took his time, stroking the satin roundness and nuzzling the tight nipple before drawing the tip into his mouth.

She moaned, her grip on his hair tightening.

Tongue and lips, the spare rasp of his teeth, he loved her breast until her breathing grew uneven and wavering. When she climbed onto his lap, her towel fell to the floor. Now she sat, straddling him, and there was no way she could miss just how much he wanted this—wanted her.

He stood, lifting her to roll her onto her back. She gasped as she landed on the mattress, staring up at him, the fire in her passion-glazed eyes mesmerizing. She smiled, her eyelids fluttering as she arched against him.

"Felicity," he ground out.

Her hands slid down his side, gripping his hips and holding him still as she rocked against him. This time, he arched forward, grinding them together. Her broken moan was the sexiest thing he'd ever heard.

She reached between them, fumbling with his pants. But her fingers were shaking, and she ended up giving up with a giggle.

He smiled, holding her gaze as he unfastened his pants. "One second." He stood, stepping out of his pants and boxers. With an impatient sweep of her arm, she sent the pillows flying. She pushed him flat on his back, and then she was climbing on top of him.

He ran his hands over her, exploring every dip

and curve. The feel of her, skin on skin, stopped him from saying anything else. This was an intimacy he'd forgotten. A shared silence. A soft touch. Tender and sweet. Real and deep. She was all those things. And his hands were driving her mad. He watched every quiver, soaked up every whimper, and ached to be inside her.

He wasn't prepared. "I don't have…anything."

"Anything?" she murmured, distracted by his hold on her breast.

"Condoms." He cleared his throat, lifting his hand. "Protection."

"Oh." Her eyes flew to his. "Right." She blinked. "Do we… I mean, I've only slept with Matt." She shrugged. "And, you know, I can't have any more kids. Unless you need to wear…something?"

"No. I'm clean." He was still stuck on the fact that she'd only slept with Matt. Before Julia, he'd had several girlfriends. After, well, there'd been no interest.

Her smile was back as she bent forward to kiss him—with enthusiasm.

But the kiss grew fierce. He rolled over her, loving the way her fingers tugged his hair, loving the way her leg wrapped around his hip. Nothing prepared him for the feel of her body hot and tight around him. The slow, broken sigh that spilled from her lips when he slid deep rocked him to the core.

She moaned, staring up at him—stunned and lost.

He felt it, too. Lost. And found.

But her legs wrapped around him and her fingers, tangled in his hair, tugged him close until their lips sealed together. Gripping her hips, he thrust into her, a groan tearing from his throat.

She moved without restraint or inhibition. It was incredible to watch. So incredible that he knew he wouldn't last long. But, dammit, he would make her happy first. He concentrated on breathing—on her—anything but the dangerous tightening inside. Thrusting and withdrawing, teasing her until she was breathless and grinding against him. But the second she tore her mouth from his and her cries rang out, he let go—thrusting into her as his climax slammed into him.

He gasped for air, and she was smiling and beautiful and reaching up to smooth the hair from his forehead.

He didn't want to move. Didn't want this to end. The sex was incredible, but the connection, the tenderness she stirred in his blood, was more potent than he'd anticipated. Or been prepared for. He'd always cared for her. Known she was important. But now—

"You okay?" she asked, her hand pressed to his cheek.

That was the question. If she was talking about this? Yes. "Okay" didn't begin to describe it. Everything about tonight had been incredible. "Yes." He smiled, lying by her side and pulling her close.

If she was talking about his heart? He wasn't so sure. It had taken a hell of a long time to piece it back together. He couldn't give it away, not without a fight. No matter what it wanted.

• • •

Nick did his best to act like he didn't give a shit about the fact that Lane's hand was sliding along Diana's skinny legs. She wasn't his problem. If she was, she wouldn't be glaring at him like that or giving him the cold shoulder. So why did he feel so damn protective? It's not like she was Honor. They were *not* family. Thank God she was not his sister. Having Diana as a sister would be like waking up daily to being kicked in the balls.

"Nick?" Fran offered him her half-charred marshmallow.

"Thanks."

"I didn't drop this one." She giggled, leaning against him. "You want a beer?"

Hell no. He was done drinking. Forever. "No. This is good." He leaned forward to bite the melty-sticky marshmallow from the skewer.

"Oh my God, Nick!" She squealed as he leaned in to kiss her. "You are covered in marshmallow."

He hesitated. They'd kissed before, once or twice, but never in public—surrounded by their friends— and never when she was in a bikini. But she was in a bikini, and he was having a hell of a hard time ignoring that fact. Or the fact that her overflowing top was pressed against his arm. And he had some view. His gaze slipped from her face to her cleavage. *Damn it.* Fran's breathing picked up, her gaze falling to his mouth—and shooting blood to parts of his body that could make this whole thing way awkward and potentially embarrassing.

Just fricking awesome.

She was kissing him. That was a first. "Missed you," she whispered, winding her arms around his neck, which put those hella-soft curves against his bare chest.

"Wanna walk?" he asked.

But her eyes went wide. "Oh? You... Walk where?"

He shrugged, draping his beach towel around his neck for camouflage, and stood. "Along the shore." At least until he wasn't pitching a half tent.

Fran glanced around the fire, her knees drawn to her chest. "Just you and me?"

He frowned. "Yeah?" That's when he realized they had an audience. And why Fran was freaking out. Some people might be cool hooking up in the woods when there was a crowd of people close by, but that wasn't him. Cheesy or not, he wanted his first time to be...cool. But he wasn't going to tell her that here—now. "For a *walk*."

She didn't believe him. From the giggles and whispers around the bonfire, nobody did. Not that they mattered. Fran did. She couldn't look at him— she was too busy pulling on her swimsuit cover-up.

What the hell? Didn't she know him? He wasn't out to screw her. Is that what she thought of him? That he was like...like Lane?

"Okay." Fran stood, red-cheeked and nervous.

"Looks like someone's getting lucky." Lane laughed.

It took everything he had not to say something. His jaw hurt from how hard he was clenching it. But he wasn't going to pick a fight, because Lane was an asshat. He'd want to fight here, in public. Make a scene. Make Nick look like a tool. Not happening.

"You okay, Fran?" Diana asked, coming around the fire. She stood there, looking back and forth between him and Fran like Fran needed rescuing.

Is Fran okay? What the hell? He glanced at his girlfriend—sort of girlfriend. She didn't look okay. She looked freaked out.

And it irritated him. A whole hell of a lot. "Fran, just forget it." He sounded pissed. And he was, but not at her. Not really.

"Cockblocked!" Lane laughed, louder this time.

"Are you kidding me?" he snapped, rethinking the whole restraint thing. Using Lane as a punching bag sounded pretty damn good at the moment.

Fran grabbed his hand. "Come on, Nick." She stood, tugging him away from the fire. "Let's walk."

But Nick was seeing red. "It's fine."

"No, Nick, come on." Fran yanked on his hand. "Please."

Nick blew out a long, slow breath. "Fran…"

She stood on tiptoe to kiss his cheek. "Come on. We're walking."

He resisted for a few seconds, then let her lead him away from the fire, the crowd around the bonfire, and Lane. After ten minutes of walking, he said, "All I want is to walk." He cleared his throat, hoping he'd sound less like an asshole. "Not…that. What he thought."

"That guy really gets to you." She threaded her fingers with his.

He nodded.

"Because he's a jerk?" She paused. "Or because of Diana?"

He stopped walking then. "What?"

"You seem sort of really hung up on her," she whispered.

"No. God, *no*. We grew up together." He shook his head. He frowned, unable to think about Di that way. "More like the pain-in-the-ass sister I never wanted sort of thing." All true. He didn't want to think of her that way...so why did he? *Dammit*. Because unlike Honor, she didn't have someone looking out for her. And, clearly, she needed someone looking out for her. And, for some reason, he felt like he was that person. *Fuck.* "She's a screwup. She and her dad have had a rough time. I don't get why she wants to make it worse." Didn't he though? He hadn't exactly been easy on his mother.

"That's all?" Fran stared up at him.

She was seriously gorgeous. "That. Is. All." Maybe she didn't get how into her he was?

"Okay." She was smiling. "I'm glad."

Now who's the asshole. He tugged her close. "Believe me. You're the reason I'm out walking in the dark. Your bikini?" He shook his head. "Seriously dangerous."

She was smiling. "You like it?"

"I like *you*, Fran." He swallowed. "And, yeah, maybe the bikini, too."

"Good." She rested her head against his chest. "For the record, I didn't think you wanted to, *you know*, out here. I was freaking out because my bikini strap broke. That's why I had to put on my coverup. And fast." She tugged the fabric down, drawing his attention to her broken strap.

Nick swallowed hard. "Oh." So much for walking it off. He adjusted his towel, very thankful for her cover-up, his towel, and that his girlfriend was pretty awesome.

CHAPTER EIGHTEEN

Graham unzipped the suitcase and pulled out the smaller one inside. "These two should work. Need anything else?" he asked, sitting on the couch to go through the inside pockets.

Diana's hands rested on the back of his chair as she leaned forward over his shoulder. "Perfect."

He smiled at her. "I'm glad. Looking forward to the trip?"

"I hope Felicity changes her mind." She pushed off the chair.

He didn't say anything. He'd told her Felicity had been touched by the offer but that there was too much happening for them to join them. Which was the truth. *I wish she'd change her mind, too.*

After last night, everything was different. Before midnight, he'd reluctantly slipped from her bed. She hadn't made it easy on him—her kisses almost changed his mind. Instead of hurrying from the house, he'd stood watching her—smiling when she sleepily told him to be careful driving home—wondering what a future with her would look like. Wondering if it could be as good as he imagined it to be. He'd pressed a final kiss to her forehead, peeked in on Jack, and left the house—tripping over Pecan on the way out.

As appealing as the idea of them all vacationing together was, he wouldn't push. Felicity's devotion to her children was fundamental to who she was.

He'd never push her to go against that. Not that he'd walked away. He'd never be able to walk away from her, not if she needed him. Last night was incredible, and he had no regrets, but he knew better than to think that what happened would take precedence over her kids. When things with Nick and Jack and Diana had settled, they'd find a way to make time for each other. When, not if. Until then, the chances of last night happening again anytime soon were slim.

"You look tired," Diana said. "Didn't sleep well?"

He shrugged. "Did you have fun last night?" he asked, hoping to steer conversation into neutral waters.

"I did. I met a really nice girl. Fran." She shrugged. "She's sort of obnoxiously popular but still cool."

"That's good?" he asked.

"It's different."

"Good different?" he asked.

She nodded. "Until Nick showed up. He was acting like a total dick. Giving me the cold shoulder and being a cocky asshole to Fran. I told her she could do way better."

He frowned. "That doesn't sound like Nick." Then again, he'd never thought Nick would ask Felicity to give up a chance at happiness. At least, he'd like to think he could make her happy.

"Don't worry. I set him straight." Her eyes flashed.

He could imagine. Graham stared at his daughter then—She was stunning. No eyeliner. No dark smudges. Just Diana's spiky lashes and hazel eyes. "You look pretty," he said.

Her cheeks turned red. "Whatever." But she was smiling. "You don't want to hear what I said to him?"

"Who?" he teased.

"Dad." She crossed her arms and frowned.

"Go ahead." He waited.

"I told him he was worse than I was, keeping his mother from being happy. And you know he is— after the way he acted." She stuck her chin up. "I said he couldn't call me a screwup and then do something like that to her."

Graham was more than a little proud of her. He stood, staring down at his daughter. "You're not a screwup, Diana."

She rolled her eyes. "What are you smoking?" She flopped into the office chair he'd vacated. "We both know that's a lie. I'm a screwup." She shrugged, spinning the chair. "A recovering screwup."

He laughed.

Diana peered around him. "Who is that? Is that Miss Takahashi?" She slipped from his chair and ran across the room, peering between the sheer curtains. "She has a cake."

"Miss Takahashi?" he asked, heading to the door.

"The assistant principal who booted me out of school?" Diana reminded him. "She was all moony-eyed over you." She ducked. "Shit, she's waving."

He frowned right back at her. "We can't exactly hide, Diana. She saw you."

"So," she argued, crouching beneath the

window. "I say we hide anyway. She'll get the hint."

He didn't mention her phone call or the fact that he hadn't called her back. It hadn't been intentional, he'd just forgotten. Now he felt like an ass. And his daughter wanted him to hide? He owed the woman and apology. And some honesty.

Her sharp knock had Diana waving him away from the door. "Don't do it. Don't." She pretended to be choking and flopped onto the floor.

He was trying not to laugh when he opened the door.

"Graham," the woman gushed, holding a Bundt cake wrapped in cellophane. "I was in the neighborhood." He recognized her then. Attractive woman. Great smile. Chin-length black hair. Amazing child advocate—something Diana hadn't appreciated. But she wasn't Felicity.

"You didn't have to do that." He tried to ignore Diana twitching on the floor.

"I did. I promised Widow Rainey I'd hand deliver this." She handed him an envelope.

"What is it?" he asked.

"An invitation." She smiled. "An adoption party for the Buchanans. You know, Felicity is taking in Matt's son? Have you ever heard of such a thing?"

"No." He could honestly say he never had. "But I know Felicity. She has a huge heart." That was why he was so drawn to her.

Miss Takahashi shifted from foot to foot.

"I'd invite you in, but Diana is sick, and we're heading to the doctor." He shot her a look. "I'm very worried about her."

"Oh dear, I hope it's not serious."

Diana sat up and rolled her eyes.

"I was hoping we could get that coffee date on the books?" She smiled, batting her eyes. "Remember?"

"I do. I apologize for not calling you back." He nodded. "But right now is probably not the best time." Honestly, this was a conversation he'd rather have without his daughter present. "May I call you later this afternoon?"

"I'm feeling better, Dad," Diana singsonged, trying not to laugh. "Go ahead." She smiled at him, up to no good.

"Oh." Miss Takahashi's smile grew. "How sweet of her."

"That's Diana. A real peach." But he was smiling anyway.

"So, coffee. What would be good for you?" she asked.

What the hell. "I'm going to be honest with you, Miss Takahashi. You're a lovely woman. But I can't." Because of Felicity. He swallowed. "I mean… I happen to…" To what? Care for? No. More. *Dammit.* "I am…in love with someone else. So, having coffee with you would be wrong for you and me and *her*."

Miss Takahashi stared at him. "Oh. And this woman? Does she reciprocate?"

Did she? And, if she did, would her son accept it? He shook his head. "I don't know. But if she doesn't, I plan on doing everything I can to change her mind."

"I appreciate the honesty, Graham." She offered him the cake. "It's refreshing."

He took the cake. "Thank you again."

"I wish you the best of luck, Dr. Murphy." Her smile wasn't nearly as bright but there no doubting her sincerity. "Take care." She waved and headed back to her car.

He nodded and closed the door. "Here."

Diana took the cake, staring at him. "That was the single coolest thing you've ever done, Dad."

"I have a feeling I'm going to seriously regret it."

"No. No way." Diana shook her head. "She'll tell Widow Rainey and Widow Rainey will tell everyone. Felicity will know, and Nick will realize he's a tool, and everything will be okay." She eyed the cake. "And we'll go on vacation at the beach house, and it will be good. You'll see."

He watched his daughter carry the cake into the kitchen and hoped like hell she was right.

• • •

Charity was surrounded by the widows' group. It was her mother's month to host and, since the cabin was too small for them all to gather, they'd converged around the large wooden farm table in Felicity's kitchen. They enjoyed her hospitality while gossiping and whispering and dropping the name of every bachelor in Pecan Valley in the hope either sister would react. Charity sipped cups of tea, ate too many slices of her sister's lemon pound cake, and was content to be healthy—for her baby to be healthy.

Her late-night trip to the ER had been the single most terrifying event of her life. The very real possibility that something was wrong with her baby had been…devastating. In the time it had taken for the doctor to run her urinalysis and figure out it was an infection, she'd accepted that this baby was hers.

More than accepted. Wanted. She wanted this baby. Whoever was in her stomach, she couldn't wait to meet them.

With a plate of lemon cake in hand, she marveled as Felicity smiled and nodded and occasionally added something neutral like, "Really?" or "I hadn't heard that," or "My goodness." So far, Filly had said "my goodness" five times more than the other two combined. Charity stroked Pecan, rubbing the giant golden feline behind the ear as she devoured her cake.

"Pace yourself," Felicity whispered, handing her a dainty etched glass plate piled high with finger sandwiches and delicately sliced vegetables.

Charity wrinkled her nose at her sister and passed the plate. She was the only one sitting here who wasn't a widow. Surely that earned her the right to a couple—or three—pieces of cake.

"Aunt Charity." Nick peeked in and waved her over.

"Excuse me." She hopped up, dumping Pecan from her lap. "The nephew calls."

"Sheriff Martinez is here," Nick whispered, grabbing her arm. "Did he change his mind? Am I going to get arrested in front of Mimi's widows' group?" His voice wavered.

"Breathe. Relax. Did you invite him in?" she asked.

"I tried. He's just…standing there." He pointed to the entry hall.

Braden Martinez filled up the space, his expression as fixed as ever.

"Sheriff," she said, smiling up at him. "What brings you around?" His steadfast presence throughout her nightmare hospital trip had guaranteed Braden Martinez the Nicest Guy Ever award—if there was such a thing.

He stood there. "Checking in."

"He's doing well, I promise." She lowered her voice. "I haven't been with him every second of every day, of course. But he hasn't broken curfew, and the party he went to at the lake had a lot of adult chaperones so I'm pretty sure—"

"On you." His gaze swept over her and held.

She couldn't blink. He was staring at her. Making eye contact. Really, honest-to-goodness *seeing* her. And she had no idea what to do. *Say something. Anything.* "My goodness," she whispered.

He cleared his throat. "Here." He thrust a brown paper bag at her. "I'm…" He glanced at her, glanced beyond her, and froze.

"Sheriff Martinez?" Widow Rainey. "My, my, my. Won't you come in? We have all sorts of deliciousness that Felicity made."

"Thank you, no." His answer was civil, if short.

"Not even for five minutes, Sheriff? I'm sure the ladies would love to hear all about your latest adventures."

His gaze flickered her way—wearing a look that reminded her of Pecan or Praline when they were being stuck in the cat carrier for a trip to the vet. Trapped. Panicked. Ready to gnaw off a limb to get away. "Just got off a double." He eyed the door.

"You should go, get some sleep," Charity suggested, hoping to help his escape.

"Now, now, if you're just getting off, you should eat." Widow Rainey hooked arms with the sheriff and all but yanked him inside.

Charity stared after them, a wave of sympathy washing over her. That didn't mean she wasn't about to laugh, a lot, but she felt for Braden all the same.

"What's in the bag?" Nick asked, still freaking out.

She peered inside. "It's…ice cream."

"That's a lot of ice cream," Nick said, pulling the two tubs out. "Two more in there. Who likes cherries jubilee?" He frowned, dropping the containers back into the bag.

She did. It was her favorite. "He remembered." The tiniest flutter teased her stomach. She smiled, running her hand over her stomach. "I can't believe it, either."

She carried the bag into the kitchen, ignoring the widows as she packed her beloved ice cream into the freezer. Braden Martinez had grown into a *strange* man, in a good way. He wasn't a talker; that was clear from the way he was staring into his tea, stoic, while the widows chattered on around him. And no one would ever accuse him of being the emotional sort. But there was something real about the man. Solid. And good. He was a decent guy—so decent he'd stayed with her until she'd been released from the ER, taken her back to her car, and followed her home.

Decent, as in checking on her *and* bringing several surprise tubs of cherries jubilee ice cream.

If she stole a glance his way a few times, it was only because she wanted to thank him. And he was hot. Like big, brooding, muscle-y, quiet, and manly sort of hot. She fanned herself with the kitchen towel in her hand.

Pregnancy hormones.

Her father hurried into the kitchen, carrying a bag of brisket. That coupled with the overpowering scents of perfume and tuna salad, and the claustrophobic heat of extra bodies in what suddenly felt like a small space was all it took to have her running. She had no choice. There was no way she'd make it to the guest bathroom. So right there, in front of the widows, Sheriff Martinez, and pretty much her entire family, she threw up her sister's lovely lemon pound cake into Felicity's pristine sink.

She was vaguely aware of many *My goodness*es being declared, but that didn't stop her vomiting. Oh, so much vomiting.

"Charity, honey." Her mother pressed a cool cloth to her head. "You ate too much."

"Want some water?" Felicity asked.

She shook her head, cupping water and splashing her face. "I'm so sorry."

"Don't be sorry, Charity girl." Her father was all concern. "You're under the weather."

"Let's move our party to the dining room," Widow Rainey announced, encouraging the others to carry tea and cups and all the plates of dainty finger foods Filly had made for them. As soon as the room emptied, Charity could breathe.

And that tiny, delicate little flutter happened again. She smiled, running her hand over her stomach. She glanced at Felicity, too excited by the flutter to hide it.

Felicity was all smiles.

"What is it?" her mother asked. "What's going on? I can tell when you two are up to something. And you, Charity Ann, are definitely up to something."

She shrugged. "I guess I am. I'm not sick. Mom, Dad...I'm pregnant."

"My goodness," her mother gasped, sinking into her chair.

• • •

There was a long stretch of silence. Felicity held her sister's hand, more than a little surprised that she decided to share her news *now*. It would have been nice to have some sort of heads-up, to prepare. But there was no angry outburst, were no tears. There was more silence. Her mother sat, staring vacantly at the tile floor. Her father kept opening his mouth, then closing it—a deep furrow creasing his brow.

"It will be fine," Felicity interjected before her parents could collect themselves. "She has a job; there's plenty of room here for them both. We're going to share baby duty, with Jack and whoever else joins the family."

"The father?" Their dad looked devastated.

Charity shook her head. "No."

Felicity squeezed her hand, relieved the rest of the story could wait. One thing at a time. Besides, it's not like it would change anything. Charity would still be pregnant and raising this child alone. As far as Felicity was concerned, those were the only two things that mattered.

"Clearly there was one," her mother argued. "Unless… Don't tell me you went to one of those, those sperm places, Charity Ann."

"Maybe we should hold off on questions for now," Felicity suggested. "Especially since Widow Rainey is here."

"What does that mean?" her mother asked.

"The woman can't keep a secret," her father answered, nodding.

Hands on her hips, her mother faced her father. "Now, Herb, she's a delightful woman. You be nice."

"She *is* a delightful woman. But she can't keep a secret to save her life." He patted her on the shoulder. "Filly's right. This can wait. Your guests won't." He held the door wide for his wife.

But her mother hesitated, looking more than irritated.

"He's right, Mom." Felicity smiled. "Let's get a few things figured out here before we share Charity's news."

Her mother sighed, scowled at her husband, and left—their father following.

"That's done." Charity sighed, looking relaxed for the first time in weeks. "And the baby's moving." She pressed her hands to her stomach.

"Or I have serious indigestion.." She shrugged, laughing.

Felicity hugged her tight. "Enjoy every second."

"Except the throwing-up part." Her sister wrinkled her nose.

"Except that," she agreed. "You okay?"

Charity nodded.

"Should I be worried that Sheriff Martinez was here?" Had Nick done something else? It was always there now, that doubt and fear. He seemed less angry and more in control of his emotions since he'd started working out with Owen. But the potential was there.

"Only if you have a fear of cherries jubilee ice cream," Charity answered. "He brought some to me."

"Your favorite." Felicity studied her. Did she know what Braden Martinez had been through? As much as she adored Charity, her sister's experience with real relationships was limited. Poor Braden deserved more than another broken heart. "Your vomiting has earned you a get-out-of-widows'-group pass. Go directly to your room."

"I'm fine." She grabbed a plate of lemon pound cake and disappeared.

Felicity picked up the chocolate éclairs and backed through the kitchen door, heading for the dining room.

"Éclairs?" Nick followed.

"For the ladies." She held the tray aside, out of his reach.

"Are you joining us, Nick?" Her mom smiled up at Nick and patted the seat beside her. "We could use some male companionship to balance out all the estrogen in the room—now that Sheriff Martinez all but ran out of here."

The women laughed.

Felicity couldn't. Poor Braden. When it came to an emergency situation, there was no better person to have around—that's why he'd been promoted to sheriff at such a young age. That, plus his absolute dedication to the job. But noncrisis hero situations had always made him uncomfortable. Something Charity had been completely oblivious to when they'd been dating.

In high school, Charity had dragged him home for a few family dinners. If not for her ability to fill silence with cheerful banter, things would have gotten super awkward superfast. As it was, he'd blushed, limited his responses to one-word answers, and stared adoringly at her sister until the dessert plates were cleared away.

Now, faced with the widows, Nick wore an expression similar to the one Braden Martinez frequently sported: absolute panic. The struggle between his desire to escape and his need for sugar was plain to see. "You got this." Felicity winked at her son, then handed him a plate with three éclairs.

Nick smiled, grinned at his plate, and settled back in the chair beside his great-grandmother.

"I'm not sure who he was talking about," one of the women was saying. "All I know was he said he was in love and he couldn't possibly go for a coffee with anyone else."

Felicity made the rounds, placing the éclairs on the table and refilling cups.

"Thank you, Filly, dear," Grams said, patting her hand. "Do you know who it might be?"

"I need more details. Who might be what, Grams?" she asked, passing the small ceramic pitcher of cream around the table. "I'm late to the conversation."

"Romi Takahashi told me that she'd stopped by Dr. Graham Murphy's house—with a cake, mind you. She's set her cap for him. Very determined, let me tell you." Widow Rainey shook her head in disappointment.

Graham? They're talking about Graham? Tightness pressed in, making it hard to breathe.

"Graham turned her down," Grams finished.

Breathing. I remember how to do that. First a deep, cleansing breath, followed by an intense urge to smile. An urge she had to fight. She had to. But couldn't.

"He didn't just turn her down." Widow Rainey covered her mouth with her napkin, enjoying another bite of éclair before adding, "He told her he couldn't go for coffee because he was in love with someone."

In love? Knowing Graham, he was looking for a way to dodge Widow Rainey's good intentions. If there *were* someone he was interested in, what happened between them wouldn't have happened. He would have said something. Unless... She suspected she knew the answer to that.

Oh God. Oh God. Don't ask. Do. Not. Ask.

"He... He said that?" Felicity almost dropped the sugar bowl Grams offered her. "That he's in a relationship?" *Stop talking. Don't act interested. Just*

smile and nod. Say, "My goodness" or something.
But the words kept coming. "With this mystery
woman?"

"No, no, he said something about doing whatever
he could to win her over." Widow Rainey sighed.
"Now that is a true romantic for you. I always said
Graham Murphy was the sort of man a woman
would be lucky to have."

Felicity set the sugar bowl down and wiped her
hands on her skirt. He was kidding. He must be. It
was a way to avoid this Miss Takahashi and her
cake. He was not, under any circumstance, talking
about her.

"Any ideas?" Grams asked again.

"Me?" she asked, beyond flustered. But if he
was serious… They'd *never* talked about feelings.
What had happened between them was wonderful.
Incredible. No, he was being smart. But, because he
was smart, he'd know putting that sort of puzzle out
and about would have the widows' group on the
hunt. They would never rest until they knew who
he was talking about. "No." But she was chewing
the inside of her lip, her mind spinning and her
heart… Her heart…

Graham. The pressure was back, warm and fluid
and full of hope.

Her gaze darted to Nick, who was watching her
like a hawk.

"No. But I wish him well," she added.

"You know…" Widow Rainey leaned closer to
her. "I once had high hopes that your sister would
wind up with Graham. They'd be a good match, I
think."

Would they? She couldn't picture it. Probably because she didn't want to picture Graham with anyone else. Anyone other than her.

Pull it together, Filly. This was not the time to let her emotions get the best of her. Not with the widows watching—and Nick. She forced a smile. "More tea?"

"No, Filly, I think we're all set." Her mother smiled. "Can you sit a while?"

"I'm going to check on Jack." There was no need. He was a champion napper. He napped for two hours every day but still had trouble at night. But she needed a moment to process what she'd just heard and what the hell she was feeling. Because there was a very real possibility that she might want, more than anything, for Graham Murphy to be in love.

With me. And... *I love him.*

"I'll go," her father offered.

Great. She wanted to argue but couldn't think of a thing. "You sure?"

He nodded. "You sit and enjoy your company."

"Thanks, Dad." She sat, smoothing her skirt into place, then fiddling with the end of her apron tie.

Nick was watching her. She knew it.

And if she started acting weird, he'd get suspicious. Sometimes, Nick was too intuitive for his own good. Like now.

She wouldn't lie to him. She would always pick her son first, always. But that didn't stop the way her heart reacted. When it came to Graham, there were a lot of reactions. Some of them she wasn't sure she was ready to deal with yet. Others, she welcomed. With Graham, she was happy. Was it wrong to want happiness?

"Where is Honor?" Grams asked.

They chattered on about Owen Nelson, his impending departure for boot camp, and what solid stock the Nelsons were. Felicity liked Owen well enough but worried a long-term separation would lead to her daughter's first heartbreak. They were so young. And college and the military were different worlds.

But there was no denying he loved Honor—all she had to do was look at Owen to see it. Her daughter deserved to have someone look at her that way, every day for the rest of her life.

"What about you, Felicity?" one of the women asked. "Wilma's niece's cousin works for Mr. Klein. Word has it he's sweet on you."

Great. Wonderful. It shouldn't be a surprise. They'd had dinner in public, after all. Word traveled fast in Pecan Valley.

"A lawyer." Grams snorted. "Money-grubbers, the lot of them."

She swallowed a giggle. "No. I mean, Mr. Klein is a very nice man but… No." She sipped her tea.

Once more, Nick was watching her. She smiled at him, but he didn't smile back. He was studying her closely, too intent, too serious for a boy his age. She nudged his knee with her own and winked at him—earning her a reluctant smile.

"Filly, if I could offer you one piece of advice, it would be to grab on to happiness with both hands whenever it comes your way." Grams took her hand and cradled it in hers. "I know losing Matt took a toll on you. But he'd left you before he was gone. Things are harder now, complications all over the place — I know. Life's like that, up and down and every which way. But you hang in there, you keep smiling, and when you find something good, you protect it. You hear me?"

"I hear you." She pressed a kiss to her grandmother's cheek, squeezing her hand. "Wise words, Grams."

"Because I'm a wise old crone." She slapped her thigh and laughed. "I read a lot of fortune cookies."

CHAPTER NINETEEN

Nick sat on the blanket his mother had spread along the shoreline. Jack was beside him, stacking up cups, knocking them down, and stacking them up again. He was pretty cool that way—low maintenance. Poor kid, sitting in that cast, dripping sweat in triple-digit heat. But his mom, always prepared, had brought a canopy, and that—with the breeze off the water—made it bearable. Sort of.

But being inside on the Fourth of July in Pecan Valley wasn't an option. Everyone drove up to the lake; hit the marina shops; rented sailboats, paddleboats, and tandem bicycles; then ate Popsicles and ice cream until the sun went down. Once the campfires sprang up and the s'mores and hot dogs came out, everyone was ready for the big finale: fireworks over the water.

Jack knocked the cups over and clapped, looking to Nick for approval. Nick grinned. That kid was too cute to resist.

A quick glance around told him Dr. Murphy's black SUV still wasn't here. They were late. Diana said she'd have her dad here by five. It was almost six. He sighed, running the back of his forearm across his forehead. After three days of texting, and a lot of patience on his part, he and Diana had come up with a way to make absolutely sure that the two families would run into each other.

From there, it was up to his mom and Doc

Murphy. He was pretty sure he knew what was going to happen. He was pretty sure his mother was in love with Graham Murphy. And she was missing him.

Because Nick was being a prick.

What the hell was wrong with him? Or, as Diana put it, what gave him the right to stop his mom from being happy? All the bullshit excuses were just that: bullshit.

Graham was the best thing that had happened to his mom—and their family—in a long time. He kept his cool, rolled with whatever life threw at him, and he looked at his mom like she was the only woman in the world.

Had that bothered him? Hell yes, it had, in the beginning.

But that's how any man who deserved her *should* look at her. When Diana finally came clean about the level of hell she'd put her father through, Nick had a whole new level of respect for the man. His daughter was messed up, but Doc Murphy would never give up on her. Ever. He loved her, no conditions, no leaving—no matter what.

His mom deserved that. Someone who would always love her.

It was all thanks to Grams. While he'd been stuffing himself on éclairs, she'd been setting him straight. He might be young, but he wasn't stupid. Grams might use fortune-cookie speak sometimes, all vague declarations and philosophical mumbo jumbo, but other times she was a freaking genius. Like the tea party.

Bottom line, life was hard. But going it alone was harder.

Having Jack at home only proved how much love his mom had to give. Were his mom and Jack getting close? Yes. And he was glad. The little dude needed a mom. And there was no better one in the world.

And then there was Di. He'd texted her after the bonfire—told her Lane was a dick and she could do better and since their parents were hooking up she needed to get used to him being a pain-in-the-ass big brother. She'd texted back "Fuck off." Then texted "Okay. Cool. I'm good with that."

"Hey, man." Owen sat on the blanket. "Hey, Jackman." He high-fived the toddler and chuckled. "Love the shades."

Nick bought Jack a pair of plastic aviators so they could match, and Jack wore them constantly. "He looks cool. Like his big brother."

"They here yet?" Owen asked.

Nick shook his head. His sister, Owen, and Aunt Charity were all on board with the whole Mom and Graham thing. Now all they had to do was get his mom and Graham here, and hopefully they'd take it from there.

"But Di knows this is where to be?" Owen asked.

"I told her. We always camp in front of the flagpoles." They came to the same spot, year after year. Granddad said it was the best view. Nick leaned back on his elbows, trying to relax. It wasn't working. "She'll get him here."

If Diana wanted something, nothing was going to stop her. She wanted this. Her dad was in love with his mom; she *knew* it. According to her, he was sad and missed being with her—and the family—a lot.

Besides, as Diana liked to point out, as soon as

they got their folks together, she went from being an only child to having two brothers and a sister. Which, Nick had to admit, was cool. Diana was messed up, but that was who she was. She was going to be a hell of a complicated sister, but she'd fit right in.

If this was what his mother wanted.

Honor arrived, a lemon freeze in each hand. "Here ya go." She offered one to Owen and Nick swiped the other. "Hey, that was to share with Jack."

"I'll share with him," Nick said, spooning some of the tart sweetness into Jack's mouth.

Jack's lips tightened with a loud smack. His hands waved and his little face screwed up into a ridiculous expression, making them all burst out laughing. Jack laughed, too.

"What did I miss?" Mom joined them, sitting between Owen and Jack. "What's so funny, Jack-man?"

Jack grinned a sticky grin and clapped his hands.

Nick, still laughing, held up the lemon freeze.

"You did *not* feed him that?" his mother asked, digging in her monster purse for a wipe. "Nickie, that's too tart for him."

"He liked it," Nick managed.

"You're terrible." She shook her head, but she was smiling.

When she smiled, everything felt like it was going to be okay. He really wanted that for her. For her to be more than okay. He wanted her to be happy. "You look pretty, Mom," he said, really looking at her.

"Thank you." He'd surprised her, in a good way. "You're sweet."

"Being honest."

"He wants something, Mom," Honor cut in. "Look at that face. He is up to something."

Nick shot her a look. He *was* up to something, and she knew it.

"Are you?" his mother asked.

He shrugged. "I might have rented a paddleboat for later. Maybe this time, we'll make it back without a tow."

"Story?" Owen asked, sliding his arm around Honor and leaning forward for a scoop of lemon freeze.

"The last time he rented a paddleboat…" His mom shook her head. "Though, to be fair, it was his grandfather who rented it. He was supposed to take Nick out, but he had a few too many beers and ended up with a killer headache. Nick's dad was on call, and I wasn't about to disappoint my son, so I decided I'd do it." She sighed.

"We almost got to the middle of the lake when the cotton candy and corndogs and lemon freeze kicked in." Nick nudged her. "I started puking all over and crying."

"He wouldn't let me move—to paddle back in—so I'm floating around, covered in gunk." She laughed. "You were so pathetic Nickie."

"Where were you?" Owen asked Honor.

"I was sitting right here with Mimi and Grams, making s'mores and laughing at them." She covered her mouth.

"Who gave you a tow?" Owen asked.

"Dr. Murphy," he and Honor answered in unison, and both of them glanced at their mother.

She was staring at the wipe, twisting it in her hands, a smile on her face.

"He's always been around?" Owen asked.

"Always," Honor agreed. "He's the sort who sticks, you know?"

"Like me?" Owen asked, wrapping his arms around her and pressing a kiss to her cheek.

It still floored him that Owen was this into his sister. The dude was…his hero. Honor was his sister. Which meant it was awesome because they might be family someday. Or he'd have to kick his hero's ass on behalf of his sister.

Or not.

They didn't talk about it, but they all knew what was coming. In a few weeks, Honor was going off to college and Owen would be at boot camp. That was going to hurt both of them. Like, really hurt. It sucked that they waited so long to get together, now that they were both leaving.

"Speak of the devil," Honor said, pushing Owen aside and standing up. "Diana! Hey," she called out, waving her hands.

Finally. Nick relaxed, ruffling Jack's curls and glancing at his mom.

"Honor." His mother shushed her, casting a nervous look his way.

"It's cool, Mom," he said, catching her hand in his. "We've got room."

She chewed on her lower lip—it was what she did when she was stressing out. *He* was the reason she was stressing out.

"Hey." Diana was out of breath. "Hi. Happy Fourth of July, people." She dropped to her knees.

"Jack. How's it going? Cool shades, little dude."

"We match. My idea." Nick grinned.

"He looks good. You?" Diana wrinkled her nose and shrugged. "Looks like you're trying to be like him."

"I got the cup-stacking thing down." Nick pointed at Jack's handiwork.

Diana laughed, peering back over her shoulder. "Dad. You coming?"

Graham Murphy was taking a hell of a long time with the unpacking. Stalling, maybe? "What did you bring?" Nick asked, pushing off the blanket. "I'll help." He headed across the sand to the grass, then the parking lot beyond. "What can I carry?"

"I'm good." Graham held a small ice chest and towels, shouldering the straps for two beach chairs. "Thanks."

"Here." He took the chairs. "We've got room. Diana's there." He headed off before the man could argue. Because he was going to argue.

Chaos ensued while they rearranged the canopy, making sure everyone had shade and room, doling out drinks, then rearranging the chairs so that everyone would see the fireworks when they started.

Graham didn't say much. But the way he looked at his mom—it said enough. His mom was all jumpy and red-faced, trying to avoid Doc Murphy, both tense, barely looking at each other or talking to each other. Because of Nick. He felt like shit. He'd done this to them. In a sick, twisted way, it was seriously cool that they'd sacrifice their happiness for him.

He'd messed this up. Tonight, he was going to fix it.

• • •

Graham threw some dry sticks on the fire he was building, watching the embers dance to life. The sun was going down, and the fireworks would start soon—just not soon enough. He'd missed Felicity, and this was killing him.

Every time her green eyes met his, he was reminded of all that could be and should be between them. Their kids together like this, laughing and teasing, made it that much harder. Because he loved them all. Felicity, yes, but her kids, too. He'd missed them all.

"You're awful quiet," Diana said, nudging him. "What's up?"

He smiled. "Thinking."

"About what?" she asked. "Right this second, spit it out. Don't think."

He laughed. "The fire."

She frowned. "What about the fire?"

"Is it big enough for s'mores?"

She rolled her eyes. "You're so full of shit."

"Di, language." He glanced at Jack, close enough to hear.

"Fine. You are full of piles of poo."

He laughed again.

"You want to leave?" she asked, her enthusiasm wavering.

He shook his head.

"Liar." She sighed.

"What is he lying about?" Nick asked, offering him a soda.

Graham took the can. "Thank you."

"What he's thinking about," Di answered.

"Can I talk to you about something, Dr. Murphy?" Nick asked, catching him by surprise. "Alone, Di?"

Di's brows rose. "Is this *the* talk? Go easy on him, Dad. He's young and innocent and all." She headed back to the canopy.

"She's something," Nick said.

Graham nodded, curious—and wary as hell. Still, if Nick needed someone to talk to, he wasn't going to turn his back on him. "What's up?"

"You know being a teenager sucks, right?" he asked.

Graham laughed. "I remember, though it's been a while. Just so you know, being a teenager's parent can suck, too."

"I owe you an apology, I think." He cleared his throat, running a hand through his blond curls. "You like my mom?"

Graham froze. Was this a trick? Diana had taught him just how dangerous questions could be. Nick wasn't as manipulative as his daughter, or as desperate, but he had more than his fair share of rage. And if his answer was going to trigger an episode here and now, he wasn't sure what the hell to say.

"I mean, you love her?" Nick's voice was low, a little shaky.

He looked at the boy. This was important to Nick—knowing.

"Like, *love* love her?" Nick pushed, jaw clenching.

With a sigh, he gave up. "I'm in love with your

mother," he clarified, a little more firmly than he'd intended. "Very much."

Nick blew out a long, slow breath. "I thought so. And I got in the way." Nick raked the sand with his toes. "I really screwed up. I'm sorry for being an asshole, Dr. Murphy."

"Graham," he corrected him, the weight he'd been bearing since he'd left Felicity easing a little.

"Graham." Nick nodded. "I'm super protective, you know? She's special—not just because she's my mom. And my dad… He destroyed her, almost. She wants us to think she's tough, and she is, but still, you have no idea. She cried all the time. Every night. What he did—" He broke off.

Graham nodded. "He hurt you all." There was not a damn thing he could do to change that. But he'd do everything he could to help him move past it. But that's not what this was about. This was a son needing confirmation that Graham loved his mother—that he *got* how special she was. And Graham did so he said, "He gave up the best part of himself when he let her go."

Nick's eyes searched his, a sad smile forming. "Yeah."

He blew out a deep breath. "I'll never do that to her."

"I know." Nick nodded. "I know you're always going to love her. And take care of her. And be there for her."

He nodded. "For all of you, maybe."

"Maybe?" he asked, frowning.

"We haven't really talked about a future, Nick." He shook his head. "You know more than she does."

"Oh." Nick glanced at his mother. "No shit?"

He laughed. "Nope. I have no idea how she feels or what she wants."

"Well, that sucks."

"It does?" He couldn't help but smile.

"Yeah, I figured you two would work everything out, she'd be happy, and Diana would get off my back."

"Diana?" His gaze drifted then. Di was lying on her stomach beside Jack, his stacking cups piled up on her head.

"She's all pumped about moving into our house."

"How do you feel about that?" he asked.

"If Mom's happy, and you don't screw it up, I'm fine with it." He shrugged. "Just don't screw it up, okay? She can't go through that again."

None of us can.

It was unspoken but there—Nick, trusting him to love his mother and take care of his family. Graham's heart thumped heavily, humbled beyond words. "I promise."

"Nick," Honor yelled. "We're going to get Jack's face painted."

"And ice cream," Diana sounded off.

"Coming." Nick handed him a paper ticket. "Here, I got the six thirty time slot. Girls like that sort of thing, right?"

Graham glanced at the ticket. "Paddleboats?"

"It's a start, Doc—Graham." He winked and ran back to the canopy. "Hey, Aunt Charity, bring the graham crackers?"

"Yes. They were the only reason you invited me, weren't they?" Charity teased, hugging Nick.

From here, he could see the slight swell of Charity's stomach. Once her family wrapped their head around it, she'd have more support than she knew what to do with. Knowing Charity, she'd rely on Felicity. She was everyone's rock. He knew that loving her meant loving them all. But loving him meant taking on Diana. No denying it—he was getting the easier deal.

"Graham." Charity waved, heading his way. "Are you the keeper of the fire?"

He glanced at his watch. "I got it started. Can you keep it going?"

"Me?" She eyed the small blaze. "Um…"

"Please?" he asked, glancing Felicity's way.

Her eyes went wide, and she smiled. "Does your request have anything to do with publicly wooing my sister?"

"It might."

She took the long stick he'd been using to stir the flames and crouched on the sand. "Off you go. Make me proud, Graham."

He winked at her. "Thanks."

Felicity sat, staring out over the lake. The breeze lifted her strawberry-blond curls, making them dance around her neck and shoulders. But the tension in her posture had him suspecting she was just as aware of him as he was of her. With any luck, that meant she loved him the way he loved her.

• • •

She was too old to feel this way. Nervous. Excited. Achingly aware of the man talking to her sister.

Apparently, all that was required to send her heart thumping was his presence. His dark-haired, broad-shouldered, warm-smiling presence. And when he laughed, it warmed her from the inside.

She missed his laugh. She missed talking to him. She dreamed of being in his arms with the beat of his heart beneath her ear.

"Felicity?" Owen offered her an ice cream. "Honor said it's your favorite."

"Thanks." She took the cone, the scoop of mint chocolate chip already dripping along the waffle crust.

"No prob." He flopped onto the blanket.

She smiled at the boy. He was a man, really. A man who made her daughter happy. "When do you ship out?" she asked.

"One week." He swallowed hard, the muscles in his throat working. "I was all fired up and ready."

"Not anymore?" she asked.

He looked at Honor. "I don't want to leave her."

She still wasn't used to his honesty. "She's leaving, too, you know."

He rested his arms on his knees. "Not for another three weeks. That's fourteen more days than what we've got now."

"Then it sounds like these seven days need to count triple." Her brows rose. "You better write to us. And when you get back, I expect us to be the second stop you make."

"Because I'll be heading to Austin first?"

She nodded, unwilling to ding the confidence of first love. It was fierce and passionate, she knew that. She'd married hers. But time and separation could take a toll, and she didn't want either of them to feel bad if it didn't last. The memories they made this summer were special, no matter what.

"Thanks for letting me be part of your family, Mrs. Buchanan. With my dad deployed and my brother...having a life, it's been nice."

She reached out and squeezed his shoulder. "We tend to nag, get in each other's business, tell each other what to do now and then. And we have little to no respect for personal space and quiet time. Fair warning."

"Sounds perfect to me," he murmured, his gaze following Honor as she steered Jack's stroller along the water's edge. With a grin, he pushed up and ran down the beach to join them.

Honor smiled at him, tilting her head back for the kiss Owen gave her. It was quite a kiss. Intimate. Too intimate for a mother to watch, so she stared at her ice cream, running her tongue along the cone to catch the drips before they landed on her bare legs. A slight tilt of the cone and the scoop rolled off and splatted into her lap.

She squealed and jumped up to wipe the cold stickiness from her legs. "Oh, great."

"You okay?" Graham was there, his concern vanishing when he saw the smear of green running along her leg. "Ice cream incident?"

She laughed, awkward. Nick was close. The day was going so well; she didn't want to jeopardize it. But she couldn't exactly ignore him. She didn't want to. "You could say that." With the ever-useful pack of wipes, she managed to make her legs mostly ice cream–free, babbling, "The mosquitoes will love me."

He smiled then. Oh, how she loved that smile. The real one that made the corners of his eyes crease.

And he stared at her, hard. "I have this." He held up a ticket. "For six thirty." He pointed at his watch. "Which is in five minutes. If you want to ride with me." He never looked away.

"Ride?" she managed, a little breathless.

"Paddleboat." He'd moved closer. "Will you go with me, Felicity?"

She shook her head. "I can't, Graham."

"Nick gave me the ticket." Another step nearer. It knocked the air from her lungs. "For us."

"He did?" She'd seen them talking earlier. No matter how Nick felt about her and Graham's relationship, she'd hoped he'd consider Graham an ally. He needed a man in his life. And she couldn't think of a better role model for her son than Graham. But she'd never in a million years thought they'd been talking about her.

"How about it?" he asked.

Her gaze darted around, searching for any excuse to turn him down. She needed one, desperately. Because she really wanted to go with him.

"I've got the fire," Charity called out. "Honor's got Jack—and Owen, too, from the looks of it."

"Diana? Nick?" she asked, combing the shop fronts.

"Getting their faces painted." Graham stared at the ticket. "You can say no, Felicity. It's a choice."

Her heart pounded wildly when she faced him. "I don't want to say no, Graham. I want to go with you. I want to spend time with you. I want…" She could touch him now; his heat and scent surrounded her. She wanted to touch him—but she didn't.

"What do you want, Felicity?" he whispered.

She shook her head. "It doesn't matter. I made Nick a promise. After everything he's been through, I can't break it. No matter what happened between us—or what I want."

He was smiling broadly.

"Why are you smiling?" What was there to smile about? She was in love with the one man she'd sworn off.

"Your unwavering loyalty to your family." His hand cupped her cheek, sending an alarming shudder down her spine. "It's one of the things I love about you."

She blinked, his words jarring her. "What?"

Both hands now, cradling her face. "I love you."

"Graham." Her breath hitched, hard. "You can't say that."

"I just did." His thumb ran along her cheek. "And since Nick has given me his blessing, I'm going to say it again. And again." He tilted her face back. "Whenever and wherever I feel like it."

With each word, her hope grew. Nick had changed his mind? Graham loved her? Here, in front of everyone—and she knew *everyone* was watching—he loved her.

"I love you," he whispered again. "And even though the kids think you love me, too, I'd feel a hell of a lot better if you said something right now."

He was worried. Here he was, baring his heart to her, a heart that had been just as broken as hers. Still, he put himself out there—for her—and she hadn't said a word.

The words came rushing out. "I love you, too."

He was kissing her then. He didn't care what sort of gossip followed. It would be worth it. He smiled, resting his forehead against hers and breathing hard.

"You scared me," he confessed.

"I'm a little shell-shocked myself." She slid her arms around his waist.

They stood there, wrapped up in each other. Content.

"Hate to break this up," Nick said, running toward them. "But if you're not going to use this, Di and I are."

Graham let go of her long enough to give Nick the ticket.

"We're good?" Nick asked. "You two, I mean? I was right, Graham? It looks like I was right." He was all smiles.

"You were right," Graham agreed.

"Aren't you glad we booked the bus now, Dad?" Diana yelled from the sidewalk. "Come on, Nick." She waved him over.

"Better go before we lose the slot." Nick shook his head and ran to Di, the two of them racing down the sidewalk to the pier and the paddleboats.

"Bus?" she asked.

"To drive to the beach house." He smoothed the hair from her forehead. "She wanted the big one—in case you changed your mind."

"I'm glad. I've changed my mind." Her smile demanded her kiss her again.

He did, pausing between kisses to ask, "You're sure? I don't want to rush this—"

"How big?" she asked, distracted by the curve of his lips.

"Big enough for all of us. Charity—probably a couch for Owen somewhere, if you think it's safe?" he asked, casting a concerned glance at the young couple.

"I don't know if there's anything safe about love." Burying her face in his chest felt right. "Besides, he's leaving in a week. If they want to spend every second of that together, I'm not going to stop them—they're good kids. Smart kids. I trust them."

His arms tightened around her. "Okay."

"When do we leave?" she asked.

He sighed. "After the adoption party? If you want to go?"

She rested her chin on his chest and smiled up at him. In two days, they'd take their first family vacation. The first of many. Whatever life threw at her, at them, they'd face it together. "I want. There's nothing I want more."

EPILOGUE

Owen had this way of looking at her that made her feel beautiful. He said it, too, a lot, but sometimes—when he looked at her—she *was* beautiful. Tomorrow they would leave for the coast, all of them. Her mom hadn't bothered asking her if she wanted Owen along. She'd just invited him. It was like her mother knew how important he was and how little time they had left.

"Isn't that adorable?" Grams asked, holding up the tiny baseball mitt and glove someone had brought for Jack.

Nick eyed the baseball gear with contempt. "He's going to play soccer."

"He can play more than one sport," Mimi argued.

Owen spoke up. "I played baseball for a while."

"And ran track. And played football." She shook her head. "You're what they call an overachiever."

"But you love me anyway." He caught her hand in his.

"I do." She squeezed his hand. Knowing he was leaving soon scared the crap out of her. It wasn't like he was taking a semester abroad or going on safari.

He was joining the Marines—the front line.

Uncle Zach's letters were few and far between. They hadn't seen him in years. She didn't want that for Owen—she'd miss him too much. And the fear of things like guns and explosions and injuries was enough to give her nightmares. Every time she thought of Owen out there dealing with that, it hurt—enough that tears kicked in before she could stop them.

And it could happen at any time. Like right now. "Be right back," she said, needing an escape before the crying started.

She hurried up the stairs and into Jack's nursery, taking deep breaths and shaking her hands. It was supposed to calm you down, according to Diana. She had a whole arsenal of ways to "calm down" and "decompress" and not all of them included smoking pot.

"What's up?" Owen had followed her.

She shook her head, avoiding his gaze. He'd know. And as bad as it was for her, she knew it was eating him up, too.

"Talk to me." He caught her hand and pulled her against him. "Talk." He kissed her nose. "To." Her forehead. "Me." Her lips. He clung long enough for her to sway into him. "Did I do something?"

"No." She gripped his T-shirt, holding on tight. "No. You're here."

He nodded, instantly understanding. "I'm coming back."

"You promise?" she whispered, hoarse.

"I promise. I'll write. I'll call when I can." He smiled. "You'll be so busy at school, you probably won't have time to miss me."

"Don't, Owen." She frowned. "You know that's not me. Thinking about next week—" Her voice broke.

"Then don't." His hands tightened. "Right now, it's all about us. You and me."

She nodded. "You and me."

"I'm coming back." He kissed her with everything he had.

. . .

Braden Martinez was a man of few words. Charity had taken to spouting off random bits of trivia just to see what reaction she could get from him. Not much. He remained ever aloof but ever present. And currently, he carried several large trays of finger foods into the dining room.

"Does he know about your condition?" her mother asked, watching the silent sheriff place the trays on the table, then straighten them before stepping back.

She nodded.

"Does he?" Her mother glanced back and forth between them. "You be careful, Charity Ann."

"It's not like he can get me pregnant, Mom," she teased.

Her mother swatted her shoulder. "I wasn't talking about you. And that wasn't funny. Not in the least."

Charity popped a powdered-sugar-covered wedding cookie in her mouth. "Who were you talking about?"

"Sheriff Martinez." She sighed, exasperated. "He's seen his fair share of hurting. Now you're back and he's just as smitten as ever."

"What are you talking about?" Charity knew her mother had a flare for the dramatic, but she was being ridiculous.

"You were so determined to get out of Pecan Valley, you never stopped to look around you. That boy followed you around since grade school, not that you ever noticed." Her tone was sharp.

"Mom, we dated…sort of. I was never mean to him." Was she? She hoped not. She'd never have intentionally hurt him.

Her mother's look was disapproving. "You left; he moved on. Married, settled down, and expecting."

Charity stopped eating. Braden? Married? A father? "What?"

"Not anymore. Sad story, really. Too sad for today." She paused, shaking her head. "I think we've had enough sadness for now, don't you?"

"Mom, you can't start to tell me something like that, then stop." Besides, she needed to start breathing again.

"They died, honey." She sighed. "Let's leave it at that."

Charity stared at the man talking with her father. "How long ago?" she asked.

"Six years? Eight?" Her mother shrugged. "He hasn't shown a bit of interest in a woman until now." Her mother tipped her chin up, her gaze brutal. "Now you're back, pregnant and alone, and he's still following you around. I'm not worried about you, Charity—you've got us. I am worried about *him*. He's lost enough. You be careful with him, you hear me?"

A hard, jagged knot settled in Charity's throat. Poor Braden. Her hands skimmed over her stomach, imagining the bump and flutters going away forever. It hurt too much to imagine. Braden had lost that and more. Children and his wife? Her stomach rolled, and she sat heavily in one of the dining room chairs.

Braden was up before she could stop him, offering her a glass of lemonade. "Charity?"

"Thank you." She took a small sip before she smiled up at him.

But there it was, just like her mother said. A flash of warmth, concern—tenderness even. Then it was gone. She'd never have suspected he cared about her if her mother hadn't said something. She was pregnant, after all. Wasn't that sort of a huge deterrent for a single guy? A too-hot-to-be-single guy… Then again, her mother loved to read between the lines and extract what she wanted to see. But, if there was the slightest chance her mother was right she'd be extra careful with Braden. Besides, she could use some friends that weren't related to her. And she got the feeling Braden could use a friend, too.

• • •

Felicity pulled a package of clear plastic plates from the pantry. When Widow Rainey said a few people were coming for a quiet gathering, she'd believed her. Instead, most of Pecan Valley was here. Now she was scavenging for cutlery and food and working her refrigerator's ice machine overtime.

"Need a hand?" Charity asked. "I brought reinforcements."

Braden Martinez was there, looking as uncomfortable as ever.

But Graham slipped in behind them, and her

tension melted away. His smile did that. And, boy, was he smiling.

"That tray, please." Felicity nodded at the tray piled high with fresh chopped veggies and a home-made dip. "Can you take that one, too? With the sweets? But tell Nick to stay away from this one; it has pecans." She put the tray with candies and cook-ies in Braden's hand.

"Right. The whole *allergic* thing." Charity laughed. "It is a good way to get out of eating stuff, I guess."

Graham stood back, his warm brown gaze watch-ing her. The sooner she shooed her sister and Braden out of the kitchen, the better.

"Anything else?" Braden asked.

"This, too?" she asked, adding a package of cutlery and plates. "Got it?"

He nodded.

"Let's go, Sheriff. But try not to drop anything," Charity said, pushing open the kitchen door and shooting him a cheeky grin as he led the way. "Hey, I got you away from Widow Rainey. You can thank me later." The door swung shut.

She grabbed Graham. "I was wondering when you were going to get here."

"Diana." He kissed her. "She wanted to dress up." He kissed her again. "An actual dress."

Felicity pushed off him. "Really?"

He nodded, pulling her in for another kiss. "I've been wanting to do this since I woke up."

Her tongue traced the seam of his lips, pulling a full-bodied shiver from him. "Some things are worth waiting for."

He pressed her against the counter, his hands sliding up her back to tangle in her hair. "I'm not a fan of waiting." His lips traveled to her neck—as the kitchen door swung wide.

"Felicity, Charity needs—" Widow Rainey stood, staring.

Graham stopped kissing her, but he didn't let her go.

Widow Rainey kept staring.

"What can I get you?" Felicity asked, trying, and failing, to wiggle free of Graham's hold.

"Uh-huh. I heard rumor of something happening between you two. I'm assuming Felicity is the woman you told Miss Takahashi about?" Widow Rainey asked, smiling.

Graham nodded. "She is."

"And I'm assuming from the goings-on in this kitchen that nuptials are soon to follow?" she asked, brows high.

"We haven't gotten around to discussing nuptials yet. We're still very involved in the wooing and, what did you call it? *Goings-on?*" Graham's smile was mischievous.

Widow Rainey's brows shot higher, but she disappeared from the doorway without another word.

"Everyone in Pecan Valley will know we're an item now, Dr. Murphy." Felicity shook her head.

He sighed, brushing her hair from her shoulder. "That was the plan." He smiled her favorite smile. "Now, about the nuptials…"

ACKNOWLEDGMENTS

I am blessed to have the love and support of so many talented and nurturing people.

To Allison Collins, Jolene Navarro, Joni Hahn, Storm Navarro, and Marilyn Tucker, for being the first to welcome the Otto-Buchanan family onto the page.

Thank you Teri Wilson, Julia London, K.L. White, Frances Trilone, and Maria Rodriguez for suffering through early drafts and loving me anyway.

I am thankful for my wonderful, strange, unique family—by blood or by choice. Thanks for always having my back!

To my Cowboy and my kids - I love you more than you will ever know. Thank you for giving me the chance to chase my dreams and cheering me along the way!

Turn the page to start reading the latest
heartfelt, small town romance from
New York Times bestselling author
Victoria James.

Cowboy for *Hire*

CHAPTER ONE

"Stop! You can't go out there!"

Sarah Turner jolted back from the door, sending her coffee swishing over the rim of the mug as her housekeeper, Edna Casey, burst into the office. The older woman was panting, clutching a folded newspaper to her small frame, her eyes as wide as the antique wagon wheels leaning against the barn.

Sarah glanced around, half expecting a herd of angry cattle to be barreling their way, but the area was clear of immediate danger. "What's wrong?"

Mrs. Casey shoved the newspaper at her. "There's been a horrible mistake."

Frowning, Sarah took the paper. "Is there a problem with the ad I placed?"

Mrs. Casey made a strangled noise and nodded, her eyes still wide.

Dread pooled in Sarah's stomach. She'd checked the online version of the ad, and it had been perfect. So perfect, she'd already received quite a few calls about the new ranch foreman position. It wasn't even eight o'clock in the morning, and she had a dozen interviews ahead of her. This time tomorrow, she'd be able to hire a new foreman and get the family ranch up and running again.

She inhaled sharply as she read the only ad that boasted the ranch's phone number. The ad that Edna must be referring to. The ad she never, ever, in a million years would have placed.

A bead of sweat trickled between her shoulder blades, and she put her coffee mug down with a *thud* on the desk. Squeezing her eyes shut, she said a quick prayer that maybe when she opened them again, the ad would be correct. She opened one eye, and a wave of nausea hit. Nope. The "horrible mistake" was still there.

Cowboy for Her: Experienced and skilled cowboy companion for lonely young woman. Duties include social engagements, long walks, and romantic evenings. Excellent compensation, full benefits, and paid time off. Call for interview.

"No. No, no, no. It was supposed to say 'foreman for hire,' not…what even is this?" She clutched the newspaper. "Experienced and skilled…social engagements…romantic evenings… It sounds like I'm hiring an escort!"

It was so bad, it was almost laughable. Except it wasn't.

Mrs. Casey was standing so straight, she could have been a sergeant. Her thin lips were pursed, hands on her narrow hips. "Your parents would be mortified!"

Her parents were the least of her problems right now, especially since neither was alive. Sarah rubbed her temples, deciding not to respond. This was her first act as owner of the family ranch, and while Edna was like family, this was all on Sarah.

She looked at the paper again and groaned as she read the ad for a foreman—*her* ad—below the disaster in question, noting that it listed the wrong number. "They must have mixed up my ad with someone else's. Of all the stupid errors…"

She marched across the room to her computer, brought up the page, and breathed a sigh of relief when she saw the correct version was still in place.

Ranch Manager/Foreman: The ranch manager is responsible for all aspects of operating the ranch. Experience necessary, full benefits, immediate start date.

Wait. So were the calls she'd been getting in response to the online ad or the print version? She glanced out the windows and swallowed hard. All those men out there had to be applying for the foreman position. *Right?*

Sarah put her elbows on the desk and rubbed her temples. This was so bad. "How could they have printed this? I don't even understand who would *write* an ad like this."

"They should be fired. All of them at that two-bit paper," Mrs. Casey said, her outrage clinging to her words like honey on a spoon as her loyalty shifted back to Sarah. "Are you getting a migraine? You keep rubbing your temples." She squared her shoulders and nodded once. "I'll take over. This is too much stress for you."

Sarah stopped the temple rubbing. "No. I'm fine, and I know what I can handle. This is my ranch, and I'm going to find a way to run it."

"There is a reason your father never wanted you in the ranching business—it's no way of life for a woman. Alongside all those men out there day in and day out…" Edna shook her head.

If they kept this conversation going, Sarah *would*

end up with a migraine. It wasn't a new topic, but it was one that always ended in an argument. "You know that's not true. There are plenty of women ranchers, despite this myth you and my parents kept clinging to. This is the twenty-first century, and even if it wasn't, that kind of thinking is and has always been backward."

"It's prudent, it's wise, and it's realistic."

"It's a bunch of lies that even my father didn't believe. Before Josh—" She rolled her shoulders and forced back the immediate pang of grief. "Before Josh died, Dad knew that we'd be the ones to take over this ranch when he was gone, and he had no objections. The whole 'women shouldn't be in the ranching business' was a front. A cover-up for his fear that something might happen to me. I'm not living that way any longer."

Mrs. Casey pursed her lips, coming at it from a different direction. "You know you could sell this place; it's what your mother wanted. You could sell and afford to buy a house without all this land and live a comfortable life." Her eyes ignited with hope.

"No."

Mrs. Casey made a *harrumph* noise and squared her shoulders. "This is an argument for another day. For now, we must come up with a solution for the hooligans outside."

Sarah almost laughed at the hooligan remark, but it also reminded her of just how out of touch Mrs. Casey was with the modern-day world. The poor woman had been with Sarah's family for more than two decades and was the epitome of straitlaced, black-and-white-movie era, sheltered, small-town elderly lady. This ranch had almost become a compound in the last decade, keeping them away from the neighbors and friends—and progress. While Sarah wasn't exactly living a wild life out here in rural Montana, she considered herself worldlier than Edna Casey.

By the end of this year, all that would change.

"Okay, let me think. Those men out there…they must have read the online ad, right? I mean, who reads the paper these days anyway? And who in their right mind would even think that ad was real?"

Mrs. Casey adjusted the blinds and peered outside. "No proper man would respond to an ad for an escort. I will address the men out there and whoever so dares to admit to being here for an escort position shall receive a blistering lecture from me."

Sarah resisted the urge to rub her temples again. "*I* will deal with the men outside. This is my ranch. I'm the one doing the interviews. I'm more than capable of handling a few cowboys, regardless of the position they're here for."

Sarah joined Mrs. Casey at the window and took in the appearance of the men outside. There was nothing odd about them; they all looked like the typical cowboys she'd grown up around on the ranch with their well-worn cowboy hats and jeans, fit and strong bodies.

"I'll be fine," she told Mrs. Casey. "You go back to the house. I'm optimistic that most of them are here to apply for the foreman position. They all *look* like real cowboys." She slanted the blinds and peered out the window again, trying to convince herself as well as Edna.

"Well, if not, they should all be ashamed of themselves, and I don't mind telling them on my way back to the house."

Sarah placed her arm around Mrs. Casey's thin shoulders and gently nudged her in the direction of the door. "I've got this. You go on about your day. I'll be in for dinner."

Mrs. Casey gave Sarah one last look, as though she wondered if she'd ever see her again, before opening the door and walking out.

"Everything will be just fine," Sarah called after her, feeling like the biggest liar ever.

• • •

Hours later, Sarah slowly lowered her head to the desk, her hand on a bottle of Tylenol, ready to be done with the ranching business after one day. This was a disaster.

She was a disaster.

It appeared the small town of Wishing River had an exorbitant amount of cowboys who were ready to trade in their chaps for roses and wine. It also appeared the cowboys here did, in fact, still read the paper.

This couldn't be happening. Or happened. It was over. All of it. Her career as a rancher was done before it even had a chance to start, because there was no way word wouldn't get out about this. But hey, at least Sarah knew that there were six cowboys willing to take her around town and romance her—if she paid them.

She banged her head against the desk. So stupid.

After her family's long-standing foreman, Mike Ballinger, walked off the job last Friday without any notice, she'd been left hanging. Thankfully, the other cowboys knew their jobs and were capable of continuing, but the role of ranch manager was essential to an operation this size. She needed someone immediately.

The knock on the door was the final straw. How many men were available for escort services in this town? She stomped across her late father's office and whipped open the door to find…one of the most breathtaking men she'd ever seen in her entire twenty-six years.

The sun was setting in the distance behind him. Typically the sight of it disappearing over the mountains would make her pause and take it in, except tonight it was him she was noticing. If she were part of the Montana tourism board, she'd be hiring him to stand there, just like that, with the mountains in the backdrop, the sun casting a glow over his perfect…everything.

He must be an escort. Was that bad of her to assume? The bizarre thought that maybe she should rethink her whole position on hiring an escort crossed her mind for the briefest of moments.

She forced herself to focus. He was in his late twenties or early thirties. His worn cowboy hat dipped low, but not low enough that she couldn't admire the aqua-blue eyes that stood out against his tanned skin. Light stubble highlighted a strong jaw and lean features. His dark-blue-and-white-checked shirt was rolled up midway to his elbows and revealed strong, tanned forearms. His jeans were worn and clung to his lean but powerful-looking body. He was a man who could make her nervous just by standing there.

He was probably very good at his escort position.

"Good afternoon, Miss. I'm here for the advertised job. I'm sorry I'm late—I had an emergency situation I needed to deal with at my current position."

She had no idea escorts had emergency situations. Whatever. That was none of her business. She clutched the doorknob, prepared to close it on him and the rest of the terrible day. "That's okay. There was a bit of a mix-up in the ad, so I'm afraid you came all the way out here for nothing. This is for a ranch manager position."

He gave her a nod. "Right. That's what I'm here for. I saw the ad online last night."

Relief swept through her. *Online*. He'd seen the online version. She smiled and held out her hand. "Oh. Well, in that case, I'm Sarah Turner."

He grasped her hand firmly, and she tried to maintain eye contact, but this man had an entirely different effect on her than anyone had before. His large hand was warm, slightly rough…a working man's hand, and his gaze was that of—

"Cade Walker."

She pulled her hand back and opened the door wider. "Nice to meet you. Come on in and have a seat," she said, gesturing to the chair on the other side of the worn oak desk. Since she'd had no use for her notes, they were all still neatly lined up on the wooden surface.

Swallowing down the sudden slew of nerves and

emotions, she settled into the large leather chair that somehow seemed too big for her, as though she were still the little girl playing in her daddy's swivel chair when visiting him at lunchtime.

She blinked a few times. The days where she and her brother would race across the office, trying to beat the other one to get first dibs on the chair... those days were over. She avoided the framed family photos, because that family hadn't existed in well over a decade. It was all up to her now.

"Here's my résumé," he said, handing her two pieces of paper. She scanned them, quickly taking in the relevant points, relieved that he seemed to have so much experience.

"So you've been ranching a long time," she started, trying to act as though she held interviews all the time.

He crossed one leg over the other. "Yes, since I was sixteen. The last six years, I've been the ranch manager at the Donnelly ranch here in Wishing River."

She nodded. "That's great. I see you've also listed your references."

"Yes, feel free to call them. Martin Donnelly is my current employer."

She furrowed her brows, trying to rack her brain, but she'd been so out of the loop that she couldn't place it. "Donnelly... That sounds very familiar."

He smiled. "Not far down the road at all."

She wasn't surprised she didn't know any of the local ranchers by name. Little details like who their neighbors were hadn't been important enough for her father to share. She cleared her throat and gathered up her notes. "So as I'm sure you already know, the ranch manager is responsible for all aspects of operating the ranch, including: the preparation of our annual operating budget and our long-term rolling business plan, a grass-fed beef operations strategy, a pasture maintenance plan, care of livestock and feeding, pasture in summer, adverse weather conditions planning, hay in winter, health checks, calving, irrigation, ranch staff, leadership…"

He raised his eyebrows. "I'm very comfortable and familiar with all of that. It's very similar to what I've already been doing."

She took a deep breath and forced herself to get to the last part, the one that kept her up last night and, well, every night since she decided to step up and take over the ranch. "The ranch manager also must be able to train me."

If he was surprised, he did a good job of keeping his features neutral. "Train you?"

She placed her forearms on the desk, folding her hands together, trying to look as though it were perfectly normal that a rancher's child wouldn't know a thing about how to run a ranch. "Yes. I'd like to be able to share certain aspects of the ranch manager's job by the one-year mark."

A flash of surprise flickered across those eyes. "That would be fine."

She nodded, her shoulders relaxing slightly. She spent the next fifteen minutes giving him a rundown of their ranch. His questions demonstrated how knowledgeable he was, and his genuine interest in her vision was promising.

"I guess the last thing to tell you is that our ranch

manager left abruptly last week, so this position needs to be filled as soon as possible."

He ran a hand over his jaw, drawing her attention again to his perfectly sculpted features. "Okay. If I were hired, I would have to make arrangements. I know the Donnelly ranch is in good hands and they'll be fine without me, but I don't want to leave them in a bind. I would like to ask them how soon I could leave."

She nodded, trying not to look as desperate as she felt. Calling his references was definitely a must, but other than that, he had a dream résumé for this position.

They continued talking for the next half hour, and she found herself drawn to his voice, the way he spoke. He had a way of making his confidence known, and he handled himself as someone of authority, which was perfect for this position, but he also didn't patronize her. She stood slowly, wiping her palms on the front of her jeans before she shook his hand again. "Thanks for coming out. I will make my decision by tomorrow."

He gave her a nod before turning and walking to the door. Somehow he managed to make the small office seem even smaller, like his presence sucked out all her oxygen. "It was nice to meet you, Miss Turner."

"Sarah."

"Right." He pulled open the door and stepped outside. She held the door, ready to close it, when he turned back around, his cowboy hat shadowing his eyes slightly. "I forgot to mention, if you need any help with that escort service, I'd be glad to oblige."

Fire stormed through her body, but before she had a chance to sputter out a response, he gave her an utterly charming half smile, perfectly timed with a small tip of his hat, before turning around and walking away.

Sarah slowly shut the door, torn between laughing and dying of humiliation.

All the weirdness of the afternoon aside, this was the first step in taking over the ranch. The next step was going to be in Cade Walker's very capable hands.

Cowboy for *Hire*

Look for it everywhere books are sold!
Visit www.victoriajames.ca

Wedding cakes never tasted sweeter in
USA Today bestselling author
Cindi Madsen's small-town rom-com full
of laugh-out-loud moments.

alwaysa
bridesmaid

Violet Abrams may have been a bridesmaid no less than seven times, but her wedding day was near—she could feel it. Until her longtime boyfriend left her for someone else. That's just fine—she has her photography and a new project redesigning her sister's bakery to keep her happy and fulfilled. Fast-forward to the day of his wedding, though, when Violet might have accidentally, totally not on purpose, started a fire. And... Officially the worst day ever.

Firefighter Ford Maguire thought he'd seen it all. Until he's called out because someone tried to set the local bakery on fire...with a wedding magazine? The little arsonist might be the cutest woman he's ever seen, but he's too career-focused to consider something serious. Still, Violet seems like a great person to help him navigate his upcoming "man of honor" duties in his best friend's wedding.

Pretty soon, not only is Violet giving him lessons on all things weddings, she's helping him train his latest rescue-dog recruit puppies and weaving her way seamlessly into his lone-wolf lifestyle. But forever is the last thing on Ford's mind, and if there's one thing a perpetual bridesmaid knows, it's the importance of a happily ever after.

USA Today bestselling author Ophelia London brings a sweet, heartfelt, and surprisingly funny take to the popular Amish romance canon.

NEVER
an
AMISH
BRIDE

Everything changed for Esther Miller with the death of her beloved fiancé, Jacob. Even years later, she still struggles with her faith and purpose in the small, tight-knit Amish village of Honey Brook—especially now that her younger sister is getting married. All she wants is to trust in the Lord to help her find peace...but peace is the last thing she gets when Lucas, Jacob's wayward older brother, returns to town.

Lucas Brenneman has been harboring a secret for years—the real reason he never returned from Rumspringa and the truth behind his brother Jacob's death. Honey Brook still calls to him, but he knows his occupation as a physician's assistant must take precedence. With sweet and beautiful Esther he finds a comfort he's never known, and he feels like anything is possible...even forgiveness. But she was Jacob's bride-to-be first. And if she knew the truth, would she ever truly open her heart to him?

From the author of *The Last Letter*, a gripping, emotional story of family, humanity, and faith.

BY REBECCA YARROS

How do you define yourself when others have already decided who you are?

Six years ago, when Camden Daniels came back from war without his younger brother, no one in the small town of Alba, Colorado, would forgive him—especially his father. Cam left, swearing never to return.

But a desperate message from his father brings it all back. The betrayal. The pain. And the need to go home again.

But home is where the one person he still loves is waiting. Willow. The one woman he can never have. Because there are secrets buried in Alba that are best left in the dark.

If only he could tell his heart to stay locked away when she whispers she's always loved him, and always will…

Great and Precious Things is a heart-wrenching story about family, betrayal, and ultimately how far we're willing to go on behalf of those who need us most.

16086